A Cup Full of Midnight

ANOTHER JARED MCKEAN MYSTERY BY JADEN TERRELL

Racing the Devil

A JARED McKEAN MYSTERY

A Cup Full of Midnight

JADEN TERRELL

THE PERMANENT PRESS
Sag Harbor, NY 11963

For information, address:
    The Permanent Press
    4170 Noyac Road
    Sag Harbor, NY 11963
    www.thepermanentpress.com

Library of Congress Cataloging-in-Publication Data

Terrell, Jaden–
    A cup full of midnight : a Jared McKean mystery / Jaden Terrell.
        p. cm.
    ISBN 978-1-57962-225-1
        1. Private investigators—Tennessee—Nashville—Fiction. I. Title.

PS3620.E753C87 2012
813'.6—dc23   2012013711

Printed in the United States of America.

CHAPTER ONE

The call came three hours into the stakeout, just as the man in the cowboy hat pulled up to the curb in a red Lexus so polished it looked like it had been dipped in molten glass. It was a wet winter afternoon, and a flat gray sky spat sleet and ice onto the windshield of my black and chrome Chevy Silverado pickup. A sweet ride. Not so sweet in the middle of winter with the engine off to keep plumes of exhaust from drawing attention.

Shivering behind the wheel, I blew on my hands to warm them. Then, ignoring the phone vibrating in my cupholder, I lowered the window and reached across the seat for my camera. With the office rent due and Christmas a few weeks away, the two hundred dollars a day plus expenses my client was paying for surveillance shots said whoever was on the phone could wait.

It buzzed again, rattling against the plastic like a hornet against glass. Holding the camera to my eye with one hand, I felt for the phone with the other and pressed a button on the side, cutting the connection.

Across the street, the man in the cowboy hat—small-time record producer and big-time philanderer Richie Barron—clambered out of the driver's seat and waddled to the passenger side, the tails of his leather duster flapping around his calves. The hat was a prop. He was built like a groundhog, and if he'd ever even been on a horse, it was being led in circles at some kid's birthday party.

As he reached for the handle of the passenger door, I adjusted the lens and snapped a photo. The phone buzzed again. This time, I glanced over at the caller ID on the illuminated screen. My niece, Caitlin. I frowned. She wouldn't risk losing her phone privileges to call me in the middle of a school day unless she had a serious problem. But why call me, instead of my brother or his wife?

Fingers numb with cold, I lowered the camera and fumbled for the phone. Flipped it open and held it to my ear.

"What's going on, Katie-Bear?" I said. At fourteen, she was too old for the nickname, but as her favorite—and only—uncle, I got a special dispensation.

"Hey, Uncle Jared." Her voice was almost too soft to make out, so I shifted the camera and put a finger in the opposite ear to hear better. "I'm not supposed to have my cell phone out, but . . ."

"But?" Phone tucked between my jaw and shoulder, I aimed the Sony and snapped another picture as Richie slung open the passenger door of the Lexus. Snapped another as a woman in black tights and stiletto-heeled boots emerged, looking like she'd stuffed the bra beneath her fur cape with casaba melons. A minimal background check had identified her as Destiny Mirage, a twenty-two-year-old stripper with musical aspirations. Gypsy Rose Lee meets Dolly Parton.

Caitlin said, "I have to tell you something."

Across the street, Destiny planted a kiss on Richie's cheek, leaving a smear of lipstick behind. I snapped another picture and said, "So. Tell me."

"I'm not sure if I should."

"If you're not sure you should—"

"It's just . . . Well . . . Josh . . ."

At the quaver in her voice, my mouth went dry. Overreacting, maybe, but in the past six months, Josh had given us reason to worry. Moody. Withdrawn. Flirting with danger. This past summer, he'd come out of the closet and run away from home to live with the pushing thirty son of a bitch who'd seduced him.

The son of a bitch, Razor, had been murdered a few days ago—butchered by the group of vampire wannabes he'd gotten Josh involved with—and even though Josh hadn't seen the man in months, the murder had hit my nephew hard.

And now . . . ?

A series of disasters flashed through my mind. Pictures of my nephew crumpled in a spreading pool of blood. Shot by a classmate. Knifed in the high school cafeteria. Crushed in a smoldering tangle of tortured metal that had once been his mother's Camry. Nothing simple like a nosebleed or a broken arm. Caitlin wouldn't have called me for that.

I said, "What happened to Josh?"

"I don't want to be a snitch, you know?" she said, and my chest loosened up a notch. Josh wasn't hurt; he was into something Caitlin didn't want to snitch about.

"Are you snitching or helping?" I said.

"Helping, I think."

"Then tell me."

Silence.

As the couple across the street picked their way up the slippery walkway, I finally remembered what I was supposed to be doing and snapped another photo.

The silence on Caitlin's end of the line stretched on. I blew out a long breath that fogged the windshield and formed a cloud around the bobble-head Batman on my dash. A gift from my brother, Randall, who had a matching Superman on his. Batman wore a piece of tinsel around his waist in honor of the season.

"Okay," I said to Caitlin. "This is where you tell me about Josh."

She let out a sigh and said, "Maybe it's nothing."

"Or maybe it's something. Tell me, and we'll figure it out."

"I don't know. You know how you and Dad always say no tattling unless there's destruction involved?"

"Yeah. So?"

"What if you're not sure?"

"Then you tell."

She was quiet for a moment, maybe thinking about it. "I don't know where to start."

At the door of the condo, Destiny rubbed her upper arms with her gloved hands while Richie jiggled the key in the lock. I snapped another shot.

"Start anywhere," I said. "Is Josh into drugs or something?"

"No. I mean, I don't think so."

"What *do* you think?"

Another silence. I imagined her, hand cupped over the phone, face scrunched with worry and concentration. The same look she'd worn when she was five and I put her on my palomino Quarter Horse for the first time. Finally, she said, "It's just . . . A couple of cops came and talked to him while we were at lunch. And then—"

"Wait a minute. Cops came and talked to him? Without Randall or your mom there?" No need to wonder what they'd discussed. Razor's murder had been brutal; the police would have questions for everyone who'd known him or his killers. I didn't like it that they'd talked to Josh. It wasn't illegal, but it pissed me off anyway.

Caitlin said, "They were just asking some questions. But then, when he came back to the cafeteria, this guy named Kevin called Josh a faggot and a criminal and sort of shoved him, and they . . . sort of got into it."

I glanced up at the condo. Richie and his lady friend had disappeared inside. Nothing to see but the blank face of the door and a half-dozen thick-curtained windows.

"Is Josh all right?" I asked.

"He had a bloody nose. So the principal sent him to the clinic and then to detention."

"What'd he do with Kevin?"

"Nothing. It was so totally not fair."

"So Josh is in detention."

"No, he *was* in detention. But about five minutes ago, I was in Algebra, only I was looking out the window—because who could listen to one more boring word about integers, you know?—and I saw him running across the parking lot. And when he got to the street, he just jumped in the middle of the road and stopped this truck—it almost hit him—and then this big guy got out and they talked for a minute, and then Josh climbed in and they drove away. So I told Mrs. Taylor I had to go to the bathroom, and I came out here and called you."

"You're sure it wasn't a friend's truck?"

"I never saw it before. It had one of those camper tops with a picture on the side, so I'd know if I'd seen it. Something with an eagle."

"Why didn't you call your mom or dad?"

"I told you. I don't want to get Josh in trouble. But he looked—" She hesitated.

"He looked what?"

"I don't know. It scared me. Would you go and check on him, Uncle Jared? Please? What if he got in the truck with some kind of psycho?"

I'd worked too many homicide cases not to know it was possible. The odds were with him, but they'd also been with every kid we'd ever pulled out of a shallow grave.

"I'm sure he's okay," I said, though a worm of anxiety squirmed low in my belly. "But if it will make you feel better, I'll check it out."

She whispered a quick thanks and a more detailed description of the truck Josh had gotten into, and the connection broke.

I dropped the camera onto the passenger seat and started the engine. A blast of cold air burst from the dashboard. I punched the accelerator without waiting for the engine to warm up and squealed away from the curb. Best-case scenario, I was wasting my time. Worst-case scenario . . . No point thinking about that.

I skidded on a patch of black ice and swerved to avoid the front bumper of a tricked-out Mustang with a Confederate flag on the hood. The driver blasted the horn. Shot me a salute with his middle finger. I started to flip him off, then gave a "whatever" wave instead and eased off the accelerator. I'd be no good to Josh wrapped around the front grille of an eighteen-wheeler.

From Music Row, I shot across Chet Atkins Place, hit Broadway and then I-40 heading east toward my brother's place in Mt. Juliet, a bedroom community about sixteen miles east of the city. Twenty minutes after Caitlin's call, my tires crunched onto the gravel drive-way of Randall's split-level white brick house. No one answered my knock, so I used my copy of the key, pushed open the door, and called Josh's name.

No answer.

A light blue backpack lay on the hall table, zipper half open, a half-naked, scythe-wielding winged man sketched in black ink across the front of the pack. It was homoerotic as hell, and I knew Josh and Randall must have fought bitterly about it. It bothered me some too, but a bubble of pride rose in my chest anyway. It was a damn fine drawing.

The backpack meant Josh was here, or had been here. Maybe alone, perhaps with a friend. Maybe with Caitlin's hypothetical psycho, though the odds were against it. A serial killer wouldn't have brought Josh home. Probably.

More likely, I'd find Josh in bed with some other boy from school. Or maybe an older man. At the thought, my fists clenched. Razor was dead, but there was always some other lowlife ready to take advantage of a kid in crisis.

The kitchen and the living room were empty. Nothing in the hall but smiling family photos, a spectrum of blond. Wendy's platinum, Caitlin's butter, foster daughter Rina's cornsilk, Randall's and a younger Josh's matching buckskin. All that gold, broken by an older Josh's artificial black.

At the foot of the stairs, I called my nephew's name again. Listened for the frantic scrambling of two kids about to be caught screwing around. Heard nothing.

Up the stairs, quicker now, glancing into each room as I passed. Guest room, master bedroom, Caitlin's, Rina's. Rapped my knuckles on Josh's door, got no answer. Pushed it open.

Empty.

The bathroom door at the end of the hall was closed. I knocked. No answer. Tried the knob. Locked.

I pressed my ear to the door. "Josh?"

Silence.

Wrong, this was all wrong.

I took a step back. Pivoted sideways, rocked my weight onto my right foot, and had a moment to wonder how I'd explain the broken door if Josh was inside wearing headphones and jerking off to some heavy metal Goth punk band. Then I drove the heel of my left boot into the particleboard just below the doorknob. A blade of pain shot through my calf, the ghost of a bullet wound that would probably have healed by now if I'd had the patience—or maybe the discipline—to stay off it. The wood trim around the lock splintered with a sharp crack, and the door swung inward.

The crack widened in slow motion, and the room swept into view. Polished ivory tiles, a white porcelain toilet with a thin brown crack along the base, a set of monogrammed towels folded neatly over a ceramic bar. An old-style, claw-footed tub filled to the rim with what looked like watered wine.

The air in the room seemed to thicken. For a heartbeat I stood paralyzed, unable even to breathe. Then I was moving, cell phone in hand, punching 911, my voice detached as if I were calling in a robbery to Dispatch. Not thinking, no time to think, but the details catalogued themselves into my brain all the same.

Josh slumped inside the tub, fully clothed except for his sneakers, which were neatly aligned on the bathmat, navy sweat socks tucked inside. Beside them lay a package of Schick double-edged razor blades, flap open. On the edge of the tub, a bloody half-handprint stood out like a flare against the white enamel.

No time.

I hauled Josh out of the still-warm water, cell phone trapped between my ear and shoulder, giving the operator my brother's address with one part of my brain while another part gibbered like a madman. Praying, praying without words, because the only words my brain would form were in answer to the operator's cool tones. Reddened water sloshed over the side of the tub, streamed from Josh's hair and his shirt and his blood-darkened jeans, soaked my shirt through to the skin.

Too late, the madman whispered. My stomach felt lined with lead. *Too late.*

But sometimes, in His infinite mercy, God allows us to save the things we love.

Blood still trickled from Josh's wrists, a good sign, even though his skin was so white he looked bleached. Only the living bleed. His skin had a waxy sheen, but his chest rose and fell almost imperceptibly.

The phone, useless now, clattered to the floor. I snatched the towels off the bar, pulled Josh's arms above his head, and pressed a towel to each wrist. I held them there until the paramedics pulled me away.

CHAPTER TWO

We gathered in the family waiting room of the ICU, a cracker box of a room with a soda machine and a pea-green vinyl couch and matching chairs. A round card table wobbled in the center of the room, and against the far wall, a flimsy wooden shelf overflowed with outdated magazines and jigsaw puzzles in split-cornered boxes. Someone had taped a line of paper candy canes along one wall, a pitiful attempt at holiday festivity.

Randall's wife, Wendy, sat stiffly on the sofa, one arm around their foster daughter, Rina, and the other around Caitlin, who slumped in her seat with a spiral notebook in her lap. She was writing her name over and over, every spelling she could think of, in neat, loopy letters with hearts over the i's. Caitlyn. Kaitlin. Kaitlyn. Caitlin. Maybe deciding who she'd be tomorrow. Maybe taking her mind off the fact that her brother had just tried to kill himself.

Across the room, my wife . . . my ex-wife . . . Maria and her new husband, D.W., clasped hands across the arms of their chairs. Her other hand rested on her swollen belly, beneath a *Baby on Board* sweatshirt. Cross-legged on the floor in front of them, my son, Paul, built something indefinable from Legos. He looked up at me and smiled, a slant-eyed Buddha in thick glasses and a Batman T-shirt. He could have been a Down syndrome poster child.

I wanted to punch something, seeing them like that, the three of them posed like a family photo. My family photo, with D.W. sitting in my place. He was a good guy. A safe guy. The kind who never came home with blood on his shirt and stitches in his head.

Maria had said of our marriage, *I couldn't live that way, never knowing when they'd bring you home in a body bag.* And later, when I'd offered to change careers and sell insurance or repair motorcycles, *It's not what you do; it's who you are. You're a hero waiting for something to die for.*

I guessed she didn't have to be afraid for D.W.

Randall stood in front of the Pepsi machine, one fist pounding lightly but steadily on the fiberglass front. I walked over to him, laid a hand on his shoulder and said, "He'll be all right."

He gave the machine a final punch and swiveled to face me, eyes red, face drawn. It wasn't quite like looking in a mirror, but it was close. At forty, he was four years older than I was and topped my six feet by two inches. His nose, broken during basic training, veered slightly off center just below the bridge. I had a small vertical scar across my lower lip and another above one eyebrow—reminders of bad men in bad places. But we had the same buckskin-colored hair, the same gray eyes, the same rangy build we'd gotten from our father.

I repeated, "He'll be all right."

"You don't know that," he said.

"We got to him in time."

"You don't *know* that."

Caitlin looked up from her notebook. "Uncle Jared," she said, a tremor in her voice. "You have blood on your shirt."

I looked down at my chest, where the edges of my jacket framed a dark stain on my still-damp shirt. Pulled the zipper up to hide the stain and realized the cuffs of the jacket were splashed with rust. It was my father's jacket. A leather bomber jacket he'd worn in the war. I felt bad that the blood on the cuffs bothered me, but it did.

"You should soak that," Wendy said. "Use cold."

Randall turned away from the Pepsi machine. "For Christ's sake. What difference does it make?"

She started to speak, then bit her lip and looked down at her lap.

Caitlin sniffled, wiped her eyes with the heels of her hands. I kissed her on the top of the head, then pulled one of the chairs over and slid into it. Paulie came over and crawled into my lap. His hair smelled like oranges. Like Maria's. He squirmed against my chest, and I realized I was holding him too tightly. Reluctantly, I loosened my grip.

The clock on the wall ticked on, still no word about Josh.

My left calf throbbed, probably from kicking in the bathroom door. I shifted in the chair, careful not to unseat Paul. Stretched the leg out in front of me and flexed the muscle. Despite the dull pain, it felt strong. I flexed again and thought about close calls and bad choices.

Wondered what was taking so long.

Randall came over and sat on the arm of the couch beside Wendy. She shifted away from him, ever so slightly. I wondered what that meant. Maybe nothing. It bothered me all the same.

Time inched ahead. More waiting, more wondering, and finally, a doctor with a smudge of beard on his chin and a stethoscope around his neck pushed through the door. He looked barely old enough to drive, let alone to hold Josh's life in his hands.

"How is he?" Randall said.

The doctor tipped his head toward Randall. "He's out of immediate danger. He's lost a lot of blood, but he's stable for now."

"For now?"

"All indications are, he's going to be fine. Physically, at least. We have a psych consult lined up."

"When?"

"Today, I hope. They have a heavy load this time of year." He flashed a rueful smile. "Which one of you is Uncle Jared?"

I slid out from under my son and stood up. "I am."

The doctor said, "He wants to talk to you."

I looked at Randall, who read the question in my eyes.

"Go ahead," he said roughly. "It's what he wants."

I glanced at Wendy. She turned her face away, jaw tight. I looked back at the doctor and said, "All right."

He led me down the hall and through a set of swinging double doors. Our footsteps sounded loud on the polished tiles. A pretty blonde nurse in scrubs passed, pushing a cart piled with disposable pill cups and paper-wrapped syringes. She glanced up as we passed, gave me a sympathetic smile. I nodded back, feeling like an impostor. Stealing sympathy that should have been my brother's.

"Here we are," the doctor said. He glanced at his watch. "You have ten minutes."

I took a deep breath, and the sharp smells of antiseptic and ammonia stung my nose and throat. I pushed open the door. Josh lay on his back, eyes closed, an IV dripping a clear liquid into his veins. Even against the white of the pillow, his face looked pale. The dark smudges beneath his eyes and the faded charcoal of his dyed hair seemed to float above the over-bleached blankets. He looked too young for sixteen. And too old.

He needed a haircut. He needed . . . I wasn't sure what.

I moved to the bedside, watched him breathe. The bands around my lungs loosened, and I let out a quivering breath. He opened his eyes and said, "Hey."

"Hey." I closed my fists over the metal handrail to keep my hands from trembling. There were a thousand things I wanted to say to him—*What were you thinking? Why didn't you call someone? Why didn't you call me?* And the million dollar question, *Why?* None of them seemed right.

None of them seemed like enough.

I settled for, "You had us worried there for awhile."

His lips strained upward in a smile that stretched the skin across his bones. "I had me worried too."

I cleared my throat and said, "Your family is outside."

"You're my family too," he said.

"Josh—"

He lifted a hand to silence me. Winced as the IV needle pinched the skin. "I wanted to talk to you first."

"Why?"

To hurt my brother and his wife? He'd already done that. I glanced at the IV line, followed it down to the bruised flesh at the bend of his arm and then to the bandages taped tightly around each wrist. Tried not to think about what was beneath the bandages.

He saw where I was looking and turned his palms toward the mattress.

"I need a favor," he said. "Not an Uncle Jared favor, a P.I. favor."

I frowned. What did a sixteen-year-old kid need with a private detective? "What kind of favor?"

"I have $160 at home. I know it's not enough, but . . . I want to hire you."

"You don't need to hire me. If you need something, all you have to do is ask."

"I know. But this is, like . . ." He made a helpless gesture with his hands and winced again. "Huge."

"Try me."

"I want you to find out who killed Razor."

My mouth suddenly tasted sour. Before I could stop myself, I blurted, "That son of a bitch."

"It's okay." He gave me a weak, sardonic smile. "Tell me how you really feel."

Razor's mother had named him Sebastian Edward Parker. Razor was the name he gave himself. Sharp. Bright. Dangerous. It was an affectation. He was a predator, but like a hyena, he preyed only on the weak. His sexual preferences ran to teenaged boys. Fifteen, sixteen. Give or take. Vulnerable. Alienated. Horny young guys drowning in confusion and testosterone.

Boys like Josh.

"He molested you," I said.

He looked away. Plucked at a frayed edge of the blanket. "I knew what I was doing."

"You were fifteen."

"Old enough."

"And he was pushing thirty."

"He wasn't pushing thirty. He was only, like, twenty-five."

"He told you that, he lied. He was on the downhill side of twenty-nine. Too old to be——"

"Stop," he said. He wiped the back of his free hand across his eyes. "Just . . . It doesn't matter now."

I let go of the bed rail and stalked to the window. Looked out through the shatterproof glass into not much of anything. A parking lot frosted by halogen lights, a black-silhouetted tree line, and beyond that, the lights of the apartment complex behind the hospital. They looked like scattered stars.

"Please, Uncle Jared," Josh said. "I need to know what happened to him. Why it happened."

It happened because he was a shit, I thought. *Because sometimes bad things happen to bad people.*

It happened, maybe, because in spite of legal loopholes and sleazy lawyers, there was sometimes justice in the world.

I turned back to the bed and said, "The police already have a suspect. Some girl he knew. Laurel O'Brien. She confessed."

A snort escaped him, something between a laugh and a sob. "Gimme a break. You met her. You really think she could—" He stopped. Closed his eyes and swallowed hard. "Do you think she could do what they said?"

"When did I meet her?"

"That time I ran away and you went looking for me. You know. She told you her name was Absinthe."

"Ah." I remembered her then. An overweight girl in Goth makeup and a black satin gown too tight across the chest. Beneath her obnoxious façade, there was something about her I'd liked. "Why would she say she did it if she didn't?"

"I don't know. But I need to know. What if it was—" His voice broke, and tears shone in his eyes. "I just need to know. Please, Uncle Jared?"

Maybe I should have needed to know too, but the truth was I didn't care who'd killed Razor. I just wished it had happened six months earlier, before he'd gotten to Josh.

I said, "Those cops who came to your school—"

"Don't tell Mom and Dad. Please."

"What did they say to you?"

"They think . . ." His mouth trembled.

"They think what?"

"The day he . . . Razor . . . died, I ditched school."

He didn't have to put it together for me. A cannonball settled in my gut, and suddenly I cared who had killed Razor. I cared a hell of a lot. "They think you were with Absinthe. That you were in on it together."

"They didn't say it, but I could tell, yeah."

"And that's why you . . . ?"

He turned his head away. "I don't want to talk about that. Promise you won't tell Mom and Dad about the cops."

"Josh, they're going to find out."

"Not if you catch the guy first."

The room was silent except for an irritating buzz in one of the fluorescent lights. Josh gnawed at his lower lip. I thought about my brother, how he'd feel if he found out I'd kept a thing like this from him. I sneaked another glance at Josh's wrists.

"All right," I said finally. "I'll see what I can do."

The corners of his mouth tugged upward. "Thanks, Uncle Jared. You won't be sorry."

I thought of my brother again. Forced a smile and kept my mouth shut.

I was already sorry.

CHAPTER THREE

At eleven-thirty the next morning, I pushed through the double doors of the West precinct house and flashed my ID through the safety glass of the information booth in the lobby.

"Frank Campanella," I said.

The guard inside, a skinny acne-scarred kid I'd never seen before, gave me a curt nod and went back to his dog-eared paperback. He'd get reamed for that if anybody who mattered caught him, but I wasn't anybody anymore.

Frank Campanella, my former partner, should have been in charge of Nashville's Murder Squad. Instead, the new police chief had disbanded the unit, leaving only a small core of investigators to carry on as the Cold Case Division. Frank and the rest of the Homicide and Murder Squad detectives were sent to other precinct houses and served an entrée of break-ins and vandalism with an occasional murder or missing persons on the side. It was like feeding a grizzly on nothing but tofu and alfalfa sprouts.

The idea was to make everybody equal, put an end to specialized investigations, get the guys out in the neighborhoods where they'd be working. It sounded good on paper.

Frank's new sergeant was a thirty-four-year-old green-eyed redhead named Kelly Malone. Until the shake-up, she'd never worked a homicide, but she was brassy and ballsy and looked good on the six o'clock news, where my ex-girlfriend, local anchor Ashleigh Arneau, made syrupy references to her as the "Debutante Detective."

Frank had the highest solve rate on the squad and more years on the force than Malone had been alive, but nobody cared about that. He was Old School, which meant he was Old News.

His cluttered cubicle was two doors down from Malone's office. He looked up and scowled when I rapped my knuckles on the edge of the cube. He had an open file in front of him and a Styrofoam cup in one hand. The cup had holly leaves printed on the side.

"Let me guess," he said. "You need a favor."

"What makes you think I didn't just come by to visit an old friend?"

"Don't make me laugh." He closed the folder and pushed it away. "I know that look."

I took the seat across from him, a black vinyl office chair with stuffing peeking from a split seam, and said, "I need to see the Parker file."

"The Parker file."

"You know. Sebastian Parker. Vampire wannabe. Ritual killing. Called himself Razor."

"I know who he is. What I don't know is why you think I'm gonna get myself fired for giving you case files when you don't work for us anymore."

"I'm not asking you to give it to me. I can look at it right here. We could go in the copy room and lock the door, if that will make you feel better."

"Not even if I wanted to." He slumped in his chair, raked his fingers through his silvering hair. "I don't have it. It's not my case anymore. Malone gave it to Gilley and Robbins."

"Who the hell are Gilley and Robbins?"

He barked a bitter laugh. "Fucking parking meter detectives. Part of some master plan to make us do the things we suck at." He plucked a fat file folder from a sloppy stack of papers and shoved it across the desk at me.

I picked it up and rifled through it. Peeping Tom. "You gotta be kidding me."

"Do I look like I'm kidding?"

I slid the file back toward him. "So they get the homicides, you get the scut work?"

"Malone sent them on a new case today. Dead guy on the porch, pissed-off wife with a shotgun. The Parker case, Gilley lost his lunch, and Robbins broke down and cried like a baby. So she sends them out to see some poor schmuck with his brains all over the porch."

"Amateurs."

"Don't get me wrong. They're good investigators. But what do they know about homicide? You know what our solve rate is these days? Forty percent."

Before the big upheaval, it had been eighty. You couldn't blame Malone or the precinct commanders for that. Not entirely. There were other factors. Politics. A new police chief who didn't understand that homicide was a different kind of crime and homicide detectives a different breed. I'd seen good beat cops broken by the sight of a butchered body, unable to leave their own houses without getting the shakes. Not the guys in homicide. In homicide, we know how to detach.

"When it gets down to thirty," I said, "maybe you'll get your office back."

"If it gets down to thirty, I'll die of shame and they can have the fucking office."

"But then I'd miss the pleasure of your scintillating conversation." I leaned forward, put my hands flat on his desk, and said, "Frank, I need to see that file."

His eyebrows bunched together, wild silver bristles that made him look like a disgruntled badger. "I just told you, I don't have it."

"But you could get it."

"Sure, if I wanted to spend my golden years saying, 'Welcome to Walmart.'"

I looked down at my lap. I knew Malone would pounce on an excuse to cut him loose, and I was asking him to risk both his pension and his reputation and give her one. It was a lot to ask. "I know I'm putting you on the spot," I said. "But you know the case. I need to know what angle your guys are working."

"My guys?"

"Your guys, Malone's guys. Whoever they belong to, two of them went to Josh's school yesterday and questioned him about Razor's murder."

Frank raised an eyebrow. Rocked back in his chair. "S.O.P. You know that. He was intimate with the victim."

"He was molested by the victim."

"Okay." His voice softened. "I misspoke. But he hung out with the guy for a long time. You don't think he could shed some light?"

"They called him out of the cafeteria in front of the whole school and then they made him think he was a suspect."

"You think they crossed the line?"

"He went home and cut his wrists. What do you think?"

His face went perfectly still. "What?"

"He's going to be okay, probably. If he doesn't try it again."

"My God."

"So I need to know, Frank. Is he a suspect?"

He rubbed his hands over his face, as if he'd just walked through a cobweb. "My best guess?" he said. "Probably. The O'Brien girl didn't kill Parker and pose him on that pentagram all by herself. She had to have help. And witnesses place Josh and the girl together near the victim's house an hour before the murder."

I tried to keep my expression neutral, but he knew me too well. He said, "Josh didn't tell you about that?"

"He told me he ditched school."

"That's all?"

"He didn't do this, Frank. You've known him since he was, what, seven? You know he isn't capable of this."

He gave a slow nod, as if his head were too heavy for his neck. I wiped my palms, suddenly clammy, along the outside seam of my jeans. I wondered if he was remembering, like I was, the scrape-kneed, sunburnt, laughing boy Josh had been. If he was imagining, like I was, what prison might do to that same boy charged with a vicious crime and old enough to be tried as an adult.

Then, "Wait here," Frank said.

A few minutes later, he came back and handed me a thick manila folder. "Do something with that and come on," he said. "I gotta get out of here."

I stuffed the folder under my coat and zipped it inside. The coat was an Australian duster with a fleece lining. I liked the bomber jacket better, but I couldn't get the bloodstains out. "What about Malone?" I asked.

"Fuck her," he said. He leaned across the desk and picked up the Styrofoam cup, downed the last of his coffee and crumpled the cup into a shapeless wad. "For this, I need a beer."

CHAPTER FOUR

We pushed out onto the freshly salted sidewalk and into a skin-chapping cold that briefly glued my nostrils shut. The sky was a bitter gray, and needles of sleet stung our bare faces. I looked at Frank and said, "Where to?"

"Let's go to Tootsie's. You drive."

Tootsie's Orchid Lounge was a famous dive on Lower Broadway in the heart of downtown. We parked the Silverado in a public lot four blocks away. In good weather, it was a pleasant stroll. Today, the wind knifed through my coat and brought tears to my eyes. Halfway across the street, my ears were already numb.

"You're gonna give me pneumonia," I groused. "Worse, you're gonna *get* pneumonia, and then Patrice is gonna kill me."

His wife's name evoked a grudging smile. "Damn straight. Can't you hear it? 'What were you thinking, dragging an old man out in the cold like that?'"

"Not so old," I said, trying to count it up. What was he? Sixty, sixty-one? Didn't they say fifty was the new thirty? That would make sixty the new forty. Which would make me, what? The new sixteen?

After awhile, he said, "I always thought I'd die in the traces."

"Things get too rough, you could come and work with me," I said.

"I've seen your office. That damn desk. It should have its own country. There's not enough space for me and it in the same room."

"I love that desk," I said. "It's got character."

"So did Margaret Thatcher. But I wouldn't want to share my office with her."

We pushed open the front door of Tootsie's, and a gust of warm air rolled over us. It smelled of beer and grease and a hint of old cigarette smoke. The musicians at the front, a Dixie diva and a concrete cowboy, were singing a decent version of Garth Brooks's "I've Got Friends in Low Places" to a half-empty room. They nodded in acknowledgement as we stuffed a pair of fives into the tip jar and made our way to a table for four at the back. We shook the sleet out of our jackets and tossed them into the extra seats. Then we both moved our chairs so we could see the exit.

I plucked a handful of napkins from the dispenser and dried my hands and face as well as I could, then waited until the waitress had taken our orders—a Bud and an order of fries for Frank, onion rings and AmberBock for me—before taking out the file and opening it on the table between us. A full-color photo of Razor's butchered body lay on top of the stack, and it suddenly occurred to me that maybe it was a good thing we'd come at a slow time.

The photo showed a naked young man stretched across a pentagram drawn in blood. His own blood, according to the lab results. Drawn postmortem—though how you could sacrifice a guy who'd already bled out was beyond me.

The next photo was a candid shot taken a few weeks before Razor's death. He had high cheekbones and a straight, narrow nose and, except for a few faint lines at the corners of his eyes, he looked younger than his years. Thick hair dyed onyx juxtaposed with blue-white skin and a sullen, effeminate mouth that had probably seduced dozens of boys like Josh.

I studied the picture, trying without success to muster some sympathy for the dead man, but all I could think was, *Flirt with the devil, and don't be surprised if he asks you to dance.*

Suddenly queasy, I shoved the photograph to the bottom of the pile. Sifted through the haphazard stack of papers. Crime scene photos, the medical examiner's report, police reports, transcriptions of interviews, including Absinthe's confession. Razor's death, laid out in front of me like a hand of cards.

"How about an overview?" I said.

Frank took a swig of beer, took his time swallowing. "We found traces of blood in the tub," he said, finally. "Looks like they carried your buddy Razor upstairs and hung him up to drain the body."

"Hung him up where?"

"Chin-up bar in the upstairs hall. We found a little spatter on the wall there. We think they drained the blood into a bucket and rinsed it out in the bathtub when they were finished with it. They disinfected afterward, but you know how that is."

I knew. Chemiluminescent compounds could reveal traces of blood years after the fact. The newer ones worked just like Luminal, only better.

Frank went on. "After they drained the blood, they went downstairs and drew the pentagram with it, splashed the rest around the room, posed the body, then used some kind of vacuum on the couch and carpet."

"They leave the bag?"

"I wish. They did leave a couple of footprints—looks like somebody stepped in the blood and tracked it around some—but even if we could pull prints from the carpet, they're too smeared to be of any use. Can't even tell what size they were."

"You think they smeared the prints on purpose?"

"We're pretty sure they did."

I picked up the next photo, a close-up of Razor's forearm, arcane symbols carved into it, dark slits between whitened edges of skin. "Ugly," I said.

"Aren't they all?" He tapped one of the symbols with a forefinger. "Some of these are defensive cuts. The symbols were carved on top of them later. Like somebody didn't want us to know he fought."

Somebody. Not Absinthe. Not Josh. Just somebody. The muscles in the back of my neck loosened a bit.

I rummaged through the stack and plucked out the medical examiner's report. Cause of death was a jagged throat wound. Its size and shape showed that the blade had gone in straight, then jerked sideways, slicing through the jugular; but there was no way to tell whether the killer had planned it that way, or whether Razor had widened the wound in an instinctive attempt to pull free of the blade. The forensic pathologist called it a compound wound. Like the defensive cuts, it indicated a struggle.

The other wounds—the occult symbols, the long vertical slash that opened his gut like a dressed deer, and the one that had severed his genitals—had occurred postmortem.

My better self was glad he hadn't been tortured. The rest of me wished I'd killed the son of a bitch myself.

I dropped the report on the table and picked up a photo of the blue ceramic bowl found beside Razor's body. The inner curve of the bowl was streaked with black, and in the bottom of it, three charred lumps lay in a pool of something that looked like tar but wasn't. A wisp of smoke curled from a stick of incense propped between the lumps—Razor's shriveled genitalia and his blackened heart.

Just looking at it made my nuts draw up.

"Gotta hate someone a lot to do a thing like this," I said. "Even as part of some ceremony."

"It wasn't a ceremony. Before the girl confessed, we talked to an occult expert. This isn't an authentic ritual. Just bits and pieces patched together from books and horror flicks. Look." He handed me a picture of the pentagram. "It's just a star inside a circle. Satanists draw the star upside down."

"Somebody trying to make it look like a satanic killing?"

"Or trying to invent one. Kid was a role player. Vampires and all that crap. But then, you knew that." He paused, then added, too casually, "Josh used to play with them, didn't he?"

I said, sharply, "Not for a long time."

"Don't bark at me." He held up his hands in mock surrender. "You know I have to ask."

"So now you've asked."

"Relax, Cowboy. Just dotting the i's."

I nodded. Drew in a calming breath and opened the fists I hadn't known I'd clenched. When I felt like I could speak, I tapped a finger on the medical report. "You think role players did this?"

"Why not? You remember that bunch from Kentucky a few years back."

I remembered. Young family on their way home from a church retreat. Stopped at the wrong rest area and met up with a bunch of vampire wannabes high on PCP. It was the last mistake they'd ever make.

"I thought vampires were passé," I said.

"Check out the internet lately? Ninety-five million hits, give or take. You got vampire chat rooms, vampire web sites, vamp support groups. Orientation meetings for teenagers who think they're vampires."

"Jesus."

"Sanguinarius. The Sanguinarium. The Temple of the Vampire." He ticked them off on his fingers. "Nutcases 'R' Us."

I scanned the M.E.'s report again. "Traces of drugs? Alcohol?"

"Not enough to knock him out." Frank tipped his chair back and ran his hands through his rumpled hair. "A little beer and pot from the night before. Lots of stuff stashed around, though. Uppers, downers, Ecstasy, Rohypnol." My jaw tightened at the mention of the date rape drug, and he added, "Lotta kids take it just to get high. But from what I hear about our boy Razor, he coulda found a lot of uses for it."

"Any chance this was a drug-related killing?"

"Naw. Too much imagination."

His cell phone rang, no fancy tones, just a plain old-fashioned rotary phone ring. He pulled it out of his jacket pocket and grimaced at the caller ID.

"Malone," he growled, and tucked it back inside his jacket without answering.

Our waitress came out of the back carrying a tray with our food and more beers. I slid the photos into the file and flipped it shut just as she reached our table.

"Hiding your dirty pictures?" she asked, nodding toward the folder. "Not that it's any of my business."

"Trust me," Frank said. "It's nothing you want to see."

She hovered around for a minute or so, fiddling with the salt and pepper shakers, casting furtive glances toward the file. Frank and I opened our beers, took turns whacking ketchup onto our plates from an old-fashioned glass bottle. After awhile, she heaved a sigh and went back into the kitchen.

When she'd gone, I said, "What about the O'Brien girl? What've you got on her?"

"You mean besides the confession? We got her fingerprints on the knife. Right thumb and index finger. She definitely handled it."

"You're sure it was the murder weapon?"

"You know how knife wounds are. They get all stretched out of shape. But we think so." He dropped the legs of his chair to the floor with a thud, shuffled through the sheaf of photographs, then shoved a picture of a small, curved dagger across the table toward me. "It's called an athame." He pronounced it a-THAW-may. "Some sort of ritual knife. It belonged to the victim, but we're pretty sure the initial slashes and some of the symbols were carved with this."

"You gotta be kidding. Those ritual knives won't even hold an edge. They're just for show."

"Not this one. Your boy Razor bought the real deal. Top grade. And he kept it sharp."

"Pretty pricey for a showpiece. How'd *my boy Razor* afford a thing like that?"

Frank's nose wrinkled. "Family money. And what can I say? Mama loved her little boy."

I picked up another photo, this one of Razor's chest and belly opened from sternum to navel. I said, "You can't crack a rib cage with a knife like that."

"No. M.E. thinks they did that with some kind of tactical or survival knife." Frank held his hands about a foot apart. "Big hunting knife they use to dress deer."

I knew the kind of knife he meant. A heavy-duty blade. If you knew what you were doing, you could perform most of an autopsy with it. The only thing it wouldn't do was cut through the skull. You needed a saw for that.

I took a sip of AmberBock and said, "Tell me about the girl. What about her friends? People she hung out with? Anything there?"

"She hung out with Razor and a little group of his vampire friends. The rest of them all alibi each other." He picked up the report, tapped a line somewhere in the middle of it. "There are four of them. The O'Brien girl, Laurel. Medina Neel, twenty-one. Calls herself Medea."

"I've met her. Back in the fall, after we found out about . . . Razor and Josh. She seemed a little high-strung."

"If high-strung means as crazy as a Betsy bug, you got that right." He swirled a French fry in a pool of ketchup, popped the whole thing into his mouth.

"You said four. Who's number three?"

"Older guy, close to the victim's age. Barnabus Collins. Just like the guy from *Dark Shadows*. Says so on his driver's license."

"Five bucks says it didn't say that on his birth certificate."

"Sucker bet. No thanks." He looked back at the report. "The last one is a kid named Dennis Knight. Sixteen. Everybody calls him Dark Knight, even his mother, who confirms the group was hanging out at her place."

"She reliable?"

"Didn't strike me that way. House smelled like pot, and there was alcohol on her breath. Twitchy, too. Betcha fifty bucks she's using, and that would be a sucker bet too." He took a swig from his bottle and said, "Parker's new boy toy found the body."

My jaw tightened. "How old?"

"Fifteen."

"Son of a bitch." I didn't mean the kid.

"Kid's name's Byron Birch. Says he was at the gym. Logbook there backs him up."

"And the girl?"

His phone shrilled again. He pulled it out, glanced at the caller ID, rolled his eyes, and put it back in his pocket.

"Malone again?"

"Suspicious bitch."

"Should we get back? I don't want to jam you up."

"Little late for that, don't you think?" He cleared his throat and said, "The girl. Not talking. She definitely handled the knife. But whether she took a few whacks at him, or whether she just watched, I couldn't say. She wouldn't give us any details, just kept saying she did it alone. Which, as we know, is bullshit."

"Why confess and then not talk?" I picked up the arrest report and scanned it. "Says he was killed between twelve and two in the afternoon. Odd time for a blood sacrifice. Especially for a bunch of vampires. That all you have on the girl? The fingerprints and the confession?"

The musicians started a new song, a bastardized Christmas carol. *On the first day of Christmas, my true love gave to me . . . a fifty-inch HD TV.* Frank took a swig of Bud and said, "It was enough to hold her. If she's whacked enough to kill this guy, she's whacked enough to keep killing."

"Remorse?"

"Judge for yourself." He rifled through the folder, found the transcript of the girl's confession, and tossed it across the table.

I skimmed the report. When I'd finished, I said, "As confessions go, it's not much."

"I've seen flimsier." He popped another fry, took his time chewing. Finally, he said, "You were a cop for a long time."

"Long time," I agreed. Uniformed patrol officer to undercover vice officer to homicide detective to outsider. Nose to the window like a homeless, hungry kid.

He said, "You're gonna make the whole department look like a bunch of schmucks."

"That's not my intention."

"But?"

"But I will tear this department apart if that's what it takes to get Josh out from under this thing."

He sighed. "I thought you might say that."

The phone in his jacket shrilled. This time he reached in and turned it off without looking. An angry flush spread upward from beneath his collar.

"You gotta get back," I said.

"Guess so." He stared glumly at his nearly empty bottle.

"I might need to ask you for a few favors. Run a tag, match a fingerprint."

"We'll see. I'm not saying no. I'm just saying, don't count your chickens. See where it leads."

"Let's start with this, then. You don't think it was a ritual killing, do you? Not even a made-up one."

"I don't know, Cowboy." He downed the last of his beer and thunked the bottle down on the table. Gave me a dour grin. "Take away the trappings, and there was a lot of random stabbing. This one feels personal."

CHAPTER FIVE

We stopped at Kinko's and made a copy of the file. I put it in my glove compartment, then zipped the original under my coat and headed back to Frank's office. Malone met us in the lobby, lips pressed together, arms folded across the chest of her tailored black pantsuit. Even angry, she looked damn good. She shot me a scowl and said, "I heard you were trouble."

I forced a grin. Mr. Innocent. "You shouldn't believe everything you hear."

She rolled her eyes, then turned a chilly gaze toward Frank. "You. Campanella. In my office. Now."

He reddened, gave me a cursory nod, and stalked, stiff-backed, toward her office. When he'd gone, she leveled her gaze at me and said, "You're not doing him any favors."

"Neither are you."

"He's a pigheaded dinosaur. It's not my job to do him favors."

"What is your job?" I asked.

She flashed me a middle finger and strode back toward her office.

I waited until she turned the corner, then went back to Frank's cubicle and tucked the Parker file under the Peeping Tom folder. On the way out, I waved at the skinny kid behind the glass, but he didn't wave back. Immersed in his book.

With ice crusting the streets and the traffic in a snarl, I decided to shower and shave at my office, one of six suites in a renovated building that had begun life as a boarding house a few blocks from Vanderbilt Hospital and University. One of my co-renters had wound the porch columns with strands of plastic lights shaped like jalapeño peppers. The place looked like the bastard child of a Victorian dollhouse and a cheap Mexican restaurant.

We were a mismatched lot, but the rent was reasonable. 1-A was a counselor to battered women. Her clients passed me in the hall from time to time, some timid, some defensive, most stepping wide to avoid me as if I were a water moccasin. Across from her, a group of aging hippies called themselves the Society for the Legalization of Psychotropic Substances and occasionally slipped pro-LSD flyers through my mail slot. On the second floor, a nondescript man who shuffled nondescript packages to and from Bangkok and Shanghai worked across the hall from an elderly woman who ran a quaint little business called "Strip-o-Grams." I saw her ladies on the stairs sometimes too, sequined and feathered as they headed out to work, or scrubbed fresh in jeans and oversized sweatshirts after. Sometimes they were the same women I saw in 1-A.

My office, Maverick Investigations, was on the third floor across the hall from an empty suite. Two doors led from the outer office, where my desk sat, to the rest of the apartment—shower, kitchenette, and a former bedroom that now housed surveillance equipment, a hodgepodge of indispensible gadgetry, and a walk-in closet for extra clothes and my theatrical kit.

After exchanging my damp jeans and chambray shirt for a gray suit and a blue silk tie, I looked through Razor's case file for the name of Absinthe's attorney. Aleta Thomas.

I stared at the name. Five feet nothing on her tiptoes, with wrists the size of wishbones, Miss Aleta was nothing but bone and gristle beneath a seventy-five-year-old veneer of southern grace. Many a hapless prosecutor had cause to regret mistaking her wry charm for weakness.

I found her name in my Rolodex and punched in the number. After the usual half-dozen transfers, someone finally took pity and put me through. A moment later, she drawled, "Laws, child, I didn't expect to hear from you again."

"I know, Miss Aleta. Life's funny that way."

"Life's funny a lot of ways. But you didn't call me to talk philosophy."

"No ma'am. I called you to ask if I could talk to one of your clients, Absi—" I stopped myself. "Laurel O'Brien. The Parker case."

A brittle note came into her voice. "Now, what might a man like you want with Laurel O'Brien?"

"A man like me?"

"Take that any way you want, honey." She chuckled softly, without humor. "You boys in blue spend your whole lives finding ways to make folks look guilty—"

"We don't *make* anybody look guilty. We just prove it when they are."

"That's how you see it, I guess. My point is, what would make me think you got my client's best interests at heart?"

"She was with my nephew that morning," I said. "They skipped school, must've met somewhere. You can imagine how that looked when she confessed to Razor's murder."

"And this should ease my mind, why? Don't tell me you wouldn't toss Laurel to the hogs if you could pin this on her instead of your nephew."

"I don't need to pin anything on her," I said. "She pinned it on herself. But Josh wasn't part of this, and if she was with him, she wasn't part of it either. Anything I learn that could help Josh is going to help her too."

"If they were still together when the victim was killed."

"Look," I said. "You and I both know that girl did not slash Razor's throat, hang him up to bleed, and then pose him on that pentagram. But somebody did. I can find him for you."

"All by your lonesome."

"Just let me talk to the girl. You can be there if you want."

"Oh, I will. I surely will." She heaved a long-suffering sigh. "Tomorrow morning, then. Ten sharp. Don't be late. And if I catch even a whiff of a double-cross, I'll shut you down faster than a hound on a ham bone."

I assured her there would be no double-cross and hung up. A few minutes later, I eased the Silverado onto the highway and headed south between a battered Ford pickup and a fuchsia minivan that skidded across the yellow line at every curve.

Perfect weather for a funeral.

CHAPTER SIX

I'd expected Razor's funeral to be delayed because of the autopsy. Sometimes it took weeks to get the tests done and the body released, but the Parker case was high profile and the Parker family well off, and for once, the wheels of justice spun like they'd just been oiled. Maybe they had.

The funeral home was a venerable brick building with a modern extension that stretched toward the surrounding memorial gardens like a prosthetic arm. A knot of kids in Goth garb crowded around the front door. A young woman in a scarlet evening gown and black hooded cloak stood nose-to-nose with an older woman, a slim brunette who was under-dressed for the cold in a tight black skirt and matching bolero jacket. Long legs, narrow hips, small waist. Behind her, a twenty-something guy in an expensive suit shuffled anxiously from foot to foot. The woman's features were delicate, the young man's coarse. They looked like they'd been sculpted by the same artist, but one of them had been left unfinished.

I touched my fingertips to my chest, where the Glock in my shoulder holster made a barely perceptible bulge in my coat. I probably wouldn't need it. But my father hadn't thought he'd need his piece either when he went out to buy cigarettes and walked in on a convenience store robbery. Died a hero, the newspaper said, but maybe he wouldn't have died at all if he'd had a Desert Eagle under his jacket.

I swung out of the Silverado. Gasped as my left foot skidded on the gravel and a needle of pain lanced through my calf. Annoyed, I took a moment to let the pain ebb, then crunched across the parking lot toward the clot of disenchanted youth.

The girl in the cloak and scarlet gown gestured angrily toward the building. I recognized her thin face and wild, mascara-rimmed eyes. She called herself Medea, after some nutcase from Greek mythology who murdered her children to spite her cheating husband.

Sweet.

Like Razor, she fancied herself dangerous. She reminded me of a rabid kitten. "We were his friends," she said. "We have a right to be here."

"A right?" The dark-haired woman arched a perfectly shaped brow, a careless gesture belied by the frayed tissue clenched in her fist. She had the figure of a co-ed, but a spray of faint lines around her lips and at the corners of her eyes betrayed her age. The icy mist had ruined her makeup and flattened her hair. "You have no rights, as far as my son is concerned."

Her son. I searched her face for some clue that she'd known he was a monster. Saw only love and grief, and knew that, to her, it wouldn't have mattered. She looked a lot like Razor, I realized. Lean build, fair skin, otter-dark hair. A hint of Eastern Europe in her face, which had good angles and fine, symmetrical features.

A Goth-looking guy in tight leather pants and a red velvet pirate shirt leaned in and jabbed an accusing finger at Razor's mother. "Razor hated you," he said. Up close, he looked older. Maybe mid-twenties. I mentally ran down the descriptions in Razor's file and pegged him as Barnabus Collins.

The other boy, pimple-faced, in black jeans and a leather bomber jacket, nodded. "We were his real family."

The woman's chin quivered. "You have three minutes to get off the premises before I call the police," she said.

"You don't—" Medea began. I stepped between them, and her eyes widened. "I know you," she said.

"Time to go." I nodded toward the parking lot.

"Mind your own business, dickwad." Medea thrust out her chin and clenched her fists against her sides. "You think Razor wanted some phony-ass Christian funeral?"

"Razor is dead. This is for his family."

She crossed her arms against the cold, pressing her small breasts flat against her bony chest, then rubbed her forearms with her palms and glared at Razor's mother. "She's got no right to keep us out."

The young man in the suit, presumably Razor's brother, stepped forward and said, "The police—"

His mother cut him off with a gesture. "Stay out of this, Heath."

Heath flushed from collar to hairline, and the boy in the bomber jacket—Dennis Knight?—said with a smirk, "Police eat shit."

I nodded. Smiled. "And they're noted for their loving kindness to smartass punks who give them a hard time."

For a long moment, we stared each other down. Then Medea made a sweeping gesture that ended with a sharp jab to the air in front of my face. "Remember this," she said. "When your world falls all to hell."

I didn't believe in magic spells or voodoo curses. I didn't believe in vampires or witches or things that go bump in the night. The only monsters I had ever seen were human. All the same, just for a moment, the wildness in her face made my stomach clench.

Then the moment passed. I looked her in the eye and laughed. "Bring it on."

"You'll see," she said. She spun around and scuttled down the path with a hunching, spider-like gait. The boys sauntered after her, scowling theatrically, thumbs hitched into their pants pockets.

"Looks like I've been hexed," I said.

Razor's mother forced a smile and dabbed a finger at the wet mascara smudges under her eyes. "Thank you," she said.

"Friends of your son's?" I asked.

She made a sour face. "That would be stating it generously. First they kill him, and now they want to dance at his funeral."

"Did they?" I said. "Kill him?"

"One way or the other. I'm Elaina."

"Jared." I held the door open, and she went in first. Heath followed sullenly.

"You should see Sebastian," she said, and guided me forward with her fingertips. "Heath, would you get Mummy a cup of coffee?"

Heath bent from the waist in an exaggerated bow. "Of course. Anything for *Mummy.*"

As we stood beside the chrome-edged casket at the front of the chapel, Elaina reached into the coffin and straightened Razor's tie. "He looks beautiful, doesn't he?"

He'd been dressed in a traditional dark suit, probably the first he'd worn in years. The flesh-colored foundation and the hint of peach blush applied to his face made him look oddly more alive than he had the last time I'd seen him.

"He looks . . . peaceful," I said.

There was an awkward silence. Then Heath appeared with the coffee and handed a cup to his mother.

"Thank you, dear," Elaina said, wrapping her long tapered fingers around the cup and dismissing him with a nod. She gave me a vacant smile, scanned the room with glazed eyes. The altercation in the parking lot had probably taken everything she had. Her gaze slid to another mourner.

"If you'll excuse me," she said, and drifted away. The weight of her grief went with her, and I was relieved when she went.

I turned from the coffin just in time to see Josh slip into the chapel. He looked my way and pulled up short, eyes widening.

I watched him think it through. Had I seen him yet? Could he duck out of sight before I did? Then his shoulders slumped and he headed in my direction.

He wore a black suit with a black shirt and a red silk tie that stood out against all that blackness like a wound. He'd grown taller in the last few months, and his limbs seemed at a loss as to what to do with themselves. His eyes were watery and rimmed with red, and I thought he looked exceptionally young and vulnerable, like a newborn giraffe.

He glanced into the coffin and swallowed hard. Jammed his hands into his pockets. My gaze flicked to his wrists, where the bandages peeked out from his jacket sleeves.

"Hi," he said.

"Hi." I gave his shoulder an awkward pat. "Does Randall know you're here?"

"Are you going to tell him?"

"I haven't decided. What are you doing here?"

"I could ask you the same thing."

"You asked me to investigate."

"At his funeral?"

"You'd be surprised what you can pick up at a funeral."

He pushed a shock of hair away from his forehead. "I don't know. It seems . . . disrespectful."

"Do you want me to be respectful, or do you want me to find out who killed him?"

"Both." He reached into the casket and laid a hand on Razor's cheek. I wanted to slap it away. Knew it would be a mistake. "He would have hated this. He would have wanted to be buried in something extravagant and elegant."

The last time I'd seen Razor, he'd been wearing black trousers with laces up both sides, a white silk shirt with a ruffled front, and a crushed velvet jacket with antique brass buttons. Black lips. White foundation. He'd looked like an undead highwayman. Elaborate, sure. Memorable, even. But elegant? That was debatable.

After the service, a traditional ceremony with hymns and a sermon, we followed the shivering procession across the parking lot to the cemetery for the graveside service. The grave was a frozen gash at the top of a short slope, where the family sat in folding chairs beneath a canopy. The rest of us stood at the bottom of the slope, shuffling our feet for warmth and wiping sleet from our eyes.

"Do they always go on and on like this?" Josh whispered. When I put a hand on his shoulder, I could feel him trembling. Maybe from cold. Maybe from grief. Maybe a bit of both. It pissed me off that Razor still had a hold on him. "How can they stand it?"

I shrugged off my coat and slipped it around his shoulders. "Delaying the inevitable," I whispered back. "They don't want to put him in the ground."

I flipped up my collar and tucked my hands under my armpits to keep warm. While the preacher droned on, I scanned the crowd. Nobody looked out of place. Nobody stood up and confessed to Razor's murder. Then Josh nudged me with his elbow and nodded toward a blond boy at the back of the crowd. "That's Byron. Byron Birch. He and Razor were . . ." He rubbed his hands together and blew on them to warm them with his breath. "You know. After Razor and I broke up."

I remembered Byron's name from the police report. He'd worked out at the gym, gone to a movie, picked up a sack full of Krystal burgers, and come home to find a bloodbath in his living room.

The kid was about Josh's age, blond as an Aryan wet dream and with the kind of looks that draw predators out of the woodwork. His navy blue suit was too short in the sleeves and too tight across the chest, and his eyes were bloodshot and swollen.

"He's not Goth," I said.

"He's a jock," Josh said, as if that explained something. Maybe it did.

A man in a long wool coat, open to reveal a tailored black suit, stood beside Byron, a proprietary hand on the boy's shoulder.

"Who's that?" I asked Josh.

"Alan Keating. A friend of Razor's. From before."

"Before?"

Josh looked uncomfortable, and I knew what he meant. The only thing that really mattered. *Before me.* "Back in the old days," he said. "I think they went to school together or something."

Even with his suit damp and his dark hair stiff with sleet, Keating looked like he'd stepped out of a magazine. Sun-bed tan, conservatively styled hair, gold tips attached to his starched white collar. His tie was lavender, the tie tack embellished with a loop of gold chain. He looked to be in his late twenties, which should have made him too old for Razor's taste. Certainly, he was too old for Byron.

My fists clenched at my sides.

Josh said, "It's not like Byron was some little virgin or anything, anyway. Angel Face was hustling tricks way before he took up with Razor."

The minister finished his speech and the mourners fluttered into bunches like a flock of half-frozen but well-dressed ravens.

I made my way toward Byron, catching snippets of conversation as I passed. Josh trailed along behind me.

". . . his poor mother . . ."

"Maybe now she'll give Heath the time of day . . ."

". . . Sebastian . . . freakish, last time I saw him . . ."

". . . so very sorry for your loss . . ."

". . . so sorry for your loss . . ."

". . . so sorry."

I caught up to Byron and touched his sleeve just as he and Keating turned away. Byron looked blankly at my extended hand for a moment before clasping it in his own, and his smile flashed half a beat too late. His eyes were glazed. I thought of the pharmaceuticals found in Razor's house and wondered if Byron had been medicated. If Keating had medicated him.

"Byron Birch?" I said.

"Do I know you?"

"This may not be the best time, but—"

"I still can't believe it." His hands were trembling, and he jammed them into his pockets when he realized I had noticed. "He's the most . . . alive . . . person I ever met. How can he just be gone?"

He still spoke in the present tense, as if he hadn't fully processed the fact that Razor was dead.

A mechanical whirr interrupted the conversation as the coffin began its descent into the grave. The crowd began to disperse, and Elaina gave us a narrow look before Heath guided her away.

"She hates me," Byron said. "I don't know why. I didn't kill him."

"No," I agreed, though I had no idea if this was true. "But you probably know the people who did."

Keating shifted forward so that one shoulder edged into the space between Byron and me. Protecting a troubled kid, or staking out his territory? He said, "And you are?"

"Jared McKean." I extended my hand. His grip was firmer than I'd expected. "I'm investigating Razor's murder."

"You're a homicide detective?" His speech sounded unnaturally formal, as if he'd learned English from a dictionary. No trace of an accent. I figured the formality was an affectation.

"Private investigator. I'm working with Laurel O'Brien's attorney." This was not entirely untrue. "Is Byron staying with you?"

There must have been a note of menace in my voice, because both Josh and Byron turned startled faces in my direction. Keating shrugged and forced a smile that was more grimace than grin. "Everybody's got to be somewhere."

"You know he's a minor."

"So for that, I should make him sleep on the streets?"

Behind us, the Bobcat rumbled to life. Even amidst the subdued chatter of the retreating mourners, it sounded obscene. Harsh and ugly as death itself. Fitting, maybe, for this death, which had been especially ugly, but in general I preferred the respectful sound of shovels crunching into earth. It seemed a small enough concession, for a man's grave to be dug by human hands.

Though in Razor's case, it might have been more appropriate to dump the body in a landfill and cover it with compost.

Keating looked over my shoulder toward the sound, and his expression changed. Wary, with a touch of pity.

I turned to follow his gaze. A woman in a gray wool coat had made her way down the icy embankment and was watching us in much the way an injured bird will watch a cat.

She looked to be in her early forties. A thatch of gray-streaked curls framed a square-jawed Mediterranean face. Her deep-set eyes were the color of moss.

Keating's nod was almost imperceptible. "Mrs. Savales."

Josh and I must have registered somewhere on the edges of her radar, because she flashed us a distracted, fleeting smile as she passed. Then she leaned forward, puckered her lips, and spat onto the toe of Keating's expensive Italian shoe.

He tilted the toe up and waggled it from side to side. "I hope that made you feel better," he said.

She wiped angrily at her eyes. "What would make me feel better . . . But you can't give me that, can you?"

"No," he said. "I wish I could."

Her shoulders jerked as if he'd struck her. Then she turned and picked her way up the slope, purse clutched against her stomach, back straight. She walked stiffly, pausing between each step to pull the pointed heels of her pumps out of the ground.

"Who was that?" I said.

His smile was wry. "A fan."

"I can see that." A dozen questions tumbled into my mind, but Josh was shivering violently even beneath my coat. I took a notepad and a ballpoint pen from my jacket pocket and handed them to Keating. "Mind giving me an address and a number where I can reach you?"

"Do I mind?" Ignoring my utilitarian Bic, he drew a gold Mont Blanc pen from his pocket and scribbled something on the back of a business card. I swallowed my annoyance and tucked my disposable pen back into my jacket, letting the lapel fall back slowly enough to give him a glimpse of the shoulder rig. His eyes flicked to the gun, then back to my face. "Somehow," he said, "I don't think that's really much of a consideration. Whether or not I mind."

"I'll find out what I want to know," I said. "One way or the other."

"I'm sure you will. But by all means, give me a call." He held out the card between two fingers. "Byron, of course, will have to decide for himself."

CHAPTER SEVEN

As Byron and Keating pulled away in Keating's Buick Skylark, Josh turned to me and asked, "What was that? Some kind of pissing contest?"

"Something like that. How'd you get here, anyway?"

"Hitched. Don't say it, I know it was stupid."

It was. I opened my mouth to deliver a lecture. Closed it again. What could I say that he didn't already know? "Come on. I'll give you a ride home."

"Could we just drive around for awhile?"

"Roads are getting pretty bad."

"Just for a little while."

We drove past a mall that had been dying since the seventies, cruised through the parking lot of a movie theater shaped like a jukebox, and crossed onto Bransford past a row of specialty shops draped in Christmas lights. While I drove, Josh closed his eyes and leaned his temple against the passenger-side window. I wondered what I should say, or if I should say anything at all.

We passed the darkened fairgrounds and came back out onto I-65 on the south side of town. The city came into view, the double antennae of the AT&T Batman building stretching up past the L&C tower and the rotating restaurant at the top of the old Hyatt Regency hotel. With the ice glistening in the lights, it may have been the most beautiful skyline in the world.

I glanced over at Josh and said, "Why'd you do it?"

He lifted his head. "I wanted to see the funeral."

"No." I nodded toward his wrists. "Why'd you do that?"

"You know you're the first person who's asked me that? I mean, besides my therapist. Everyone's so freaked thinking if they ask, I'll do it again. Like I'll go right over the edge or something."

"You came pretty close to it already."

"I know. It's complicated. Like . . ." He pressed his head hard against the window. "I can't explain it."

"Can't?"

He shrugged. I wanted to ask why he hadn't told me he was with Absinthe an hour before Razor's murder, but something in his face told me this wasn't the right time. Instead, I swung onto the 440 bypass loop, then onto the West End ramp. Past Centennial Park, where the full-sized replica of the Parthenon glowed in the mist, pale pillars lit with green and red. Not for nothing is Nashville called the Athens of the South. We drove to Music Row, circled the classical nude bronze Musica statue and headed back toward the Interstate. Passed a six-foot fiberglass catfish in a cowboy hat, and a few yards away, a man playing a guitar on the sidewalk. A Weimaraner dressed in an army uniform shivered at his feet.

Josh leaned over me for a better look. "Can we give them something, Uncle Jared? It's freezing out there."

I glanced into the rearview mirror, saw there was no one behind me, and slid to a stop. Rolled down my window and waved the musician over to the truck. He slung the guitar strap over his shoulder and picked his way across the slick street. He was about sixty, stiff with arthritis, or maybe just half frozen. The dog padded behind him, tail wagging. I stepped out of the truck, motioned Josh to stay inside, and shut the door behind me. Just in case.

I handed the musician a twenty, and he pocketed it with a grateful smile.

"Bless you, sir. God bless you."

I said, "You know Kaizen? Shelter over near the bus station?"

"I heard of it. Why?"

"Guy who runs it is a friend of mine."

He nodded toward the dog. "Can't keep Charley in no shelter."

"Ask for Billy Mean," I said. "Tell him Jared sent you. He'll let you keep your dog."

"Billy Mean," he said. "I heard of him. Some kind of badass in Vietnam."

"Long time ago," I said.

"Not to me."

It was a long walk, so I loaded them into the back of the truck, drove to Billy's, and dropped them off. Randall would kill me if he knew I was picking up strangers with Josh in the truck, but I was pretty sure Josh wouldn't tell him.

The musician turned back at the door. "Bless you, sir," he said again. "Bless you both."

From the passenger seat, Josh waved goodbye, looking happier than he had in months. It had probably been awhile since he'd felt like he'd done something good, or at least caused something good to happen. He needed more of that. As we pulled away, I looked at him and said, "Can you get me into one of those vampire games? The kind Razor and his buddies played?"

"Razor didn't play. Razor just *was*."

"All right. Whatever. But the others. They told the police they were playing the day—" I stopped.

"The day Razor died. I know. But Mom and Dad don't let me play anymore. Maybe if you told them I was helping you out with an investigation—"

"Never mind. It was a bad idea."

"But if you saw what it was really like. I mean, if you told them it was no big deal—"

"Josh . . ."

He gave me a big-eyed, pleading look. When he was five, I'd bought him a big-kid bike because of it. "Please?" he said. "If you'd just check it out, I know you'd see it isn't like you think it is. It's not all weird and gruesome."

"You guys drink blood. How much more weird and gruesome could you be?"

His fist clenched against the side of his thigh. "That's not part of the game. Most of the people who play don't even do that. Razor was just a little . . ." He stopped.

"Extreme? Perverse? Sociopathic?"

"Eccentric."

I snorted, and he turned his face away, back toward the window.

"Anyway," he said, "why are you doing this if you hated him so much? Whoever killed him did the world a favor, right?"

"I'm doing this because you asked me to."

"But you think he deserved it?"

"That's not for me to say."

In the long, uncomfortable silence that followed, we swung onto Briley Parkway and cruised past the gold glass International Plaza building. It glistened like a Christmas ornament in the icy mist. Then Josh said, "Please, Uncle Jared? I've done everything they've asked me to. Ever since you brought me home last summer. I make curfew every night. I'm seeing a counselor. She's lame, and she doesn't understand about the game, but even she says Mom and Dad should check it out. They won't, I know that. But they'd believe you if you told them it was okay."

"And if I don't think it's okay?"

"You will. But I wouldn't ask you to lie. I know you wouldn't, anyway."

I thought about it. What could it hurt? Josh could be my passport to the vampire culture, and if there seemed to be anything harmful about it, I could make sure he never went back.

Never being a relative term. Once he turned eighteen, all bets were off, all influence null and void.

"I'll think about it," I said.

He turned back toward the window, but not in time to hide his smile.

—⟳—

I hadn't even stopped the truck before Randall opened his front door and stepped out onto the porch. He watched us through squinted eyes, pulled a pack of Marlboros out of his pocket, and tapped one out into his palm. I hated that he was smoking again, but ragging him about it would only make him defensive.

"Shit," muttered Josh, then cut his gaze toward me. "Sorry."

"I've heard the word before."

"He's gonna kill me." He slid out of the passenger seat and slunk toward the house, head low. I turned off the ignition and followed.

When we were almost to the porch, Randall jerked his head toward the house. "Your mom was worried," he said to Josh.

Josh bobbed his head even lower. "I'm sorry."

"Tell it to your mother."

As Josh ducked around his father and into the house, Randall turned to me and said, "You took him to the funeral."

"No. I brought him back from it."

"I didn't want him to go."

"I know."

He looked off into the distance, hunched a shoulder. "It's good you were there, I guess. He'd rather have you there than me, anyway."

"It's not about that."

"Right."

"If I was his dad, he'd be coming to you." I wasn't sure this was true. I thought I was a pretty cool dad. Way cooler than Randall, but it didn't seem like a good time to say so.

"Hell." He rolled the cigarette between his fingers, stuck it between his lips, took it out again and pointed it at me. "This isn't coming out right."

"You're welcome," I said.

He barked a short, embarrassed laugh and I laughed with him, glad of the moment. We hadn't laughed at all since I'd found Josh fading out of consciousness in that tub of bloody water. It was about time.

"You want to come in for a beer?" he asked.

"Next time."

He took a long drag from his cigarette. Then he said, "I hope you spit on the son of a bitch for me."

"Where he is, he'd probably appreciate it."

I watched him in the rearview mirror as I pulled away. He was a big man, but he looked small standing there, smoke curling from his cigarette and up into the mottled winter sky. I considered turning the truck around, taking him up on that beer.

But it was getting late, and the icy mix was still coming down, and I wanted to get home before the roads got any more treacherous. There were a thousand good reasons not to go inside and have a drink with my brother.

None of them should have been good enough.

CHAPTER EIGHT

The house I lived in, a two-story Victorian-style farmhouse with a wraparound porch, was a fifteen-minute drive from my brother's. The rutted gravel driveway wound for almost a quarter mile through a corridor of trees—white oak, red cedar, slippery elm, Virginia pine. From spring to fall, the house was invisible from the road, but now, with the hardwoods barren and only the evergreens in full foliage, you could catch glimpses of the house and barn through the tangle of branches.

I rounded the last curve, and the corridor opened on either side. The barn and pasture flashed by on my right. The horses looked up as I passed, then resumed munching on a round bale in the middle of the pasture.

Just ahead, my housemate, Jay Renfield, stood at the bottom of an extension ladder propped against the porch roof. Bundled up in a multicolored parka like some kind of pop art Eskimo, he was playing out a string of Christmas lights like a fishing line, while his lover, Eric the Viking, perched at the top of the ladder, hanging the other end of the lights along the eaves.

Jay and I had met in kindergarten, but lost touch after high school. He ran off with a bleached blond biker boy with a Marilyn Monroe tattoo, was disowned by his family, and went on to become a computer programmer, making a small but comfortable fortune designing games and graphics. I joined the force, got married, had a son. Our paths didn't cross. Part of it was that we moved in different circles, but I'd be lying if I didn't admit that part of it was a certain amount of discomfort with his homosexuality. I'm not proud of that, but it's true.

Years later, he called me up out of the blue and told me that the biker boy had left him with a broken heart, a dozen maxed-out credit cards, and a virus that would destroy his immune system.

Son of a bitch.

When I found myself divorced, unemployed, and rudderless, he offered me a place to stay. Cheap rent, swimming pool, and a place to board my horses. In return, I played chauffeur when he was too sick to drive, nursed him through night sweats and night terrors, and did odd jobs around the place. It was hard to tell which of us was getting the better end of the deal, so we just called it even.

Eric the Viking waved with his free hand as I approached the house. "Hey, Cowboy. Deck the halls and all that jazz."

"We'll be done here in a minute." Jay's breath coalesced in front of him like a disembodied spirit. "There's hot chocolate in the kitchen."

I gave him a two-fingered salute and went inside to pour myself a steaming cup of cocoa.

The kitchen smelled of sugar and warm milk. A pot of hot chocolate simmered on the stove. Draped across the back of my chair was my father's leather bomber jacket, the one I'd been wearing when I found Josh. Unwilling to part with it, I'd stuffed it into the back of the closet when soaking and scrubbing failed to remove the stains.

I checked the cuffs for blood. They were clean.

I put it on and stepped back out onto the porch.

"Hey," I said.

Jay looked up. Smiled. "You found it."

"How'd you get rid of the blood?"

"Enzymes."

I laid my hand over my heart and bowed my head in his direction. "I owe you one."

"You owe me more than one," he said, grinning. "But anyway, you're welcome."

—m—

Upstairs, I lay on my bed and studied the Parker file. Started with the police report and worked through it page by page and photo by photo. I didn't take notes. Not yet. Later, I'd attack the file with colored pens and highlighters, but for now, I just wanted to get a feel for the case.

Somewhere in the back of my mind, I registered the phone ringing, a gust of cold air, the front door smacking shut, footsteps, Jay's voice. Casual, then concerned. It was the change in his tone that caught my attention. He sounded like he'd just been invited to his own execution.

I pushed aside the file I was reading and went to lean in the doorway of the kitchen, where he was setting the receiver back in its cradle.

"Trouble?" I asked.

He tucked one hand under the other armpit and stared at the wall in front of him. His face was still red with cold and his hair was rumpled. The knit cap he'd been wearing lay on the counter beside the phone, like a deflated caterpillar.

"That was Greg." His voice sounded strained. "I don't think you've ever met him. Dylan got him in the settlement."

I nodded. There's always a settlement. After every breakup, mutual friends choose one member of a couple over the other. It happened when Maria and I divorced, and it's just as true of gay couples as it is of straight ones.

"What did he want?" I said.

He squeezed his eyes shut and gave his head a small shake. Then, "Dylan's dying," he said.

Dylan. The biker boy with the bleached blond hair. The fucking bastard who'd given Jay AIDS.

"Good," I said.

He looked at me sharply. "He's got no place to go."

"What about Greg?"

Jay picked up the caterpillar cap and twisted it in his hands. "Greg's a fabulous person, but he doesn't deal well with suffering."

"And the punk he left you for?"

– 54 –

"Bailed when Dylan started to show symptoms. Poor Dyl. I don't think anyone ever left him before in his life."

"Poor baby."

"You think I'm a sap."

"He gave you AIDS."

"He didn't mean to." He turned the cap inside out, rubbed the ribbing between his fingers. "I need to do this, Jared."

"Do what?" I asked. Jay looked at me, and it suddenly came clear. "You mean, bring him here?"

"He's all alone. There's nobody to take care of him. Can you imagine what that must be like?"

"Let his family deal with him."

"His parents are dead. Car wreck. They hadn't spoken to him since he came out." He looked away, but not before I saw the muscles in his jaw twitch. Jay's parents had washed their hands of him when he'd told them he was gay. "He doesn't have anybody else," he said again.

I ran my tongue between my teeth and upper lip and tried to think of something clever to say. Instead, "It's your house," I said. "You can bring anybody into it you want."

He said, "You'll love him, you know. You think you'll hate him. You'll *want* to hate him. But you won't."

"I guess we'll see."

"It's not all altruism." He traced an invisible circle on the blue mosaic counter with his finger. "Maybe I'm just gratified that I'm the one he has to come back to."

"I'm not the one you have to convince," I said. "Don't you think Eric might have a little problem with this?"

"I love Eric. He knows that. He'll understand."

I gave Jay's shoulder a quick pat and sauntered upstairs, leaving him to break the news to his current lover that his former lover was coming home to die.

I wasn't sure if I was being a coward or just minding my own business.

I found a pen in the drawer of my bedside table and flopped down on the bed with my copy of the Parker file. I went through it again, occasionally scrawling a note in a margin. People to interview, questions to ask.

Downstairs, voices rose and fell in tones of anger and betrayal. When the door slammed shortly after midnight and the house fell into an empty silence, I knew Jay had been wrong. Eric had not understood.

CHAPTER NINE

When Maria and I divorced, I took the horses on twenty-mile trail rides, baled hay until my shoulders ached and sweat glued my shirt to my back, sparred at the dojang until my lungs burned. Jay had a different way of coping, and I awoke to the mingled scents of dark roast coffee and blueberry muffins. If he and Eric didn't patch things up, we'd be eating cookies and cobbler until New Year's.

Blearily, I stumbled down to breakfast barefoot and blue-jeaned, scratching my stomach and stifling yawns. Jay looked up as I plopped into my chair and reached for the steaming mug he'd placed beside my plate.

"You missed a button," he said, gesturing toward my shirt. His smile was weak, embarrassed. "I guess you heard?"

I fumbled to realign my buttons. "A little."

"It doesn't change anything."

Jay set a plateful of muffins on the table between us and scooted onto his chair. A coffee cup full of immune-boosters, protease inhibitors, and Shaklee vitamin supplements sat beside his plate. He said, "Do you think I should call him?"

"Eric or Dylan?"

"Eric."

"I don't know. I guess that's up to you."

"You aren't helping."

"Jay, I'm sorry. I—"

"No, it's all right. It isn't fair of me to put you in the middle of it." He picked up a muffin, made a neat incision in it, and tucked a pat of butter into the slit. Then he set it down carefully and slid it to the far side of his plate. "If I bring Dylan here . . . are you going to walk out too?"

"You know better," I said.

I was relieved when he finally pushed his plate away and started to clear the table. I pushed away too. I had a couple of hours before I had to meet with Miss Aleta and her client. "I'll be in the barn."

He forced a smile. "Say hello to the boys for me."

The barn smelled of hay, fresh earth, sawdust, and leather oil. The sweet-sweat-and-dry-dust scent of the horses. Dakota, the rescued Arabian, arched his neck across the stall opening. I fed him a handful of oats, brushed a few stray grains from his lips, and laid my palm flat against his nose so I could feel his breath. Rubbed the scar tissue around his blind eye. Four months ago, he would have flinched. Now he rubbed his head against my palm and whickered.

I brushed the caked mud from the horses' winter coats and picked out their hooves, then returned them to their stalls, which were open to the pasture. Dakota and the Tennessee Walker, Crockett, trotted out into the pale winter sunlight. Tex, the Quarter Horse I'd run poles and barrels on when I was a kid, nuzzled my hand with his graying muzzle. I raked my fingers through his mane and plucked a burr from the pale, coarse hair. Thought of Androcles, though there was nothing lion-like about the palomino gelding. He gave my palm a long lick before plodding out to join the others. His limp, the residual effect of a damaged tendon, was barely noticeable. A lot like mine.

By the time I'd put out their hay and checked on the heating element in the watering trough, I was shivering. It would have been a good day to curl up in bed with a thick blanket and a warm woman. Instead, I shrugged on my dad's leather jacket, locked my Glock and shoulder holster in the glove compartment, and drove downtown to the juvenile detention center where Absinthe was being held. The wheels of justice had already begun to grind, and in a day or so, a judge would decide whether or not the heinousness of Razor's murder merited a transfer to adult court. If so, she'd be moved to the Metro jail a few blocks over, but for now she was still in the juvenile system.

Miss Aleta met me on the other side of the security checkpoint, her hand extended in greeting. I plucked my keys from the plastic container and stuffed them into my pocket, then clasped her proffered hand. The bones felt fragile, and I thought that if I squeezed too hard, the hand would crumble in my palm like a dry leaf.

"You remember what I told you," she said. "I'll be listening."

"I remember."

I followed her past the courtrooms and a bulletin board where rows of clipboards hung on nails announced the day's court dockets. Just beyond the stairwell was the door to the detention facility, and beyond that was another checkpoint, where I left my keys with a pleasant-looking woman behind a glass partition. She gave me an appraising smile and gestured me through the electronic security gate. Miss Aleta went around the gate and opened one of the small lockers mounted on the wall. She rummaged through her purse for a pen and a memo tablet, then stuffed the purse into the locker. The woman behind the partition buzzed us through the heavy security door, and we stepped into the corridor that led to processing.

To our left was a visitation room that doubled as a training room for new hires. We passed through it to a smaller room, bare except for a table and four cushioned office chairs, two on each side. No partition, like there would have been in the Metro jailhouse, just a plate glass window between the two rooms so the guard posted outside it could see if anything went wrong.

Absinthe, a chubby girl straining the seams of an orange jailhouse jumpsuit, was already seated at the table. Her head was pillowed on her arms like a child who's been told to put her head on her desk. She looked up when we came in, face blotchy from crying.

"Is my mom coming?" she asked. Her voice was high-pitched, girlish. She didn't sound like someone who would slash a young man's throat and gut him with a hunting knife. She sounded like a little kid lost in the woods.

Miss Aleta sighed. "Not this time, child."

For a moment, Absinthe's face seemed about to crumple. Then she lifted her chin and jabbed a finger in my direction. The black polish was chipped, the nails gnawed down to the quick. "What's he doing here?"

Miss Aleta said, "He wants to talk to you about Mr. Parker's murder. You don't have to say anything you don't want to say."

"I remember you," Absinthe said to me. She tugged self-consciously at the waist of her jumpsuit, which was at least a size too small. "You're Josh's uncle."

"That's right. Jared McKean. They treating you okay?"

She glanced at her attorney, then back at me. Shrugged. "I guess."

"You don't sound sure."

"It doesn't matter. It's just . . . The other girls are kinda mean."

Miss Aleta slitted her eyes and said, "Have any of them hurt you?"

Absinthe picked at a cuticle. "Sticks and stones."

I said, "You were with Josh the day Razor died."

Something flashed in her eyes, and she swung her head toward me. "I'm no snitch."

"Look, he told me he ditched school. Witnesses saw him with you. How do you think it looked for him when you confessed to Razor's murder? The cops know you didn't do it alone."

"I told them Josh didn't have anything to do with it. I told them I was by myself."

"You overpowered a grown man, cut his throat, lugged his body upstairs, and hung it up to drain the—"

"Stop!" She flung up her hands, as if to ward off an attack, then ducked her head and whispered, "I don't want to talk about that."

"No, I expect you don't."

In a brittle voice, Miss Aleta said, "And she doesn't have to. Change your tactics, Mister, or the interview is over."

I ignored her, directing my next question to Absinthe. "You really want to stay in here?"

Miss Aleta's head swiveled toward me. I could tell she was angry by the way her hand tightened on her pen. "Mr. McKean. That's enough."

I held up a hand, palm outward. *Trust me.*

Absinthe leaned forward and sniffled. "No. No, I don't want to stay in here. I hate it here. I didn't think it would be this way."

"How did you think it would be?"

"I don't know." She took a little hitching breath. "There's no privacy here, you know? There's like six of us in a room and the toilet is right in the same room. There's just a little wall so nobody can see, but anybody can come around the corner and make fun of you any time they want. And the girls are always picking at you when nobody's watching, but if you say one little thing back, you better believe they see that. And, like, there's nobody to talk to; half the people in here can't even read. And the beds—bunks, or whatever you call 'em—are hard and lumpy, and . . . small. You can hardly even roll over. It's like . . ." She gnawed at her lower lip, then mumbled, "Like prison."

"It's nothing like prison," I said. "This is a cakewalk compared to prison."

Miss Aleta gave her head a small shake. "Mr. McKean."

Absinthe's eyes welled. "That prosecutor," she said. "Mr. Jessup. He said he wants to try me as an adult."

"Not if I can help it," Miss Aleta said.

I gave her a pointed look. "But can you help it?"

"I'm very good at what I do."

I looked back at Absinthe. "She's right. She's very good at what she does. But you confessed, remember? And the prosecutor isn't going to let the judge forget that. He's going to pull out pictures of the crime scene and say that anybody who could do a thing like that should be locked up for the rest of her life, not just until her eighteenth birthday."

Tears spilled down her face. "I don't want to go to prison."

"Then let me help you."

"It isn't what you think," she mumbled. "I never meant for him to die."

I didn't ask how you could fillet a man by accident. Instead, I made my voice as neutral as possible and asked, "How did it happen?"

Her shoulders lifted, dropped. One hand reached up, found a strand of hair, and twisted it around her finger. The other hand was clamped tightly to her opposite hip, as if to hold herself together. I'd seen a man gut-shot once, and he'd held himself like that.

"Was it a sacrifice?" I asked.

She shrugged again.

Miss Aleta said, "Laurel—"

"I hate that name," Absinthe said. "Why won't you call me by my real name?"

"Absinthe?" Miss Aleta spread her fingers in a frustrated gesture. "Why would you want to be named after a poison?"

"It isn't a poison. It's a liqueur."

I said, "Then why not just call yourself Bailey's Irish Cream and be done with it? It's easier to spell."

"You wouldn't understand."

"I'm trying to," I said. "Look, I'll call you whatever you want, but your attorney's right. You need to distance yourself from this stuff."

"This stuff is who I am," she said.

"Laurel, Absinthe. Whoever you want to be. About this sacrifice—"

"It wasn't a sacrifice."

"Then why the pentagram? Why the symbols drawn in blood? Was this a satanic thing?"

"It's not *satanic*. It's just *magick*. It doesn't have anything to do with Satan."

"Okay." I plucked a tissue from my pocket and handed it to her. She used it to wipe her nose, then folded it over and dabbed at her eyes. "Explain it to me."

She sucked on a strand of hair, pulled it through her teeth, and carefully arranged it into a long wet curl along her cheek. "First off, the pentagram isn't satanic. Satan is a Judeo-Christian invention, and people were using pentagrams way before both those religions."

"Razor was cut open across a pentagram. It had to mean something."

She looked away, chewing at her lower lip.

I said, "Talk, don't talk. It's all the same to me. But no jury will fall for this 'I didn't mean it' crap. You can't carve a man up like a Halloween pumpkin and not mean it."

Her lips trembled, and more tears spilled down her face.

I said, "The judge won't care if you cry."

A line of snot trickled to her upper lip, and she swiped a sleeve across it, then looked at the tissue in her hand and gave a little laugh. "God, I'm a basket case. I can't stay here."

"Then talk to me. Tell me what happened."

"I can't."

"Somebody threaten you?"

"No."

"I can't help you if you won't talk to me."

She tugged at her hair again. Nibbled at a nail. I kept my mouth shut and gave her time to think it through.

"You going to get me out of here?" she said at last.

"I'm going to try."

"I can't tell you who was there."

"Absinthe, these people are not your friends. You don't owe them anything."

"I can't tell you," she said. "Because I don't know."

I frowned. Licked at the small, thin scar on my lower lip. "What do you mean, you don't know? You said—"

"I said I killed him." She rubbed at a fingernail. Flicked away a chip of black polish. "I never said I was there."

CHAPTER TEN

Miss Aleta leaned forward with a little gasp. "What are you saying, child?"

"Okay," I said. "I'll bite. How did you kill him, if you weren't there?"

Absinthe raked one ragged thumbnail across the other, scraping a thin white strip into the dark polish. Then, "Craft," she said at last. "I killed him with craft."

"Witchcraft?"

She gave a miserable nod.

"How the hell do you kill someone with witchcraft?"

"I have spell books. Real ones. They tell you how to bring harm to your enemies, even death. It's Black Magick. I never thought it would really work."

"Then what was the point?"

She looked down at her lap. "It made me feel better, that's all. But then it really worked, and when you use bad magick against someone, it comes back to you, only three times worse. It's called the Rule of Three. Whatever you wish on someone else comes back on you, threefold."

"Sounds risky."

She waved a hand, indicating her surroundings. "Ya think?"

"So why do it?"

"I was pissed at him."

"Obviously. About what?"

"It doesn't matter. It was stupid. Just some stuff about our coterie."

"Coterie. That's like a coven?"

"Duh. No. It's just a group of people who hang together. Some of us are vampires. Like Razor and Barnabus. And some of us are human servants. Only, being a witch, I was special."

Miss Aleta leaned forward again. "You said, 'human servant.' You're saying Mr. Parker wasn't human?"

I could see her angling, the way defense attorneys do. If she couldn't get Absinthe off, maybe she could make a case for an insanity plea.

Absinthe tugged at the thumbnail with her teeth and winced as a bead of blood welled up beneath it. Absently, she licked it with the tip of her tongue, then closed her lips around it and sucked at the wound. I repeated Miss Aleta's question. Reluctantly, Absinthe removed the thumb from her mouth.

"He was a vampire," she said slowly. "I don't mean he was immortal or anything. All that stuff about vampires being immortal and not being able to go out in daylight . . . that's just so much crap. A vampire is a person who can feed off of the life force of another person."

"Life force. That's blood?"

"It's essence. Life energy. Some vampires have to drink blood to get it, but for a really powerful vampire, like Razor, the blood is just a high. He could tap into the life force without that. You've heard that old saying that someone just sucks you dry? Someone who sort of saps your strength? Well, that's a vampire."

I could think of a few people who fit the description. "So all this power Razor supposedly had. What did he do with it?"

She blinked. Frowned. "Do?"

"Yeah. He didn't have a job. He didn't give to charity. So what, exactly, did he *do*?"

She scowled, scratching at the table with her index finger. "He understood people. Made them want to do things for him. Give him things. He could, like, see into people's heads."

"You're saying he was some kind of mind reader?"

"I don't know. Some vampires are."

"You aren't a vampire?"

"No." She looked at me as if I weren't completely bright. "I'm a witch."

I opened my mouth to ask another question, and she raised a hand to stop me. "You want to know how it works, I'll tell you some books to read. Write these down."

Miss Aleta pulled out her pad and dutifully scrawled the titles. Charms, witchcraft, vampires, and the player's handbook for the vampire game. She tore out a sheet of paper and made another copy of the list, which she slid over to me.

"I didn't plan on taking a course," I said to Absinthe, tucking the list into my pocket.

"Too bad." She gave me a watery smile. "You need one."

—⬥—

A few follow-up questions, and then I walked Miss Aleta to her car. There was a hint of a smile on her lips, and I could see her working out a new defense strategy. Police still had Absinthe's fingerprints on the knife and the eyewitness who placed her near the crime scene, but without her confession, the case was weak. There might be enough doubt to keep her out of the adult system. Maybe even get a sympathetic judge to award bail.

"I'll call Josh," I said. "See if I can find out where he and Absinthe went when they left Razor's. Maybe there was another witness."

"You do that," Miss Aleta said. "I'll make a date with the prosecutor."

—⬥—

The phone conversation with Josh was unenlightening.

Where did you and Absinthe go when you left Razor's?

We weren't at Razor's.

A witness put you there.

Just in the neighborhood. We didn't go to the house.

Then what—?

Just watching.

Watching what?

Nothing. Everything. Just watching.

They'd watched the neighborhood for a couple of hours. Then Absinthe drove Josh home and—presumably—went back to her place. No, they hadn't seen anything. No, no one had gone into the house. Around mid-morning, Byron had come out carrying a black workout bag and pulled away in Razor's Camaro. He was too young to have a license, but I guess that didn't mean much to either of them. Josh and Absinthe had left at eleven—more than an hour before the murder, if the medical examiner's estimated time of death was accurate. Filling in the blanks, I thought Josh had probably gone there to see Razor. Changed his mind and left when he saw Byron.

Razor had lived a few blocks off West End in a refurbished multi-level house with gabled dormers and two pinnacled towers. Half House of Usher, half Addams Family. In balmier weather, I could have walked there from my office. The neighborhood had seen better days, like an aging heiress whose milky complexion had been replaced by wrinkles and age spots. Houses that had once hosted coming out parties and champagne brunches were now considered starter homes and fixer-uppers.

The only thing the residents had in common was a deep distaste for Razor. He'd died on a Friday. According to the police report, it had been a dreary, drizzling day, and any neighbors who weren't at work were at the mall or the movies, or huddled inside watching HBO. No one had seen anything. No one had wanted to.

I spent the rest of the morning and most of the afternoon talking to people the police had already interviewed. The single mother two doors down said she was afraid to let her eight-year-old son play unsupervised in the yard. The elderly woman across the street complained of loud, discordant music and "half-dressed trollops and homosexuals." About an hour before sunset, the accountant next door, Roland Calder, pulled into his driveway. He invited me in for coffee, and told me he'd doubled the insulation in his house to keep his wife and daughters from hearing the foul language that often poured from Razor's front porch and driveway.

"Truth is," Calder said, sliding a steaming mug onto the table in front of me, "the guy was a jerk. I'm not saying he deserved what happened to him—I wouldn't wish that on anybody—but if he hadn't been killed, we'd've had to put our house on the market, it was that bad. Cream or sugar?"

"Black is fine." I picked up the mug and inhaled the rich, earthy scent of Colombian roast. "Sounds like a popular guy."

"Yeah, right." He rubbed a hand across his balding pate and patted down the long strands of his comb-over. "There's this guy who lives down the street, you know? And one night, Razor . . . he's having some kind of party or something, and this guy just goes down there and says something like, 'Hey, we're trying to sleep here.'" Calder dumped two tablespoons of powdered nondairy creamer into his mug, where it dissolved into a clotted cloud. "Not like the rest of us weren't thinking the same thing. And Razor goes, 'Well, Eff you, man. It's a free country.' Only he didn't say eff you."

"Not very neighborly."

"That's what I'm saying." He swirled his spoon around the mug, nudging the powdery clumps until they dissipated. "So this guy, Hewitt, his name is, he calls the cops and makes a complaint."

"Razor must've been pissed."

"I guess so. Because the next morning, Hewitt goes out and the air's been let out of all his tires." Calder took a sip of coffee and smiled. "Ah, that hits the spot. So anyway, Hewitt figures it's gotta be Razor that did it, and Hewitt makes another complaint. But there's no proof."

"No proof, no prosecution."

Calder raised his mug in agreement. "Exactly."

"Was that the end of it?"

"Not hardly. Razor went to Hewitt's place and told him nobody liked a rat. A couple of days later, Hewitt's dog was poisoned. The vet said it was antifreeze."

"Motherfu—"

Calder frowned, and I caught myself before I finished the word. I meant it, though. Antifreeze is an insidious poison, a sweet-tasting substance dogs lap up like gravy. It takes less than a teaspoon to kill a good-sized dog.

"The dog," I said. "Did it survive?"

"Touch-and-go for awhile," he said. "Doing fine now, though."

"Let me guess. There was nothing to connect Razor to the poisoning."

"Nothing you could prove," he said. "But everybody knew. When Hewitt went out to bring in the dog dish, there was a rubber rat in it."

CHAPTER ELEVEN

According to Calder, the conflict had dragged on. Hewitt put sugar in Razor's gas tank. Razor threw a brick through Hewitt's front window. Garbage cans were overturned. Punches and epithets were exchanged. By the time Razor died, the feud was a neighborhood legend.

When I'd learned as much as I thought I could, I thanked Calder for the coffee and walked four doors down to talk to Hewitt.

A woman answered my knock, a petite brunette in a shapeless gray sweatshirt and baggy drawstring pants. Her light blue eyes were wary, but she gave me a reflexive half-smile. "May I help you?"

"I hope so." I flipped open my wallet and held up my P.I. license, which she studied through the screen. A beagle with a grizzled muzzle peered from behind her legs. It had worry wrinkles above its eyes, but gave its tail a tentative wag. "Are you Mrs. Hewitt?"

"Yes. Judith Hewitt. Why?"

"I'm investigating Sebastian Parker's death. You probably knew him as Razor."

She squeezed her arms across her breasts and squinted up at me. "I heard his vampire buddies killed him. Sacrificed him or something like that."

"Maybe. Probably. But we still need to look into everything. What he was into. Who might have wanted him dead."

She gave an angry laugh. "Everybody wanted him dead."

"He poisoned your dog, didn't he?"

"Buddy's dog." She stroked the beagle's head. "He had her before we were married. She's the sweetest thing. But if you're thinking Buddy might have had something to do with that killing—"

"I'm not thinking that." Although I was. Some bastard hurt my dog, I might not kill him, but I'd sure as hell think about it.

"He wasn't even around. He was gone all day, hunting ducks up at his daddy's farm."

"I'd still like to talk to him."

"Knock yourself out. Him and Elgin are out back. You can go on around."

"Elgin?"

"Around back."

"I'll go talk to them. Thanks for your time." I started down the steps, turned back as the door was swinging shut. "Mrs. Hewitt . . ."

She paused, peering through a six-inch crack in the door. "What?"

"The police report said you were at home that afternoon. Did you see anything? Anybody coming or going? Anyone at all, even somebody who belonged there?"

"I told the police no. The answer is still no. And if I had seen anyone, I wouldn't tell you. As far as I'm concerned, whoever killed him should get a medal."

She closed the door firmly between us, not quite slamming it. I went around to the back of the house, where a chain-link fence separated the front yard from the back. An elongated gate cut across the driveway. On the other side, two men in jeans and camouflage jackets hunched under the hood of a maroon 1989 Pontiac Grand Prix. A plastic strap held the rear fender in place. The body of the car was flecked with silver where the paint had chipped away. The smaller of the two men, who sported a scraggly beard and an orange toboggan cap, reached for a Budweiser bottle perched on the fender and took a long swig.

Never too cold for beer.

I lifted the latch on the gate and pushed it open. "Mr. Hewitt?"

The man in the toboggan turned to face me. His breath puffed out of his mouth and swirled around the lip of the bottle. "Who wants to know?"

I handed him my license. He gave it a cursory glance before tossing it back to me. "P.I., huh?" He glanced at his companion, who ducked out from under the hood of the car and looked at me as if I were a new and interesting species of reptile. Hewitt nodded toward his friend. "Jared McKean, Elgin Mayers. Elgin, why'n't you get this guy a beer?"

Elgin shrugged and strolled over to an open cooler overflowing with ice and a variety of bottled beers. Hewitt was a little shorter than me, but Elgin topped my six feet by at least four inches, muscled but not muscle-bound, with a bushy, unkempt mustache and a long, angry scar that ran from one corner of his mouth to a place just beneath his jawline. A corkscrew of greasy brown hair whipped across his face, exposing reddened ears and a forehead pitted with acne scars. His eyes were pale blue like a husky's.

He pitched me a beer and I caught it one-handed. "Thanks."

Hewitt took another swig and leaned against the front of the Pontiac. "So. What does a P.I. want with me?"

I gave him the same spiel I'd given his wife and added, "I wondered if you saw anything. People coming and going. Unusual noises. That kind of thing."

"Can't help you. I wasn't home."

"Your wife said you were out hunting that day."

"Hard to see anything, if I wasn't here."

I looked past his shoulder at a line of starlings perched on a telephone line. "My brother and I used to hunt."

"Yeah? What'd you hunt?"

"Mostly rabbits and squirrels. The occasional quail."

"Any deer?"

"No. Never really got the chance. You?"

He gave me a hard flat stare that said a man who'd never killed a deer had no right to call himself a hunter. "Sure. In season."

"How long you been doing it? Hunting, I mean?"

"Got my first buck when I was twelve."

"Impressive."

"Not really." He nodded toward his companion. "Elgin was ten."

Elgin grinned, his pale eyes hard and feral.

I said to Hewitt, "You were hunting when Razor was killed. Where was Elgin?"

Hewitt gave a startled laugh and glanced sharply at Elgin, who took a long draw from his beer bottle and gave me a tight-lipped smile. "Come back with a warrant," Elgin said, "and maybe I'll tell you."

"I'm not a cop," I said. "I'm relying on the goodness of your hearts."

Hewitt said, "They tell you that son of a bitch gave my dog antifreeze?"

"They said they suspected he had."

"So I'll admit it. I hated the guy's guts. But I didn't kill him." He turned back and bent over the engine again. "Now, if you'll excuse me, I gotta get to this alternator."

"You dress your own deer, Mr. Hewitt?" I asked.

There was a pause before he answered. "Doesn't everybody?"

I kept my voice light when I asked my next question. Too light. I knew that in itself would call attention to it. I wanted it to. "What kind of knife do you use?"

Hewitt's back stiffened. Then he placed his palms flat on the front of the engine housing and took a long, deep breath. "You ought to go now, Mister," he said softly.

Elgin pushed his hips away from the car and shook the tension from his neck and shoulders. I took a step back, out of arm's reach.

"You have a good afternoon, Mr. Hewitt," I said. "And thanks for the beer."

"Take it with you," he said. "And go to Hell."

CHAPTER TWELVE

Since Hell was low on the list of places I wanted to go, I stopped by the bookstore at Opry Mills instead and picked up copies of the books on Absinthe's list. Crossing the parking lot, green bookstore bag in one hand, I flipped open the cover of my cell phone with the other and tapped in Josh's number with my thumb. "Anything about that game we talked about?"

He couldn't disguise the excitement in his voice. "There's one Friday night at seven. Dad didn't want to let me go, but my therapist said it would give me closure, plus she doesn't think the game's a big deal. So Mom said okay."

"Josh, your dad—"

"Wait, that's what I'm saying. They had a talk, and Dad *finally* said I could go." He sounded happy. It had been a long time since I'd heard that in his voice.

I rang off and dialed Alan Keating. He was booked for the week, he said, but could squeeze me in during lunch the next afternoon. He sounded annoyed to hear from me, but maybe that was only my imagination.

Jay's door was closed when I got home, so I took care of the horses, wolfed down a bowl of Campbell's tomato soup and a grilled cheese sandwich, then went upstairs and crawled into bed with the player's handbook for the vampire game. Lots of complicated pen and ink artwork, from the grotesque to the glamorous. A woman with a punk hairstyle opened her mouth to show elongated canines. A hairless vampire with bulging eyes sipped from the throat of a woman wearing little but a dazed expression. *Dracula* meets *Heavy Metal*.

The rules for the game were punctuated by fictional journal entries and profiles of character archetypes. I couldn't make heads or tails of it. It was a hell of a lot more complicated than Chinese Checkers.

After awhile, I closed the books and went online. Googled *Goth* and *vampire*, and spent the next few hours lurking in chat rooms and surfing the web. It was a different world, a world of shadings and subgroups—artists and poets, stylers, vampire pretenders, and vampire wannabes. A culture in flux, constantly evolving. Razor and his coterie seemed to think they were at the pinnacle.

It was after midnight before I turned out the light and settled into an uneasy sleep, so I was tired and out of sorts when I showed up at Alan Keating's office the next day at noon.

Keating worked out of a small building on the west side of town, a few blocks from St. Thomas Hospital. He shared the building with three other psychologists whose placards read, "Andrea Shilling, Child Esteem Specialist," "Tony Kent, Psychoanalysis and Hypnosis," and "Glorianna Plummer, Women's Issues and Repressed Memory Recovery." All that was missing was a placard for Madame Zelda's Voodoo Parlor.

Keating's placard said simply, "Alan Keating, Ph.D., Psychologist."

The four psychologists shared a receptionist, a sleek redhead with a pair of rings on her left hand and a smile that said maybe her *I do* had really meant *I might*.

Her lips pursed as she studied my ID and then my face. When she handed back my card, her fingertips brushed my hand. "Third door on the right," she said, her voice sultry. "I think it's open."

Keating's office was spacious, with pale walls and a wine-colored Persian rug. On one end of the room, a child-sized, kidney-shaped table surrounded by blue plastic chairs dug moons into the rug. Against the wall was a wooden shelf lined with toys that looked like they'd never been played with. At the other end of the room, behind a cherry wood desk so glossy you could see your reflection in it, Alan Keating sat in a high-backed leather swivel chair poring over a sheaf of papers in a manila folder.

He looked up when I came in. Closed the folder and stood up, fingertips absently straightening the edges. He was dressed in another pricey Italian suit. Same gold tie chain, same gold tips at the wings of his shirt collar. This time, the tie was blood red with a pattern of gold running through it. Crisp. Clean. Careful. It made me want to pitch him into a dumpster.

He gestured to the cushioned leather seat across the desk from him. "Come in. Have a seat. Let's get this over with."

I settled into the chair, pulling my jacket across my chest to conceal the shoulder holster. His eyes flicked toward it as if he knew it was there. Which he probably did, since I'd shown it to him at the funeral. I let the jacket slip a bit and said, "How's Byron?"

"Shaken. As you'd expect."

"I need to talk to him."

Keating sat. His chair was higher than mine, and he rocked back in it. Fancy. "I'm neither Byron's warden nor his social director. If you want to talk to him, you'll have to make your own arrangements."

"What about you?" I asked. "What kind of arrangement do you have with Byron?"

He glared at me. "He's fifteen, for God's sake."

"That didn't stop Razor."

"I'm not Razor."

We stared each other down like a couple of alpha wolves. It was what Josh had called a pissing contest, and it wouldn't get me any closer to what I needed. I held up my hands to signal a truce. "Okay. I was out of line."

"Damn straight." He stepped past me to a shiny black filing cabinet, yanked open a drawer marked Q–Z, and slid the folder he'd been studying deftly into place. Closed the drawer. Locked it. Then he blew out a long breath, came back around the desk, and slid into his chair. "What is it with you?"

"Something about your boyfriend," I said.

"My boyfriend?"

"You're not going to tell me you and Razor didn't have a thing going?"

His gaze slid away, back toward the files. "That was a long time ago."

"Then it won't hurt to tell me about it."

He pushed himself away from his desk and paced a path from desk to window and back again, then over to a rosewood bookcase filled with professional journals and hardbound books. Absently, he traced the titles with his index finger. *People of the Lie. The Lucifer Effect: Understanding How Good People Turn Evil.*

He saw where I was looking and said, "The psychology of evil."

"A specialty of yours?"

"More like an interest."

"Tell me about you and Razor."

He came back and settled into his chair with a creak of leather. Swiveled his chair away and looked out the window. The view was unimpressive—a narrow, cluttered alley separated from a row of dingy red-brick buildings by a sagging chain-link fence. It didn't mesh with the Italian suits and the gold tie loop.

"We met in grade school," Keating said, eyes fixed on the glass. "Mrs. DeVray's fifth grade class. We called her The Beast. She used to keep us inside at recess every day and make us write 'play is the devil's workshop' over and over again."

"Gunning for that teacher of the year award, was she?"

He spared me half a smile. "She hated children, I think. Children in general. But me especially. Maybe she thought I was weak. Or maybe she realized my parents wouldn't intervene. You can guess how the other children reacted to that."

"Open season," I said.

"Exactly. They'd jump me on the playground, chase me home after school. They called me names, tripped me up, bloodied my nose. Once they made me eat excrement." His jaw tightened. "Made me eat dog shit. They were like sharks smelling blood."

"Kids can be cruel."

"I'm not telling you this so you'll feel sorry for me. I'm telling you because it was something Bastian and I had in common—that Mrs. DeVray hated us both."

It took me a minute to realize that "Bastian" was Razor. "The other kids pick on him too?"

He gave a little snort of laughter. "They knew better. One day, I saw him playing around near Mrs. DeVray's desk. When she opened her drawer, she found a dozen black widow spiders in it."

"Jesus."

"She quit that same afternoon."

"And you thought it was Razor."

"Of course it was. While the other kids were screaming and climbing on top of their desks, Bastian looked over at me and winked. From that day on, we were friends, and the other kids left me alone."

Razor as protector. Razor as avenger. The image didn't fit. Maybe he'd been different in grade school. Then again, Keating had been a sad, vulnerable little boy everybody picked on. He was exactly the kind of lost soul Razor would be drawn to. A shark to blood, as Keating had said.

"He saved my life," Keating said, as if he'd read my mind. "Melodramatic as that sounds. Only he couldn't do it the usual way, couldn't stand up on the playground and say, 'Leave my friend alone.' That would have been too noble. He could never bear to give in to his better instincts."

"He couldn't admit he was protecting you."

"Exactly. He put spiders in the teacher's desk. Any good it did me was just a side effect. He could tell himself our friendship was some Machiavellian thing built from ulterior motives."

"That didn't piss you off?"

He waved the idea away as if it were smoke. "He was a complex man, Mr. McKean, almost equal parts arrogance and self-loathing. Have you met his mother?"

"Briefly. At the funeral."

"Completely narcissistic. Saw him as a showpiece, not a son. He was her confidant, her little hero. As if he was supposed to meet *her* needs, not the other way around. He slept with her until he went away to college. His father slept in the guest room until the day he died. He was practically a ghost." He looked at me as if to gauge my reaction. Trying to shock me?

I ignored the bait. "Distant father, suffocating mother. Possible incest. That's got to be some kind of textbook dysfunctional family model."

Keating cocked his head to one side with a bemused smile on his face. It didn't look completely at home there. "Why, Mr. McKean," he said. "You've had a psychology course."

"One or two. But I don't buy the idea that a crappy childhood justifies bad behavior."

He picked up a sleek mechanical pencil and rolled it between his fingers. "I don't justify it, but I understand it. Bastian latched onto this vampire mythology because it gave him a sense of power and control. If it hadn't been that, he would have found something else."

"Such as?"

"Who knows? Neo-Nazism, some kind of cult. Okay, so he was a little twisted. Sometimes life is twisted."

It was a strange comment, coming from a psychologist.

I said, "He has a brother."

"Heath. A senior at Vanderbilt. Philosophy and Religion. He was several years younger than Bastian and I."

"He twisted too?"

"I expect so," he said. "Though not in the same way. Bastian was Mama's little prince and Daddy's little bastard. Heath was just invisible. Was that all you needed? I have a client coming soon."

"Tell me about the woman at the funeral. The one who spit on your shoes."

"Marta Savales. What about her?"

"People don't usually spit on people they think highly of."

"They pay you to make that kind of deduction?"

"No. They pay me to make other deductions. Want to tell me why this Marta Savales thinks so much of you?"

He didn't answer. Instead, he opened the laptop and turned it on, pointed and clicked until he found what he was looking for, and scribbled something on the back of one of his business cards. "Here," he said, holding out the card between two fingers. "Ask her yourself. I'm sure she'll talk to you."

"Why would she?"

"Her son is missing. She'd talk to the devil if she thought it would help find him."

"What happened to—"

"I have work to do, Mr. McKean. I'm sure you understand that." He tapped the edge of the card against the desk.

I reached across and took the card. *Marta Savales*, it said, followed by a seven-digit number. I slipped it into my shirt pocket and said, "One more thing . . . Where were you the day Razor was killed?"

"I was here."

"All day?"

He licked his lips and glanced away, back toward the window. "I may have stepped out for lunch," he said finally.

"*May* have?"

"Sometimes I go out, sometimes I work through lunch. There's no pattern to it. Then when Heath called to tell me what had happened—" His shoulders sagged. "I could hardly think afterward."

"If you had gone out, how long would you have been gone?"

"I don't know. Forty-five minutes. Maybe more."

"You have clients all afternoon?"

"Generally."

"And your receptionist would have noticed if you'd been gone longer than usual."

"Kirsten doesn't work on Friday afternoons. Child care issues. And I don't like where this conversation is going, Mr. McKean. Am I a suspect?"

"Everybody's a suspect," I told him. "Everybody but me. One more question. This one's definitely in your bailiwick."

"I suspect you don't know anything about my bailiwick, but go ahead."

"The severed genitals . . ." He winced, but waited for me to go on. "What kind of person does a thing like that?"

"Assuming it wasn't a prescribed part of some ritual—"

"We don't think so, no."

- 80 -

"No. Well, then." He tugged at his tie. Cleared his throat. "Look for someone who felt victimized by Bastian's sexuality—Bastian or someone like him. Someone who wanted Bastian humiliated."

"So they cut off his balls."

"Exactly. Literal emasculation. It shows a lot of rage."

"Any idea who might have been that pissed at him?"

"Mr. McKean, this was way beyond pissed."

"Rage, then. Any idea who might have felt that kind of rage?"

"I don't know." His voice broke, and tears welled in his eyes. "He hurt so many people. I'd have no idea where to start."

CHAPTER THIRTEEN

I waved at Kirsten on the way out. Pretty girl, with eyes like malachite and skin the color of eggshells. Her hair was molten copper. Straight and shoulder-length, with the ends flipped up.

I had a sudden thought, veered back and laid my palms on her desk. Flashed her a grin.

She smiled up at me, a hint of mischief on her face. "Something else I can do for you?"

"Any chance I could take a look at your appointment book?"

"I don't think so." She pushed a few copper strands away from her forehead. "Confidentiality, you know."

"Sure, I get that. I just wanted to confirm some information Mr. Keating gave me. Confirm he was working a couple of Fridays ago. I guess I could wait in the parking lot on Friday and ask the patients about it as they go in." Before she could protest, I gave her the date and added, "It should be pretty much the same folks week to week, shouldn't it?"

A thin, vertical line etched itself between her eyebrows. "That's a little invasive, don't you think? If all you need to know is if he was working, I can tell you he has clients pretty much all day every day, Tuesday through Saturday, five days a week."

"But people cancel sometimes, right?"

"Sometimes. And, of course, sometimes an emergency comes up. A client in distress, a suicide attempt. Something like that."

"Tell you what, why don't you look through it, tell me what's there? No names, no problem, right?"

She leaned forward onto her elbows, lifting the hair off the back of her neck with a slender hand. "Dr. Keating is okay with this?"

"Why not? He's the one who gave me the information."

"Maybe I should call him to verify . . ."

"Sure." I smiled. Gave her the guileless look I'd used running undercover stings in Vice. Mouth dry, gut roiling, nothing but calm on the surface. "I'll wait."

She gave a little sigh and let her hair fall back into place. "Well, I hate to interrupt him when he's getting ready for a patient. I guess it will be okay." She opened the appointment book and flipped through the pages until she found the right date. "It says here . . ." She ran her finger down the page. "Looks like a full day. He was booked from nine until four."

I was disappointed, but I nodded as if it was what I'd been expecting. "Thanks for the confirmation."

"Must have been a busy afternoon," she said, still appraising the book.

"Why do you say that?"

She tapped at a name on the schedule. "One of us always initials the schedule after a session. Since I leave at noon on Fridays, he does it then, but it must have gotten crazy in the afternoon, because he forgot to initial anything after lunch."

I tried not to grin too broadly. "Thanks. You saved me a lot of work."

She handed me another of Keating's business cards and looked at me like a cat might eye a bowl of milk. "In case you need to get in touch with me about anything. Use it sometime."

CHAPTER FOURTEEN

I had no intention of calling Keating's receptionist, but I owed her a debt of gratitude. A few missing initials didn't mean Keating was guilty of anything more than being overworked, but it seemed a little too convenient that the one day he'd forgotten to sign off on his appointments was the day his good friend Razor had been butchered. I hadn't drawn first blood yet, but it was a start.

I dialed my ex-wife's number from Keating's parking lot. When she answered, I felt a familiar rush of pleasure and pain.

"Hiya, Angel," I said.

Maria gave a pleased little laugh. "Hiya, Cowboy." There was an awkward moment. Then she said, "You want to talk to Paulie?"

"Yeah. Put him on."

A few seconds later, Paul's gravelly voice came on the line. "Mama baby comin'. Gonna take care of her, my pretty baby."

"I know you will, Sport."

He was eight years old, but fate, or God, or genetics had given him the mind of a three-year-old. Just after he was born, when Maria's doctor told us he had Down syndrome, we'd thought of all the things he'd never do and wondered how we'd cope. Would he ever ride a bike? (He does.) Could I teach him to play baseball? (Yes, but not well.) Would he be happy? Could we?

We'd thought if our marriage could survive a disabled child, it could survive anything.

We were wrong. When it ended, it had nothing to do with Paul.

As I listened to my son chatter, some of the tension in my neck and shoulders seeped away. Thirty minutes after I flipped the phone closed and pulled onto the Interstate, I walked into our living room to find Jay draping silver strands on an artificial tree so tall the angel on top brushed the ceiling. His back was to me, and the droop of his shoulders said he was giving the tree such careful attention to take his mind off his problems.

I waved one arm in an arc that swept from the tree in one corner to the sterile hospital bed in the center of the room. One leather armchair had been pulled against the wall; the other squatted beside the bed. "Did you do all this yourself?"

He turned, a strand of icicle dangling from his fingers. "I put up the tree. The guys who delivered the bed helped with the rest."

I didn't ask about Eric, and Jay didn't mention him. Instead, we made small talk over dinner, then bundled up and drove across town to bring home the scum-sucking bastard who had given Jay AIDS.

Fabulous Greg, who'd taken Dylan in for the short term but didn't deal well with suffering, was tall and lean, with rugged, Marlboro Man features and narrow, bloodshot eyes. He met us halfway down the front sidewalk, a cigarette tucked between his fingers, Greta Garbo-style.

"Thank God you're here," he said. He ground the cigarette out on the heel of his shoe and curled the butt into his palm. "It's not that I wouldn't like to help him—"

"It's okay," Jay said. "We've got it."

Greg gestured toward a pair of oversized suitcases. "His meds are in the front zipper pocket, along with an instruction sheet. You know, how many of what and when."

I carried the suitcases out to the car and stowed them in the trunk. Then Greg led us down a Georgia O'Keeffe hallway and into a bedroom with starched white sheets and ivory walls accented by Andrew Wyeth prints in wooden frames.

I'd seen pictures of Dylan. Tanned. Bleached blond. Manufactured James Dean expression. The hollow-cheeked man who lifted his head from the pillow when we walked in bore little resemblance to those photographs.

Jay's expression was neutral, but his eyes gave him away. I didn't need words to know that he was seeing his own future in Dylan's ravaged face.

"So, you're Jay's latest," Dylan rasped. His voice was weak, but he still managed to make it sound smug. His thinning hair had reclaimed its natural shade of brown, and his smooth-shaven face was mottled with purple Kaposi's sarcoma lesions. One ear was crusted with scabs.

"He's not my latest," Jay said, before I could answer. "He's just a friend. A straight friend, at that. So be nice."

Dylan's laugh dissolved into a long, racking cough that made his eyes water. When he'd recovered, he asked, "When have I not been nice?"

Jay shook his head, a pained expression on his face, as if the question had rendered him speechless. I could have said enough for both of us, but it wasn't my question to answer.

Dylan met my gaze, and his smile faded. "No, really, Jay. Thanks for coming."

Jay leaned down and placed a dry kiss on Dylan's lips. He smoothed an invisible wrinkle from the Appalachian quilt pulled up to Dylan's neck, then paused and picked up a painted plastic model of Bela Lugosi as Dracula from the table beside Dylan's bed.

"You still have this," he said. He turned to me and said, "I made this for him. Before we split up."

"It's not a big deal," Dylan said. "I happen to like Dracula."

Jay looked down at his shoes.

"Don't be a dick," I said to Dylan, and he stretched his mouth into something that resembled a grin.

"Don't get your panties in a wad," he said. "Jay knows why I kept it."

Jay and Fabulous Greg bundled Dylan into flannel pajamas and a down parka. Jay slid one arm around Dylan's shoulders and another under his legs. Dylan was drawn and shrunken, but the strain of lifting him showed on Jay's face.

"Wait," I said. "I'll do it."

I carried Dylan out to the car and laid him gently across the backseat. Jay and Greg arranged pillows and an inflatable raft around him. As they jostled him, he pressed his lips together and clenched his fists.

"I'm sorry," Jay said. His breath steamed out of his mouth and hovered between them like a ghost. "We'll be home soon. Then you can rest."

"Home?" gasped Dylan, between clenched teeth. "I don't think so, Jay-o."

Jay paused and laid a hand on Dylan's cheek. "It's my home, honey. That's going to have to do."

Greg shifted from one foot to the other. "There's one more thing. Wait here." He jogged into the house and returned a few moments later, a small bundle of white and sable fur tucked into the crook of his arm.

"Good God," Jay said. "What is that?"

It was bigger than a squirrel and smaller than a rabbit, with a foxy face and a pair of oversized fringed ears that stood out from its head like wings. Greg held it out, and it licked his fingers and wagged a plumed tail.

"This is Luca," Greg said, pressing the puppy into Jay's arms. It nestled against Jay's chest and licked his chin. "A very dear friend thought he'd be good company for Dylan. God knows what she was thinking. I've been keeping him in the laundry room; it's tiled."

Jay looked at me. I shrugged. There was hardly enough of the little guy to qualify as a dog, but he deserved better than a cramped life in a grudging owner's laundry room.

Greg said, "He's a papillon. You'll love him. I thought he'd be a yappy thing, but I've never even heard him bark."

"Well . . ." Jay said.

"Wonderful!" Greg gave Dylan a quick, careful hug and scurried back into the house, rubbing his arms against the cold.

Dylan held out his arms, and Jay tucked the puppy in beside him.

"You're too good to me," Dylan said dryly, and even though I knew he was being sarcastic, I silently agreed.

CHAPTER FIFTEEN

When I left the house on Friday afternoon, Jay was sitting at the dining room table reading the comics and eating strawberry Pop-Tarts. Beside his plate were a half-empty glass of soy milk and a fistful of vitamins and prescription drugs. The sound of Dylan's rattling breath came from a baby monitor on the edge of the counter.

"Sleeping," Jay whispered, gesturing toward the living room.

"Probably good for him. You going to be all right?"

"You're the one who's out chasing murderers." He turned the page to the horoscopes. Pointed to mine. "The stars say it's a bad time to take risks."

"It always is."

The forecast called for snow, and already the freezing wind cut through my fleece-lined jacket as if it were cotton. I pulled on a pair of gloves and a knit cap and drove to Josh's high school. Found a parking spot near the front, where a wave of exuberant teens poured through the double doors and spewed out into the parking lot.

In the front hall, I found Josh chatting with his English teacher, Elisha Casale. An attractive woman. Caramel skin. Hair the color of molasses in sunlight. We'd met the summer before, and I wondered if maybe the chance of seeing her was what had made me come inside instead of waiting for Josh in the truck.

I said, "Hello, Elisha."

She smiled, but not before I saw the hurt on her face. "Jared. You look well."

"You too."

She tilted her head, searched my face with her eyes. "I thought you might call."

"I meant to. I've been—"

She held up a hand. "I know. Busy."

"Confused."

"How about now?"

"Getting there."

She scribbled something on a scrap of paper and pressed it into my palm. "I'll wait," she said, and smiled. "But not forever." With another flash of teeth, she turned and was swallowed by the human flood.

I folded the paper and stuffed it into my wallet.

Josh nudged me with an elbow. "Her number?"

I nodded.

"If you don't call her," he said, "you really are insane."

I didn't disagree.

We crunched across the gravel parking lot and he settled into the truck, pulling the seat belt across his chest and waist.

"Tell me about this game," I said. "What are the rules?"

"You've gotta be kidding. It's not Monopoly. You can't just read the rules off a box top."

"Just hit the high points. Is this the game you guys used to play in?"

"We went a couple of times—me and Razor and the rest of us. Guy named Chuck runs it. He asked Razor not to come anymore."

"How come?"

He shrugged. "Razor thought he was jealous, but I don't know. This group is pretty straight. Maybe they just got weirded out." He plucked at his seat belt. "Thing is, Razor didn't even like the game that much. It just pissed him off that Chuck said he couldn't play."

I slowed for the speed trap in Lakewood, and Josh chatted about the game for the next few miles. I made the several convolutions Map-Quest assured me would take me to the community center. Then Josh leaned forward and pointed.

"That's it."

There was nothing remarkable about it. No gothic spires or make-believe cobwebs. It was a plain rectangular building with a small gravel parking lot, as ordinary as peanut butter.

There were already a dozen or so vehicles in the lot, many of which sported bumper stickers. *I Believe in Whirled Peas, My Other Car Is a Horse, My Other Car Is a Broom, Cthulhu Saves.*

In front of the building, half a dozen women in brightly colored parkas huddled beside the door, holding up signs that said, *Beware the Appearance of Evil* and *This Game is the Devil's Work.* One said simply, *Vampires Suck.*

As Josh and I passed, I recognized a curl of dark hair and the strong, sorrowful features of Marta Savales. Alan Keating's number one fan.

I stopped in front of her and said, "Mrs. Savales, isn't it? Jared McKean. We met at Razor's funeral."

She blinked as if trying to place me, then gave a cautious nod and hugged herself for warmth. "Is this your son?"

"Nephew."

"If you love that boy at all, put him back in your car and drive him home."

"It's just a game," Josh said. "It can't hurt anybody."

"Is that what you think?" Her eyes glittered in the street light. "I wonder if your friend Razor would agree."

Josh blanched. Before he could speak, I laid a hand on his shoulder and nudged him toward the door. *Forget about it.*

Inside, people whose costumes ranged from jeans to formal wear milled about or clustered around a cafeteria table draped in black and piled with cupcakes, chips, and soft drinks.

Two men in suits flanked the door. They pretended to scan us for weapons, using flashlights as ersatz metal detectors, and waved us inside. I pretended I didn't have the Glock in a small-of-back holster under my sweater.

Josh and I tossed our jackets onto a table piled high with winter coats. Then Josh tugged me toward a stocky guy with shaggy ginger hair and a beard in need of a trim. He looked like a lumberjack.

Josh said, "Uncle Jared, this is Chuck Weaver. He runs the game."

Chuck gave me a cockeyed grin and extended a hand. "Good to have you, man. Josh says you're a virgin."

"Hardly."

"I mean it's your first time to the role-playing world. Looking for a regular game?"

"Just checking it out for Josh's mom and dad. And I'm investigating Sebastian Parker's death."

"That freak," he said, nose wrinkling. "He wasn't a player. He was a psycho."

Josh opened his mouth and I gave his shoulder a firm squeeze.

"Care to elaborate?" I asked Chuck.

"No time." He gestured toward the milling crowd. "I don't think I'd be much help, anyway. He didn't play with us that long."

"Josh told me. Why was that?"

"Look around. You'll see mostly regular folks in regular clothes. Some people dress up." He nodded toward a woman in a low-cut red ball gown that looked like it had probably had a previous life as a prom dress. "But so what? It's all just acting. The problem is when you get somebody who isn't acting."

"Like Razor."

"He wasn't playing a vampire game. He was playing at being a vampire." He glanced at his watch. "Look, I gotta get things rolling. Josh can show you the ropes."

I dug out a business card and handed it to him. "Mind jotting down your number? I have a couple of questions."

He gave the card a perfunctory glance and scribbled a number on the back before handing it back. Then he pressed past me and raised his hands for attention. Gradually, the hubbub died down.

"Hey, everybody," he said. "Good to see you all braved the inclement weather. Hope everybody stocked up."

There was a ripple of good-natured laughter. Here in the South, the merest whisper of the S-word sends people scurrying to the grocery stores for milk, bread, and jumbo packs of toilet paper. In some circles, the list has been expanded to include beer and porn.

Chuck held up his hands for silence and went on. "Okay, quick review. First, this is a community building, so let's leave it in as good a shape as we found it. Second, keep the game inside. If you want to step out for a smoke or a quiet chat, that's fine, but the last thing we need is for the locals to get all freaked out and call the cops because the vampires are acting up outside their community center."

There was another spate of laughter. Chuck waved toward the snack tables. "No rowdiness, no alcohol, no non-prescription drugs. There are soft drinks and munchies over there for anyone who wants them. There's a basket on the table for contributions, if you want to help with next month's goodies. Any questions?"

There were none.

He gave the group an overview I found hard to follow, probably because it came in the middle of an ongoing story line. There'd been an attempt on the life of the vampire prince of Nashville. Before his execution, the assassin admitted he'd been hired by someone in the city—one of the prince's own subjects.

I whispered to Josh, "The Vampire Prince of Nashville. That's what you guys called Razor."

Josh hunched a shoulder. "That's what he called himself. It didn't have anything to do with this game." He put a finger to his lips and nodded toward Chuck.

"The traitor must be ferreted out and dealt with," Chuck said. "The vampires are coming together to discuss this crisis and the best way to deal with it. Some are meeting at a local art gallery." He pointed to the center of the room, where tables had been arranged to form the boundaries of an open rectangle. A white poster-board sign on one table said *Rogue's Gallery.* He went on, "The Wall Street types are meeting in their boardroom, and the rest of you are either at Court or the biker bar, although the lower elements may be skulking in the sewer tunnels." He indicated the designated areas and raised his arms like an orchestra conductor. "Let the games begin!"

"Come on," Josh said. "I'll give you a tour." He tugged me toward the boardroom, where three men and a woman in tailored suits were discussing the nefarious plot to kill their prince. We listened for awhile. Then Josh said, "Hey, look. There's about to be a fight in the biker bar."

I must have looked alarmed, because he rolled his eyes and said, "It's rock, paper, scissors."

"What?"

"That's how we handle combat. Rock, paper, scissors. Whoever wins the rock, paper, scissors wins the combat." He led me toward the area marked *Biker Bar*, where two men, both in jeans and leather jackets, had squared off chest to chest.

"Your insolence offends me," the taller man said with a menacing glower. "In fact, your very existence offends me."

The other man, heavily bearded and mustached, sneered. "Talk is cheap, General."

"Oh, I'll do more than talk." The General cracked his knuckles loudly. "I intend to kick your hirsute Philistine ass."

Then they waited for a mediator to arrive, whereupon they did indeed engage in a round of rock, paper, scissors. The hirsute Philistine was the victor (rock smashes scissors), and the General stalked out of the bar while the others congratulated the winner. Once out of the biker bar area, the General dropped his sour demeanor and drifted toward the snack table.

"See?" Josh grinned. "No bloodshed." He was more animated than I'd seen him in months. I let him chatter, enjoying this rare glimpse of the kid I'd taught to play cops and robbers.

"It's pretty complex, isn't it?" I said.

He seemed pleased. "Yeah, it is. Lots of politics and stuff. Mostly, it's just people standing around and talking to each other, pretending to be other people."

"How is all this different from what Razor did?"

He thought for a moment, then said, "Razor wasn't playing. He ran a game for awhile because it seemed like fun, and the rest of us liked to play it, but the whole vampire world to him . . . it wasn't about pretending to be a character. He *was* the character."

"You believe that? That he was a vampire?"

He couldn't meet my gaze. "He had some kind of power. Maybe it was just charisma."

We wandered from area to area, listening to snippets of conversation. When he was sure I wasn't going to drive a stake through anybody's heart, Josh drifted away to join the artistic types and I slipped out for a breath of fresh air. The predicted snowfall had begun, and a patina of fat flakes glistened on the hood and shoulders of Marta

Savales's parka. She stood with her back to the wind, blowing into her gloved hands so the steam from her breath warmed her face. Of the half-dozen protesters, she was the only one left.

I touched her lightly on the shoulder. "Why don't you go home, Ms. Savales? The roads are getting worse."

"I'll leave when they leave," she said.

"I don't think you're going to stop anybody from playing tonight."

"Those people are dangerous, Mr. McKean," she said. "That *game* is dangerous."

"Why do you say that?"

She reached into her purse and pulled out a billfold, which she opened to a photograph of a dark-haired boy who looked to be in his middle teens.

"This is my son," she said. "His name is Benjy."

I studied the photograph. Unruly brown hair. Crooked smile with the corner of one front tooth overlapping the other.

"He looks like a good kid."

"He is. Or . . . I think . . ." She tilted her head back, eyelashes wet with snow or tears. "Maybe he *was.*"

"You think he might be dead. And you think this game has something to do with that? So why'd you spit on Alan Keating?"

"Keating is an idiot. Or a devil. Did he tell you about Chase? No, of course not." A drop of moisture trickled from her nostril. I pulled a tissue from my pocket and handed it to her. She dabbed at her nose. "Thank you."

"Who's Chase?"

"Chase Eddington. He was one of Razor's victims—and one of Mr. Keating's patients. His parents didn't know about Keating's connection to Razor." She twisted the Kleenex into a corkscrew and closed her gloved fist around it. "When they found out who Keating was, they got Chase a new therapist. A few weeks later, the boy killed himself."

I thought of Josh, of the splash of blood on white porcelain. Pushed the thought away. "You knew him? Chase Eddington?"

"No, I met his mother—Hannah, Hannah Eddington—at a meeting for bereaved parents. And—this is terrible, I know—all I could think was that at least she knew what had happened to her son."

I touched her forearm lightly with my fingertips. She gave me a bleary smile and I withdrew my hand. "Tell me about Benjy."

She looked down at her hands, where a sprinkling of snow and white tissue fibers dusted her gloves. "Sometimes I tell myself he's dead, and it would be better just to accept that and let him go. But then I think, well, if there's no body . . . You see how it is?"

"If there's no body, he isn't dead."

She wrapped her arms around herself, shivering, and nodded. He was a good boy, she said. She hadn't worried about the role playing, because her older boys had both been Dungeons & Dragons aficionados, and they'd grown up to be well-adjusted, moral men. Benjy seemed to be following in their footsteps.

Then he met Razor.

"He was confused," Ms. Savales said. "Was he straight? Was he gay? He'd never thought he was gay, but if he wasn't, then what was he doing with Razor?"

I stared out at the snow swirling across the parking lot and unclenched my teeth. "He told you all this?"

"We were very close. I told him he had to stop seeing this man, that it was bad for him."

"Let me guess. He wouldn't stop."

"No. He said he would. A few days later, I came home from work and found a note saying he needed to pick up some things of his from Razor's house. He said he'd be right back." She gave a hiccupping laugh. "He never came home. His car turned up at the bus terminal downtown. He was so proud of it, he'd just gotten it for his birthday. If he was running away, why would he leave his car and take a bus?"

She dabbed at her eyes with the ruined Kleenex. "I'm sorry. I can't talk about it anymore."

I asked for a number where I could reach Chase's parents. She gave it to me, then tucked Benjy's photo back into her purse.

"I'll find your son, Ms. Savales," I said.

"I hired a detective once. He couldn't find anything. There was nothing to find."

"There's always something to find."

I went back inside to find Josh and spent another hour watching the game. Chuck drifted from group to group, mediating and filling in gaps in the story line. Affable guy. Smart. Smart enough to stage a crime scene like Razor's?

When things broke up a few hours later, Marta Savales was still outside, lips clenched over chattering teeth, meeting the hostile glances of the gamers with quiet defiance. Josh and I walked her out to her car, wrenched open the door, which had frozen shut, and scraped the ice from her windows.

"One more thing," I said, holding the door as she climbed inside. "How well do you know Alan Keating?"

She made an angry gesture, like swatting at an invisible fly. "I went by his office a few times to ask him about Benjy. He said he didn't know anything."

"You don't believe him."

"Benjy once said that Alan Keating was the only person in the world Razor would confide in."

"Patient-doctor privilege?" I asked.

"Maybe. I used to think of psychologists as being a bit like priests in that way."

"The confidentiality of the confessional."

"That's Alan Keating for you." She gave me a bitter smile. "The Devil's confessor."

Josh and I watched her drive away, then bundled into the Silverado and inched our way home as snow spattered against the windshield and ice crusted on the streets.

By the time I dropped him off at Randall's place and made my way home, it was almost midnight. Getting ready for bed, I laid my wallet on the beside table and thought of the phone number I'd tucked inside.

Too late to call Elisha now.

I wasn't sure if I felt disappointed or relieved.

CHAPTER SIXTEEN

The next morning, I spent an extra thirty minutes chipping ice out of the horses' troughs, then drove to the office on snow-covered streets. The red light on the answering machine was flashing. Messages from two potential clients. A skip trace and a cheating spouse surveillance. Easy money, but not wanting to commit to anything but Josh, I called both back, explained that my slate was full, and referred them to one of my competitors, a former football player named Lou Wilder. Lou and I had our differences, but he did good work.

I pulled out Razor's file and sank down in the leather chair behind the desk Frank hated. Scratched and riddled with bullet holes, the massive oak piece dated from the Civil War. One side had been scorched during a Yankee raid. Its owner, a physician, had taken it by wagon train to Arizona, where it held vials of drugs and jars of liniment until the doctor passed away and his son, the local sheriff, appropriated it. Over the years, it passed from family member to family member like an unwanted foster child, until it finally made its way to Tennessee, where a client of mine gave it to me in lieu of payment.

As it turned out, I loved the thing. It made me feel like Wyatt Earp.

I sat behind it with Razor's file in front of me and jotted the names and numbers of the coterie members onto the back of a business card. Tried the first number, Dark Knight's. No answer. Dialed the number Barnabus shared with Medea, and the answering machine informed me, in a cheesy Bela Lugosi imitation, that I could leave a message at the shriek. I told Bela who I was and asked for a call back.

I pulled out the number Marta Savales had given me, leaned back in my chair and thought of Chase Eddington, the boy who had killed himself. Just by dialing the number, I would scrape these people raw.

But my nephew needed answers, and more important, the detectives who suspected him of murder needed answers. To save Josh, I would scrape the whole world raw.

I dialed the number.

The woman who answered had a pleasant voice, like a kindergarten teacher. When I told her who I was and what I wanted, she gave a little gasp and said, "Oh. I don't think . . . What could we possibly tell you?"

"It shouldn't take long," I said. "I could be there in thirty minutes."

Silence.

"You can call Frank Campanella at the West precinct house. He'll vouch for me." I gave her the number.

Another pause. Then, "All right," she said. "This afternoon. But I'm afraid you'll be wasting your time."

—◊—

They lived on a quiet street in Inglewood, a few blocks from the river, in a ranch-style brick house with rust-colored shutters and two front windows, each with a peaked gable above and a long white flower box below. Nice house, not too expensive, in a nice, not-too-expensive neighborhood, an oasis of middle class coziness in a part of town slowly going to seed. A basketball hoop hung from the garage door, a ragged net dangling from one side.

I thought of Chase and his father shooting hoops in the driveway and felt a pressure behind my eyes.

The yard was small, but it seemed to take a long time to cross it. The snow had melted and refrozen, and with each step, my boots crunched through an icy crust.

I hesitated on the front porch. Not too late to turn around and leave these people in peace.

Instead, I rang the bell.

No answer.

I rang again, then strolled around to the backyard, where a blocky man who looked to be in his early fifties and a woman maybe a decade younger stood feeding strips of cardboard into a bonfire. She was shivering in khakis and a forest-green sweater that looked like it wouldn't be much use against the cold.

An overweight black lab peered out from behind the woman's legs, tail wagging, a ribbon of drool dangling from its tongue.

The man picked up a branch and prodded at the fire. Sparks swirled up like fireflies. An ember landed on the shoulder of his jacket, and he swatted at it with a calloused hand. The woman brushed her fingertips across the spot where it had been.

I moved into their line of vision. "Doug and Hannah Eddington?"

They both looked up, her eyebrows lifting, his joining in a heavy black 'V.' They were a handsome couple, not beautiful, but they looked good together. Her chin-length bob was frosted with gray, and a web of fine lines etched the corners of her eyes. She had a fleshy angularity around the hips, the kind skinny women often develop as they age. Her waist was slim, her stomach small and round, like half a grapefruit.

Her husband was darkly tanned, with a square-jawed face going to jowl and a forehead creased with worry lines. The sleeves of his shirt were bunched at the elbows, revealing hairy forearms heavy with muscle.

"We're trying to get on with things," he said. "Yesterday, my wife laughed at a joke she heard at the Piggly Wiggly. Now here you come to pick off the scab."

"I'm sorry," I said, moving closer to the flames. "That's not my intention."

"What is your intention?"

"I don't know. Just fishing."

Hannah's smile was small, half-frozen. She rubbed her upper arms with her hands and said, "It's too cold out here for fishing. Maybe we should go inside."

Doug gave her a long look, then sighed and turned back to the fire. Prodded the blackening cardboard. It crumbled into a maelstrom of sparks and ashes. "Just about done here, anyway."

He walked over to a faucet at the back of the house and came back with a shiny green garden hose. Water hissed inside it as the pressure built. Then a spray of ice and water shot from the end and spewed onto the flames. When nothing was left but a steaming pile of ash, Eddington put a crimp in the hose to staunch the water flow.

"Get you something?" he said. His voice sounded strained. "Coffee? Something stronger? I'm a bourbon man, myself."

"I'm fine. Don't go to any trouble."

"No trouble. Coffee's made, bourbon's . . . Well, that's made too, I guess."

"Coffee, then. Black."

I followed them back to the house, kicked my feet against the step to knock off the snow and followed them in.

"Shoes," Doug said, and pointed to my feet. He pulled off his muddy work boots and laid them beside Hannah's wet sneakers on a braided rug in front of the door. I followed suit, as Hannah wiped the dog's paws with a damp cloth.

The mudroom led to a hallway lined with photographs. A plump baby girl in a lace christening gown. Another baby, this one a boy, in a white satin suit. More pictures of the boy. Taking tentative steps with one fist clenched around his father's finger. Splashing in a plastic swimming pool. Learning to ride a bike.

Eddington averted his eyes as he passed them, but his jaw pulsed. Hannah looked at each one as she passed, occasionally trailing her fingers along the frames.

In the kitchen, Hannah settled me into the breakfast nook and busied herself at the coffee maker. The dog, by way of greeting, shoved its nose into my crotch.

Doug padded over in his sock feet, a bourbon on the rocks in one hand. "Bo, stop that," he said, and the dog heaved a sigh and laid its head against my knee.

"You had questions," Hannah said to me. She brought me the coffee in a china cup so delicate I was afraid it might shatter in my hand. Her hands were trembling, and as she set the cup in front of me, some of the hot liquid sloshed into my lap.

We both gasped, for different reasons.

"I'm so sorry, Mr. McKean." She snatched a dishtowel from the counter, started to dab at the spill, then reddened and handed me the cloth. "It's . . . I've tried so hard to put it out of my mind."

"It's all right, Mrs. Eddington." I dabbed at the stain on my lap, then gave up and pulled out my shirttail to hide it. "I can't imagine how hard it must've been."

Doug pulled over a chair, turned its back toward the table, and straddled it. "God grant you never find out."

"How did it happen?"

He took a sip of his bourbon, swished it around in his mouth, and swallowed. "I wish I knew. It started with that game. At first it seemed harmless, but then he started getting more and more into it. Couldn't—or wouldn't—talk about anything else. Then he started hanging out with some other Goth kids, and I guess that's how he met this Razor."

Hannah slid into the chair across from me and set her cup on the table. "I know what you must be thinking. Where were we? Why didn't we do something?"

"We tried," Doug said. "We'd ground him, he'd sneak out. Take his car away, they'd pick him up, all hours of the night."

Hannah said, "We tried to reason with him. And when that didn't work, I begged. But it was like . . . he was under some kind of spell."

Doug swirled the ice in his glass. "You second guess yourself. I was a Marine, for Christ's sake. Maybe I was too hard on him. Maybe I wasn't hard enough."

"Hard to say," I said. "You did your best."

"Finally, we confronted him. Or I did. Hannah was never one for confrontations." He gave her a tender smile and closed his hand over hers.

I nodded. Waited.

"It was a mess," he said. "I yelled at him, he screamed at me. And finally, he said it. That he was . . . sleeping with this Razor. He wasn't even queer. It was just . . . this Razor got him all twisted around. Talking about transcendence, and higher levels of existence. All that bullshit, but I guess it sounded good coming from him."

"What did you do when you found out?"

"Went ballistic. Told Chase it would be a cold day in Hell before he saw this son of a bitch again. I'd've killed the bastard then, if I'd gotten my hands on him." He stopped, as if suddenly remembering why I was there. "Is this where you ask me if I murdered him?"

"Did you?"

"No. But I would have that night. That was when Chase fell apart. He threatened to kill himself, got a knife from the kitchen and tried to slash his wrists."

I thought of Josh, wrists swathed in bandages, and said, "Hellish."

He raked his fingers through his hair. "We took him to the hospital, got him committed. It was a short-term thing, just until he got his head together. But he wouldn't talk to the psychiatrists. He finally said he'd go to counseling if we sent him to Alan Keating."

"So you sent him."

"We didn't know what else to do. We didn't know who Keating was. Chase just said he knew one of Keating's other patients. Three weeks after he started therapy, we found out Alan Keating was Razor's best buddy. We got Chase a new counselor, and a week after that, my boy was dead."

"You blame Keating for that?"

Hannah said, "No. Yes . . . The thing is, Chase liked him. He wouldn't have felt that way if Alan had hurt him, would he?"

I said, "Keating canceled his appointments the afternoon Razor was killed."

Her cup clattered to the table, coffee sloshing over the rim. "You think Alan Keating . . ."

"I don't know."

"No. No. He's not that kind of person."

Doug said, "He was this Razor's best friend. That says something about him."

I tried to picture Doug Eddington hanging Razor from a rod, posing him on a pentagram, carving symbols into his arms. He had plenty of motive, but that didn't mean anything. Everyone who'd known Razor had a reason to kill him.

Hannah pushed her cup away. Wordlessly, Doug picked it up and carried it to the sink.

Hannah smiled. "My knight in shining armor. Did Marta tell you how we met?"

I shook my head.

"I was fourteen. He was fresh from the war and saved me from a group of boys who were tormenting me outside the Dairy Queen. Of course, I was just a child to him, but that's when I fell in love." She stroked the dog's broad head.

"It was nothing," Doug said. He brought another bourbon to the table. "Anybody would've helped."

She shook her head. "Six years later, my car broke down, right in the middle of Old Hickory Boulevard. This handsome young man stopped to help, and lo and behold, it was him."

She pushed the dog away gently and stood up to wash her hands. Doug moved aside to give her room.

She said, "It had to be Fate, don't you think? Or God, or whatever you believe in. Every time in my life I've really needed help, Doug's been there to make things right." She poured a dollop of pink liquid soap into her palm. "Do you believe in that, Mr. McKean?"

I thought of Maria and nodded.

"We were married eight months later." She held her hands beneath the faucet and scrubbed them with a green mesh puff until the knuckles were red. "Marriage we were good at. It was making babies we couldn't seem to get the hang of."

"Don't," Doug said. "You don't have to tell him this."

She went on as if she hadn't heard. "Two miscarriages and then a little boy. Jonathan. He was stillborn." She wrenched the faucet handle until the stream of water slowed to a drip, then picked up the dish towel and wiped the counter clean with it. She kept rubbing, long after the surface was clean. "Then Lucinda came along. She lived for almost a year. And after that was Chase. We must have been doing something right, because we managed to keep him alive for sixteen years."

I said, "What happened to Chase wasn't your fault."

"I'd like to believe that." She folded the towel into quarters, then turned back to face me. "May I ask *you* a question?"

"Sure."

"They say he was . . . Razor was . . . butchered."

"That's enough, honey," Doug said. "You don't want to be thinking about that."

He stood up. Gave me a pointed stare.

"Thanks for the coffee," I said to Hannah. "And . . . I'm sorry for your loss." As I followed Doug out, I glanced into the living room. Salmon-tinted walls, furniture in white and peach, glass-topped coffee table with a bowl of walnuts on it. Beside the entertainment center was a maple gun case with a four-point buck etched into the glass door.

Another hunter. I paused in the doorway and nodded toward the gun case. "You hunt, Mr. Eddington?"

"Used to. Not much time for it these days. Why?"

"You dress your own deer?" I watched his face for a reaction and got none.

"Yeah. Sure. Why?"

"Just wondered what kind of knife you use."

"Buck Crosslock. Two blades, three functions." He went over, opened the case, and showed me. "Three-and-a-quarter-inch drop-point blade, three-and-a-quarter-inch gutting blade with a saw on the back edge."

"You got a tactical knife?"

"What would be the point?" He put the Crosslock back in its scabbard and closed the door. "This one does everything I need."

That meant nothing. The Crosslock would have done the job.

We talked hunting for a while. Then I thanked him for his time, and he shook my hand and walked me to the door. "You have a good evening, Mr. McKean."

"Jared." I bent to put my shoes on.

"You have a good evening, Jared." He gave me a smile that didn't reach his eyes. "But don't come here again."

I waited for a moment after he'd closed the door behind me. Then, suspicious bastard that I am, I went over to the ashes of Doug's bonfire. The branch he'd used to prod the flames lay beside the soggy ashes. I picked it up and poked through the soot and ash.

The layer of ash was thin, as if he'd only recently begun to use the fire pit, but the extent of the charring on the rocks that lined the pit told a different story. The pit had been cleaned out recently. I tried to make something sinister of it, but the truth was, if you burned trash regularly, there was a good chance you cleaned out the fire pit regularly too.

I sifted some more. Found a few scraps of corrugated cardboard that had escaped the blaze. Nothing important. If you'd asked me what I hoped to find, I wouldn't have been able to say. I liked the Eddingtons, and I think, more than anything, I was hoping to find nothing.

So it was with a mixture of relief and disappointment that nothing was exactly what I found.

CHAPTER SEVENTEEN

Later that afternoon, I put in a call to a friend in the juvenile division. Her name was Sherilyn Cade, and though we'd only occasionally crossed paths professionally, we'd traded favors and shared a few long lunches, commiserating over my divorce and her rocky relationship with a hardware salesman named Earl. It had been two years since we'd talked, but she still recognized my voice.

"No way this is a social call," she said. "Not after all this time. So, spit it out, honeybunch. What do you need?"

"Kid named Byron Birch. Got a juvenile record. I need to know what's on his sheet."

"You know that's confidential."

"I know. I'll owe you, big time."

"Big time, huh?" She made a little humming sound. Paused for a moment, thinking it over. Then, "Buy me lunch, and I'll see what I can do."

"You're sure Earl won't kick my ass?"

"Honey, Earl would marry you himself if he thought you'd buy him a cheeseburger."

I agreed to her terms and hung up feeling restless. I thought about Byron. His dullness at the funeral, his mental lethargy. He'd been seduced by a sexual predator, come home one evening expecting to share a meal with his lover and walked into an abattoir, and now he was living with the predator's best friend.

Kid in crisis, you damn betcha.

I called Keating's house, but the machine picked up. I left a voice-mail message for Byron, left another message with Barnabus's Bela Lugosi recording, and finally called Miss Aleta. An hour and forty-five minutes later, she and I were sitting at the visitor's table again. The door swung open, and Absinthe shuffled into the training room and plopped down across the table from us. One cheek was swollen, a purple bruise forming around one eye.

Miss Aleta frowned, gestured to the bruise and said, "Who hurt you?"

Absinthe brushed the cheek with her fingertips. "Some moron at supper last night. Said I was eyeing her dessert. Pumpkin pie, with that gross artificial topping. I mean, as *if*. It wasn't even real pie." Tough words, but her eyes welled, and a patchwork of red blotches bloomed on her face.

"Are you all right, child?"

"I guess. When are you getting me out of here?"

"Soon." Miss Aleta handed Absinthe a fresh tissue and gave her a reassuring pat. "We go back to court day after tomorrow, see if we can't put a stop to all this nonsense about adult courts and no bail."

"I don't see why they don't just let me go. I took it back. I said I didn't do it."

"It doesn't work that way."

Absinthe sniffled and cut her eyes toward me. "Are you helping her get me out?"

"Looks like it," I said. "And right now I need to know about Benjy Savales."

She gave a little hiccup, and a bubble of snot popped out of one nostril. She clamped the tissue to her nose and honked into it. "God, I'm a mess. What's Benjy got to do with anything?"

"Kind of suspicious, the way he disappeared, don't you think?"

"Razor said he ran away. He and Razor had some kind of argument or something, and a few days later, Benjy just stopped coming around."

"You never heard from him again?"

"His mother came around a few times asking about him, and so did the police. But, you know, what could we say? We didn't know anything."

I leaned forward and rested my forearms on the table. "Why do you think he ran away? Did Razor do something to him?"

"Who says he left because of Razor? Maybe he left because his mother was a crazy woman." She looked down at her hands. Noticed a hangnail on one thumb and rubbed at it with the tip of a finger. "I can't believe I confessed. Pretty stupid, huh? But I really thought I'd done it, you know? That I made it happen. But I talked to Mom last night, and she said there was no such thing as witchcraft, and since it couldn't have really hurt him, I didn't really do anything wrong."

Miss Aleta clucked her tongue and said, "Oh, child."

I took a deep breath. "Say I get really mad at you, mad enough to want to kill you. So I point my gun at you and pull the trigger. Would that be wrong?"

"Of course. But—"

"The gun jams. It doesn't go off. Does that mean I didn't do anything wrong?"

She picked at a fingernail. "You're saying it doesn't matter if it would have worked or not."

"Not if you meant for it to."

"And if I didn't? If I really thought it wouldn't work?" A tear slid down her cheek. Miss Aleta pulled another Kleenex out of her jacket pocket and handed it across the table.

I said, "Then I guess you're off the hook."

I asked her about the other players in Razor's game. I had the basics from the file, but I needed more. She talked, and I scribbled the details in a pocket-sized tablet.

First was Dennis Knight, the pimpled boy from the funeral home. A.k.a. Dark Knight, whose mother had provided an alibi for most of the players. Absinthe blushed when she said his name, and I didn't have to be a mind reader to see she liked him. Then Barnabus Collins, who slept in a coffin and who had legally changed his name to that of a sixties-era Hollywood vampire.

She paused, and I said, "What about Medea?"

Absinthe's mouth twisted as if she'd tasted something bitter. "Razor met her a couple of months after he met me. At first, it was cool. Then he said . . . um, he said I was a disappointment. That I wasn't committed. He said Medea was, like, a ton stronger than me.

And since I didn't go on to the Second Ring, I had to be Medea's acolyte and do whatever she said."

"Ouch."

"Yeah."

"What's the Second Ring?"

She pressed her lips together. "Nothing. It's not important."

"It was important enough for him to make Medea his top witch instead of you."

She sighed. Sucked on the inside of her cheek. Finally, she said, "We were neonates. New initiates. Not enlightened like he was."

"Good old Razor," I said. "Just like the Dalai Lama."

She skewered me with a glance.

"Just saying. Go on."

"Razor said enlightenment was like the bull's-eye of a target, and as neonates, we were on the outside ring. We had to go up to the next level of existence. The Second Ring. Be, you know, Transformed."

"Transformed. Into what?"

"Something better."

I tried again. "This Transformation. Why did he say you weren't committed enough?"

She untwined her fingers and plucked at the fabric of her jumpsuit. "I don't know."

He'd had some reason, and I didn't buy that Absinthe didn't know what it was, but she clearly wasn't ready to tell me or Miss Aleta.

I let it go and said, "So what was it like? Was there some kind of ceremony?"

"Just a regular ritual. You know. Chanting, incantations. And we drank some blood."

"Really." I said it matter-of-factly, but the thought made my stomach turn. I thought of HIV, hepatitis, hemorrhagic fevers. Thought of Dylan, dying in a hospital bed, and of Jay, waging war against AIDS. "Whose?"

She hesitated a moment, then said, "Each other's."

"Was Benjy there?"

"No, he and Razor split up just before the ceremony."

"How about Byron?"

"It was way before we met him. Besides, he doesn't have any powers."

"Absinthe . . . Nobody has powers."

"Just because you can't see it on CNN doesn't make it not real."

"You said it was a game. You let me borrow the rule book."

"That doesn't mean there was nothing to the rest of it."

"Razor's dead. That pretty much puts a cap on the whole 'Razor was a vampire' idea."

She twirled a strand of hair around her index finger. "Maybe he isn't dead. Maybe he's on this whole other plane now, and he's, like, a vampire of the spirit."

"So you think he's still floating around somewhere, feeding on people?"

She wanted it to be true, and for some reason this bothered me. I wanted to see her as a reckless innocent swept up in a game she wasn't old enough to understand. But here she was, still flirting with the devil.

"You don't get it," she said. "He was special. Being around him was like looking into the sun."

"So people say."

"He was like that angel in the Bible. You know, the one they say God loved the best."

I was no expert on angels, but I named the ones I knew. Michael. Gabriel. Raphael.

"You know the one I mean," she said. "Lucifer. The one who fell from grace."

Miss Aleta looked up from her tablet and shook her head.

I didn't argue the point. I wasn't her preacher, her therapist, or her father. Instead, I said, "When you go to court, you should probably keep that part to yourself."

Miss Aleta pushed back her chair and said, "Amen."

CHAPTER EIGHTEEN

By Wednesday, the snow had begun to melt, and scattered brown patches appeared through the white. I tried Barnabus's number again, and when I got no answer, decided to hell with the formalities and drove on over.

Barnabus and Medea lived in an exhausted antebellum mansion on Nashville's west side. I pulled into the driveway, passed between a matched set of soapstone gargoyles, and parked behind a black Mustang with a bumper sticker that said, *Honk if you love Satan.*

The front porch sagged in the middle and creaked beneath my feet. I shifted my weight to avoid a soft spot and pounded at the door until Medea finally answered, bleary eyes ringed with charcoal smudges, as if she'd slept in her mascara. She wore spiky black heels and black leggings under a dress that looked like it had been cobbled from a dance leotard and a handful of silk scarves.

Beneath the thin Lycra of the bodice, I could see the outline of her ribs and the sharp points of her nipples. Small breasts, but already sagging, as if she'd been starved.

I showed her my license, and she looked at it for a long time before a spark of recognition lit her eyes.

"Your life fall all to shit yet?" she asked.

"Not yet."

"It's colder than a witch's tit out here," she said, crossing her arms tightly across her breasts.

"Better let me in," I suggested. "Being as how you're not exactly dressed for the weather."

With a martyred sigh, she stepped inside, leaving me to close the door.

"You can't see Barnabus," she said. "He's not active in the day-time." She scuttled around the coffee table like one of Razor's black widow spiders. "And I'm not offering you anything, either. You're not a guest."

"Whatever you say." I looked around the room. Black velvet sofa and matching recliners, two straight-backed Queen Anne chairs, and a coffee table covered in a thin layer of dust. Crystal ball on the table, perched on a gold stand shaped like a dragon's claw. The walls were festooned with feathered masks, colored Mardi Gras beads, and a parade of dancing "Day of the Dead" skeletons strung up hand-in-hand like paper dolls.

The air was heavy with cigarette smoke and layers of incense.

"Why the hell would you come over here at this hour?" she said. "Me and my friends, we're night people. We don't really come alive until after dark."

"Uh huh. The vampire thing."

"At least we don't preach about love and then burn crosses on people's yards." She perched on the edge of a Queen Anne and crossed her legs. One foot bounced nervously, like a metronome. "You want to find out who killed Razor, talk to the Jesus people. Or talk to Chuck Weaver. He runs this vampire game over in Madison."

"Chuck asked Razor to leave his game."

"Ha." She gave me an ugly smile. "Chuck felt threatened, is all. Here he and his little friends are, playing vampires, and the real thing comes along. Chuck couldn't compete with that."

"You're saying it was a power thing?"

"Isn't everything? Sex. Love. Money. Charisma. Razor had it. Chuck didn't. Doesn't. Won't ever have."

"But it was his game."

"That was no reason to treat Razor like some kind of bit player." She picked up one end of a scarf and arranged it over her thigh. "But Razor trashed him good. About a week after the game, Razor came by my place—I wasn't with Barnabus then—and asked me for a piece of jewelry and a pair of panties I'd worn." She ran her hand over the scarf. Gave me a sly smile. "He asked me to pose for some photos. Nude photos."

"Did you?"

"Why not? He took about a dozen. Then he said he was going to teach Chuck life's two great secrets."

"Which are?"

"If you mess with Razor, you're going to get cut."

"That's one."

"The other is, *Nobody loves anybody*. That's what Razor always said. And he was right, too."

"How do you figure?"

"Because his plan worked. He slim-jimmed Chuck's car, planted the earring in the floorboard and the panties under the seat, spritzed some perfume into the car, and put the pictures in the glove compartment. Then he called Chuck's wife and told her Chuck was having an affair."

She fished a cigarette out of the pack and placed it between her lips. It was slim and black and smelled like cloves, and she sucked on it for a moment before pulling a book of matches from between the wrapper and the pack.

"Look," she said. "Magic." She struck the match, lit her cigarette, then held the match aloft for me to admire. When the flame licked her fingertips, she shook it out.

"I prefer pot," she said, giving me a sidelong look, "but tobacco is sacred." She drew in a lungful of smoke and held it. I tried not to envision what it was doing to her body. Cancer is an ugly death. I know. It ate my mother alive.

"Chuck," I prompted her.

"Ha. Divorced. Kicked out on his ass. Paying alimony and child support out the wazoo. End of story." She took another long, orgasmic drag from the cigarette and pushed herself out of the chair. "You want to know the kicker, though?"

I nodded that I did.

She blew a double stream of smoke from her nostrils, preening herself like a cat that had just dropped a dead rat at its master's feet. "He said he'd kill Razor if he ever got the chance."

"I'll check it out. Tell me something. You believe in the Rule of Three?"

She waved the idea away. "That's a Wiccan thing. They don't have the guts to embrace real power."

"What's real power?"

"Real power." She leaned forward, resting her palms on my chest, and stood on her tiptoes so that her breath warmed my face. "Real power is doing whatever the hell you want."

And then she licked my cheek.

"Seducing the company?" A man's voice, deep baritone with an English accent that was obviously fake, came from behind me.

I turned around to get a good look at him, and Medea teetered on her stiletto heels and grabbed my arm for balance.

He was cadaverously thin, with pale skin, sunken cheeks, and a prominent, beakish nose. Between the open edges of his black silk shirt, his chest was the color of buttermilk.

Medea gave him an exaggerated smirk. "Just having a little fun, my sweet."

"You can take him for a test drive, but I doubt he'd hold your interest long." He hooked his thumbs into the waistband of his pants and arranged his fingers so they framed his crotch. "So you're the detective."

"You must be Barnabus." I extended a hand, which he regarded with disdain. After a moment, I shrugged and lowered my hand. "Up during daylight, I see."

He took his thumbs from his waistband and sank into the velvet armchair. "I got your message. You want to know what happened to Razor. No great mystery, really. I imagine his past caught up with him."

Medea settled onto the sofa, her legs tucked under her. The scarves parted across her thighs, revealing a flash of black panties. I averted my gaze and took a seat on one of the Queen Annes, which made them both laugh.

I said, "What did you mean, his past caught up with him?"

"He had a way of alienating people. Family. Neighbors. Parents of the young men he slept with." He ticked them off on his fingers. "Then there's Byron. There's a kid with a troubled past."

"How about you and Medea? What were you doing the day Razor was killed?"

"Role-playing at Dark Knight's place. His mother already told the police that."

"Any rivalry between the two of you?"

"Razor was my Sire, but I'll surpass him soon. Medea can sense power. Razor's was waning. Mine is on the way up."

"Is that why Razor wasn't playing that day?"

"He wasn't playing because he was bored with the game. Imagine a real knight of the round table trying to play Dungeons & Dragons. It would get tiresome. And he wasn't a very good player, if you want to know the truth. He always wanted to run things."

No surprises there. "Tell me about the Transformation ritual. What did it mean?"

He smiled, revealing a row of white teeth with unnaturally long canines. He noticed my interest and pushed one side of his lip with one finger. "You like them? Porcelain. I had them custom-made."

"What did the ritual mean?" I repeated.

He blew out an exasperated breath. "It was a symbolic gesture indicating we'd given up the truths and values of our mortal lives and moved on to a new level of existence. A more honest level. One free of false altruism and shallow sentimentality."

"What? Like bloodletting and human sacrifices?"

He stretched his legs out in front of him, crossing them at the ankles. "You've seen too many movies. Bloodletting, yes. Human sacrifice? Well, that's something else altogether."

"A whole new level, right?"

"Several levels, I imagine." He stood up, stretched, and sauntered to the window, hands in his pockets. "It's about embracing the Great Darkness. Razor used to talk about it, and it was clear to anyone who knew him that he'd touched it somehow."

"The Great Darkness? Is that like Satan?"

"I read somewhere once that God is like an infinite ocean of love and light, and you can just dip into it and scoop up a cup full whenever you like. No matter how much you scoop out, the ocean is still the ocean."

"Nice analogy."

He looked pleased. "Well, Razor dipped out of a different ocean. What he called the Great Darkness. And he scooped out a cup full of midnight."

It sounded right. Razor had been steeped in toxic love since the day he was born. To him, the Light was alien, more frightening than the familiar chill of Darkness. "This next level," I said. "What did you have to do to reach it?"

"You scooped out your cup of midnight. Pledged to Embrace the Great Darkness, renounce the petty concerns of humanity, and embark on a journey of the spirit."

"No human sacrifice?"

"Afraid not." He perched on the arm of the sofa and placed a hand on Medea's shoulder. "Razor danced at the edge of Darkness, but when it came right down to it, he lacked the intestinal fortitude to leap in."

"But you don't."

"I didn't kill him." His hand moved to the back of Medea's neck. "I suppose I might have, eventually. But someone beat me to it."

"Benjy Savales disappeared around the time of your great Transformation."

His hand on Medea's neck squeezed, released. "He ran away to L.A., I think. Or maybe San Francisco. He called me once, a few months after he left. Said he was waiting tables in some little dive right on the beach. Living like a bohemian, pursuing a career in acting."

"I guess your phone records will back you up."

He hesitated, then said, "Unless they've made some mistake."

Covering his bases. I wondered why.

I asked again about the ritual, and he heaved another aggrieved sigh. "Razor made a speech about how we'd been preparing for this moment. Then we all took some vows and Razor passed around a chalice with some blood in it. It was kind of like taking Communion."

It was an ugly comparison. "Why wasn't Absinthe included?"

"She was included. She just didn't ascend, because she wasn't really serious. And hell, she's just a kid. I don't know why Razor even let her hang around."

"She said she was special to him."

Medea snorted.

Barnabus shot her a warning look and said, "I think she may have meant something to him at one point, kind of like a favorite pet. But she ended up being a disappointment, and he was sorry later that he'd bothered with her."

"Why? What happened?"

He shrugged. "Ask Razor." Then he smiled. "Oh, that's right. You can't. He's dead."

"You don't sound exactly broken up about that."

"You think I should be falling apart?" he asked. "We weren't that kind of friends."

"Besides," Medea said. "Death is an illusion for people like us."

"Immortality?" I didn't try to hide the sarcasm. "Like Razor's?"

She smiled, but there was nothing pleasant about it. "Razor made a mistake that Barnabus will never make."

"Oh? What was that?"

"He pissed off his witch."

CHAPTER NINETEEN

My reverse phone directory gave Chuck Weaver's address as a mobile home park east of the city. I eased the Silverado through a maze of broken toys, rusted-out gas grills, and bicycles leaning on their sides. It was too early for Weaver to be home from work, so I sat in the car and listened to Christmas carols on the radio until his white Toyota Corolla pulled in beside me.

He waved in my direction and got out of his car, pausing long enough to retrieve a bulging canvas bag from the backseat.

I slid out of the Silverado and went around to meet him. "Mr. Weaver." I extended a hand.

He shook it with enthusiasm. "It's Chuck," he said. "Mr. Weaver is my father."

"Chuck, then. You got a few minutes?"

"Sure, why not?" He led me up the cinder-block steps, shifted the bag while he fiddled with the lock, and pushed open the door. With an embarrassed grin, he said, "It's not exactly the Ritz."

"Bet I've seen worse."

He stepped aside and set down the bag, which was crammed to overflowing with books and papers. When I was clear of the door, he kicked it closed and said, "Can I get you a beer?"

He gestured for me to sit down, then went into the kitchen. I pushed aside a garish hand-knitted afghan and sank onto the sofa, an olive drab monstrosity frayed at the arms. I heard the refrigerator door open, followed by the clinking of glass and the hiss of air being released from the bottles. Chuck came back into the room, handed me a cold beer, and kept one for himself.

He settled into a black faux-leather rocking recliner pocked with claw marks. Bought secondhand, I guessed, since there was no other sign of a cat. Weaver saw me looking and rubbed at a torn nub with his index finger. "I know. The décor is lousy. But after alimony and child support, there's not much left for niceties." He took a swig of beer, made a face. "Oh well, at least it's cold, right?"

"Razor ruined your marriage, didn't he?" I rested one ankle on the other knee and took a sip of the beer. It tasted like cold piss.

"Guy ruined everything he ever touched," Chuck said. "It was like a hobby with him."

"I had that impression. How'd you know it was him?"

"You don't think he could do a thing like that and not take credit for it, do you? Shoot, for him, half the fun was gloating afterwards." He took a long swig from the bottle. "Maybe it was for the best, though, right? There were a bunch of pictures, but I wasn't in any of them. If she couldn't believe I was set up, we must've had a problem already."

"Maybe," I said, "but it still sounds like you had a pretty good reason to want the guy dead."

He tilted the beer bottle and watched the liquid slosh from side to side. "I won't say I didn't think about it. One of my favorites is he gets hit by a bus and despite my most heroic efforts to save him, he dies in horrific agony. You're thinking I might have killed him?"

"I don't know yet. Did you?"

"No. I can't prove it, though, I don't think. When was he killed?"

I told him the date and time.

He thought about it. "So, where was I that afternoon? I believe I went out to the mall and bought some books. A couple of Terry Pratchetts. The new Stephen King."

"Anybody with you?"

"No." He ran his finger over the rim of the bottle. "I'm currently between significant others."

"Got a receipt? For the books?"

"I doubt it. And even if I did, so what? I could have gotten a receipt from anybody. It's not like they print your picture on it."

"Good point. So, no alibi."

"I guess not. Sorry." He didn't sound especially sorry. "You don't really think I did it?"

"Why wouldn't I?"

"Because I'm a wuss, if you want to know the truth. I don't watch boxing on TV. I haven't been in a fistfight since I was eight years old—and I lost that one. I hardly even watch the news anymore, because all that violence depresses me."

"You spend your weekends pretending to be a vampire."

"So what? I like horror flicks, too. Movie gore, that's nothing. Just corn syrup and a little food coloring. The game . . . You saw it. Could it have been more bloodless?"

"I read the rules," I said. "I seem to remember something along the lines of 'embrace your dark side, because you can't defeat evil by denying it, only by embracing it and working through it.' That's not an exact quote."

"No, I know the quote you're talking about. But it doesn't mean anything. The rule books are written from the viewpoints of various characters, so you have to take all that philosophical stuff with a grain of salt."

"So it's not a manifesto."

"It's a game." He tucked his bottle between his thigh and the arm of the chair. "It's about the humanity of the characters, people pretty much like us, but in constant conflict with their dark sides. They have these powers, but there's a price. At its best, this is a game about redemption."

Yes, I decided. He definitely had the smarts to stage the crime scene. Probably the physical strength as well. I wasn't sure about the mind-set. A true psychopath could play the role of humanitarian as well as anyone. For awhile.

"What is it at its worst?" I said.

"At its worst, it's banal. Juvenile hack-and-slash role-play."

I looked at him blankly.

"Some people play their characters as inhuman monsters. Sharks in People Suits. There's a place for that, I guess, but I don't personally find it very rewarding."

He tipped up his bottle, found it empty, and heaved himself out of his chair. "I'm dry. Can I get you another one?"

There were still two inches of liquid at the bottom of my bottle. "I'm good," I said.

He disappeared into the kitchen and came back with another beer.

I said, "Some might say the game has a bad influence on people like Razor."

He shrugged. "It's just a game. If you're a moral person, it's not going to make you an immoral one. And if you're an immoral person, it won't make you a good one. Razor's group . . . well, they came to the game for kicks, but they weren't playing characters. They were living them."

I thought of Alan's fifth grade teacher, who had made them write over and over, *Play is the devil's workshop.* I didn't believe that, but maybe there was something to it. Not what you played, perhaps, but how you played it. "Medea says you threatened to kill Razor."

For the first time, his expression darkened. "Medea wouldn't know the truth if it materialized in front of her carrying a neon sign."

"So you never said you were going to kill him."

"I may have. How often do we say, 'I could have wrung his neck,' 'I was so mad I could have killed him.' But how many of us do?"

"Not many," I admitted. "But this time, someone did."

CHAPTER TWENTY

On the way home, I stopped by the dojang and sweated through an hour of kicks and punches that left me wrung out and high on endorphins. The calf felt fine, only a twinge or two to let me know it was there. Afterward, I jogged across the parking lot, damp hair freezing into clumps and the sweat on the back of my neck turning to ice. The Silverado glistened blue-black in the halogen light. A square of paper beneath the windshield wipers fluttered in the wind. I plucked it out and held it to the light.

The only good rattlesnake is a dead rattlesnake, it said. *Parker was a rattlesnake. Let it go.*

No signature.

I scanned the parking lot. Empty, except for the other students. I crumpled the note and stuffed it into my pocket. Unlocked the door and slid, shivering, into the driver's seat, then punched the door locks and cranked up the heat. When the cab finally began to feel a little more Bahamas and a little less Siberia, I swung the truck out of the parking lot and headed south on Donelson Pike, picked up speed and veered on to the I-40 ramp. Barreling fast through the curve, the Silverado canted to the right, and something tumbled out from beneath the seat and bumped against my left leg.

I shuffled my foot backward to keep the pedals clear and looked down. Two inches from my boot, a thick loop of mottled silver-gray thrashed up, then down. A wedged head coiled back, followed by an unmistakable rattle.

For a moment, I forgot to breathe.

Then I said a word my mama hadn't taught me and yanked both legs up and away from the pedals just as the snake shot through the place where my foot had been.

Holy Mary, Mother of God.

The engine hum dropped to a low drone, and the Silverado slowed, the headlights of the car behind me blooming in the rearview mirror. The snake coiled, mouth agape, for another strike.

No time to think.

Instinctively, I braced with my right foot. Snapped my left foot up and felt the snake's nose thump against the sole of my boot.

Shit.

The tires juddered on the shoulder, then bounced onto the grass. The pickup fishtailed, and I wrenched the wheel to the left to avoid the ditch, still blocking the snake with my booted foot. The car behind me blared its horn and shot past, and the snake struck again, hit hard against the bottom of the boot, and hung there, fangs embedded in the sole.

Heart pounding, I drove the boot down hard on its head and ground it into the rubber mat as I guided the truck to a stop.

The snake writhed beneath my foot, but I held it there until my heartbeat slowed and my hands, damp with sweat and clamped to the steering wheel, stopped trembling. Then I put the truck in Park, pulled up on the door handle, and pushed the door open with my shoulder. I reached across and popped open the glove compartment, pulled out my Glock and slid off the safety with my thumb.

I passed the Glock to my left hand—my off hand—and pressed the barrel against the base of the snake's skull. It strained upward against the pressure, body curling up and around my wrist. I squeezed the trigger once. The pistol bucked against my palm, and the shot boomed in the enclosed cab, loud enough to hurt my eardrums. A plug of flesh and blood sprayed from the snake's neck, and with its head half severed, the snake went limp against the rubber floor mat. I held the gun to its mangled head until long after I was sure it was dead. Then, ears still ringing, I hooked the toe of my boot under the body and flipped it out of the truck.

CHAPTER TWENTY-ONE

"A rattlesnake?" Jay snatched his cap and parka out of the hall closet and followed me out to the Silverado, which stood in the driveway with its driver's side door open. "Who does a thing like that?"

I had a bucket of warm water in one hand and a soapy sponge in the other. While Jay shrugged into his parka, I set the bucket on the ground next to the pickup and dunked the sponge into it. "Could have been anybody. I've talked to a lot of people in the last couple days."

"It's insane. Where would he have gotten it, this time of year?"

"Good question. I have another one. How'd he get it in the truck?"

"You're sure you locked it?"

"Hundred percent." I swabbed the blood from the rubber mat and rinsed the sponge in the bucket. "Whoever this guy is, he's good. No nicks or scratches around the locks. If he jimmied the door, he didn't leave any traces."

Jay tucked his hands under his armpits for warmth and said, "So what will you do?"

"Solve the case."

"Just like that."

"Why not? This doesn't change anything."

"Someone tried to kill you."

"Someone tried to warn me off. I'm not sure killing me was the point."

"*Not* killing you apparently wasn't the point either," he said. "You know, Josh would understand if you dropped the case. Let the police handle it."

"The police will handle it all right." I dabbed at a smear on the brake pedal. "Handle Josh right into a prison cell."

"Oh ye of little faith," he said, and went inside.

—⚸—

I hadn't been able to reach Dennis Knight, so the next morning, on the off chance he was home, I drove over to the run-down duplex he shared with his mother. The other half of the building housed an Asian family whose five children played Mother-May-I as I picked my way through the dismembered Barbies and half-buried matchbox cars littering the lawn. On the stoop next door, an Asian woman sat watching the children.

"Dennis Knight live here?" I asked.

They looked up. The oldest child, a girl of about eight wearing pink stretch pants and a fuzzy blue parka, pointed a grubby finger toward the left side of the duplex.

"Thanks." I started toward the door. Then, on impulse, I went over to the woman on the stoop. She scooted away a few inches and frowned up at me.

"You looking for good time, you go see *her*." She nodded toward the Knights' door.

"I'm not looking for a good time. I just wondered if her son and his friends ever play a game here on Fridays."

She sniffed. "Play game, make noise. Drink beer. Very noisy. Keep little ones awake." She put the tips of her fingers against her lips and made a spitting sound. "Ptu, ptu."

I looked back over my shoulder toward the house. "You see her here about three Fridays ago?"

"No, no." The woman shook her head fiercely. "Not home Friday. Two year, I live here. Never home Friday."

I thanked her and went next door. Took the porch steps two at a time and knocked at a warped wooden door with peeling paint.

A thin woman answered. Her hair was pulled back and piled high on her head, a few loose tendrils spilling out around her face. In the background, some raucous game show blared.

"Ms. Knight?" I asked. Then I remembered the police report and said, "Tara Knight?"

"Who wants to know?" She stepped out onto the porch, an unfiltered cigarette dangling from her fingers. The nails were long, fake, and very red, with sharp outlines where they'd been glued on.

I handed her my license and watched while she studied it.

She was thirty-three, according to the police report, a single mother who had given birth at the age of seventeen. I imagined she'd been attractive once, but now she just looked exhausted.

She handed my license back. "Private detective?"

"I'm working with Absinthe's attorney."

"Oh." She gave me a long, appraising look and stepped aside to let me in. "She's an okay kid. Hope you don't mind if I smoke."

"It's your house."

"So it is." She gave me an amused smile, took a long drag from the cigarette, and led me to the living room. There was a sour smell in the air—kitty litter, fried fish, and stale smoke. On the TV, a blonde woman in a sequined dress gestured to the stereo system today's lucky contestant might win.

Tara flopped into a tan recliner across from the TV and turned down the volume with the remote. "I guess you came to talk to Dark Knight." The nickname sounded odd, coming from his mother. "He can't help you. He was here the day Razor was killed."

"You knew Razor?"

"I know all my son's friends." She pushed herself out of the chair, stepped into the kitchen and returned with a glass of ice, which she filled to the brim with bourbon. "I just can't understand why anyone would want to kill Razor. He was a beautiful man, just beautiful. Eyes like an angel."

"If you say so."

She sucked in a lungful of smoke, held it in for a moment, then blew out a bilious cloud. "Razor was a very complicated man. He always said it was his destiny to be misunderstood."

I said, "I read the police report. You said Dennis . . . Dark Knight . . . and his friends were role-playing here the day Razor was killed. You were here the whole time?"

"Every minute."

I looked her in the eye, and she slid her gaze away. The lie didn't surprise me. Frank had thought she was a doper, and dopers always lie.

"Can I see Dark Knight anyway?" I said.

"Suit yourself." She waved me toward the back of the house and turned the volume back up on the TV.

Dark Knight's room was easy to find. It had a big-eyed girl from some Japanese cartoon plastered on the door. I tapped on it once, then pushed the door open. The room was cramped, the walls covered with comic book posters and movie memorabilia. *Nosferatu, Night of the Living Dead, Spiderman, Monty Python and the Holy Grail.* A couple of posters from bands I'd never heard of. A tattered Batman kite pinned to the inside of the door by a crooked thumbtack.

Dennis Knight sat cross-legged on his bed playing an electronic martial arts game, fingers flying at the controls as his video persona leaped and whirled. He played with his whole upper body, bobbing and twisting in concert with his avatar. His hair was a mass of dark, greasy curls. His pale skin was stippled with pink pimples across the forehead and in the crevices around his bulbous nose. The thick lenses of his heavy, black-framed glasses made his eyes look oversized and startled. The kind of kid who gets picked on in gym class, but Absinthe had blushed when she talked about him.

I showed him my license. "I'm working on Absinthe's case."

"That crazy bitch."

"What makes you think that?"

"Are you kidding? Saying she killed Razor?"

"You don't think she did it?"

"You seen her room? Stuffed animals. Teddy bears." He gave his head a disgusted shake, but a smile crept across his lips. "She hasn't got the guts."

"I thought she was a friend of yours."

He shrugged. Turned his attention back to his game. "She's okay, I guess. For a poser."

"A poser?"

"A wannabe. She pretends she's part of the scene, but it's like Razor said. She doesn't have the stuff."

I walked past a bookshelf filled with plastic Warner Brother cartoon figures and sat down at a desk cluttered with half-finished drawings and scraps of overwrought fiction.

"Hey," he said. "Who gave you an invitation?"

I said, "I'd think you'd want to help get Absinthe out of this mess. Keep her from going to prison for the next forty years. Seeing as how you're friends and all."

"It's her mess." He shook his hair out of his eyes and turned back to the screen. "But go ahead and talk."

"The ritual of Transformation," I said. "Who was there? You and Barnabus. Medea. Absinthe. Any others? Alan Keating?"

"That asshole. He wouldn't even've been allowed to come around if he and Razor hadn't known each other from way back."

"What's your beef with Keating?"

"Always passing judgment, always trying to psychoanalyze everybody. But he was no angel. Razor told me about some shit they pulled back in college."

"They went to college together?" I didn't know why that should have surprised me, but it did.

"Vandy." He smirked, whether at me or at the villain on the screen, I couldn't say. "They were both psych majors."

"Razor get his degree?"

"B.S. Started on his Master's. Then he and Alan got into some kind of trouble. Alan weaseled out of it and got to stay in school, and Razor got the ax."

"Funny. He didn't seem the kind to forgive and forget."

"Guess Alan got a special dispensation." He tapped a button on the game, and the screen went dark. He pushed it away from him. "What you said. About Absinthe and prison and everything."

"What about it?"

He got up and picked up a Bugs Bunny figure from the shelf. Turned it over in his hand and set it back a few inches to the left of where it had been. "I know who wanted Razor dead," he said.

"Seems like everybody wanted Razor dead."

"No, I mean, for real. Those people who lived a couple doors down. Hewitt. He's a nutcase. Him and his buddy, Igor."

"Elgin."

"Same difference. Big fucking bastard." He scrubbed at the dingy carpet with the toe of his sneaker.

I said, "Look, if you know something—"

"I'm getting to it," he snapped. "Anyway, she got herself into this. Why should I have to be the one to get her out?"

"Don't be a jerk," I said. "Absinthe's your friend, and she needs you."

I wasn't sure it would work, appealing to his better nature, but finally, he ducked his head and mumbled, "Hewitt's wife."

A bad feeling nestled in the pit of my stomach. "What about her?"

"It wasn't supposed to be a big deal. Push her around some. Show her our knives. Maybe cop a feel." He had the decency to look ashamed. "We were just supposed to scare her."

"But it didn't go down that way."

"Barnabus was getting all stirred up. And Medea kept egging things on." He scratched at a chip in the wooden shelf. "It just got out of hand."

Heat crept up the back of my neck. "Razor raped her?"

"He watched. He was into it, that he could just say do it and we . . ." He looked away. With his index finger, he nudged Bugs Bunny a millimeter to the right.

"Go on," I said in a brittle voice I hardly recognized.

"When we . . . when it was over, Razor told her he had an army of people who'd do whatever he told them to, and if she called the cops or told anybody, he'd send them to her house and they'd kill her and Hewitt."

Anger took me two steps forward before I stopped myself. "And what did you do? Stand by and watch it happen? Take a turn? Hold her down?"

"You think I'm proud of what happened? You think I don't think about it every single day?" A whine crept into his voice. "You don't know what it was like, being around Razor."

He picked up a Marvin the Martian figure and toyed with it. Our gazes met, and while I watched, the shame in his eyes turned to anger. I wasn't surprised. Anger is easier.

I said, "Explain it to me."

He placed Marvin the Martian carefully between Darth Vader and the Tasmanian Devil. "He made good things seem bad and bad things seem good," he said. "It was like he turned the world inside out."

"So the world was inside out when you helped Barnabus rape Judith Hewitt."

"You're so fucking curious," he said, mouth stretched in a humorless grin. "Why don't you ask your nephew? He was there."

CHAPTER TWENTY-TWO

I didn't believe him. Refused to believe him. To even entertain the thought was a betrayal.

Dennis Knight had forgotten the chip on his shoulder long enough to want to help Absinthe, but he'd also wanted to draw my attention away from his own part in Judith Hewitt's rape. I had no reason to trust Dennis Knight.

I knew Josh. He was incapable of rape.

I barreled through the afternoon traffic, fighting the impulse to haul Josh out of class and ask him what he knew about the assault. A dull throbbing started in my temples. I loved Josh like a son, but if this was true, I would never see him with the same eyes. And if it wasn't true, if I confronted him without just cause, he would never see me the same way either.

I forced myself to back off the tail of the car in front of me, cut off a guy in a red Subaru and swore under my breath when his horn blared. Skidded into the Hewitts' driveway and pounded on the door. Cursed when no one answered, and scrawled a note for them to call me. I waited in the driveway for half an hour, then, too restless to sit still, drove over to Vanderbilt's campus to talk to Razor's little brother. Philosophy and Religion, Keating had said.

Vanderbilt University and Medical Center sat on three hundred and thirty-three acres in the heart of Nashville. Declared a national arboretum in the late nineties, it was home to at least one of every tree and shrub native to Tennessee. A beautiful place, even in the dead of winter, but I was in no mood to enjoy it. Instead, I found a parking spot three blocks from campus and bulled past medieval-style buildings with arched doorways and an oak tree that had been around since before the American Revolution.

I stopped at the library and got directions to the right department, then asked around until a campus police officer gave me directions to the classroom where I could find Heath. I planted myself outside the room until the door burst open and a stream of chattering students bubbled out.

Heath was at the tail end of the stream, standing to one side as if to avoid the rush. He spotted me and frowned. Then he sighed and came over.

"You were at my brother's funeral," he said. He moved away from the other students, jerked his head for me to follow him.

"That's right."

"You were there with your nephew. Said he was one of Razor's friends."

I nodded, my throat gone tight at the mention of Josh.

"So, what are you doing here? Come to offer me your condolences? Or maybe it's some sort of payoff you're after."

"Payoff?"

His laugh was bitter. "Mother may be naïve enough to think Razor was mentoring good-looking teenagers out of the goodness of his heart. I know better. Did you file charges?"

"Josh wouldn't testify."

"They never do. And—let me guess—no physical evidence, by the time you found out. Same old story. Legal shenanigans, a little bit of hand-waving, and the shyster lawyer Mother always hires has him out on the street again by evening."

"Exactly how many times has this happened?"

"If you knew, it would make you sick. And to top it off, he never even paid a dime in legal fees. Never worked a day in his life, in fact. She poured money into him like it was water."

"Police report said he was an artist."

"Comic books and fantasy illustration. That's what he always said, but he never actually sold anything."

"You don't seem exactly broken up with grief."

He led me out a side door and headed across a wide patch of brittle grass. "My brother was a stone-cold bastard. He molested me when I was ten. Mother said it was normal. Boys will be boys."

"What about your father?"

"He made a token attempt to help, but he was a broken man by then. Mother had already eaten him alive." We came to a bench, and he tossed his notebook down on it and turned to face me. Some distance away, several young men tossed a Frisbee in the cold. "Does it surprise you that I'd tell you all this?"

"A little."

"It's part of my therapy. Coming to terms with Sebastian's death and how guilty I feel because I don't give a rat's ass."

"Can't blame you, under the circumstances."

We sat. The bench was hard, cold through the seat of my jeans.

"So if you're looking to extort some sort of payment to keep his sordid history secret, you can forget it. I might be tempted, to protect Mother. But since she'll never believe anything bad about Sebastian anyway, it would be rather a pointless gesture, don't you think?"

"I didn't come here to blackmail you."

"Oh." He looked mildly surprised. "What, then?"

I showed him my license and gave him the short version. Investigating Razor's murder.

"I don't give a damn who killed him," he said. "You find whoever did it, introduce me. I'd like to shake his hand."

"The kid who confessed didn't do it. Anything you could tell me that might help her out . . ."

He shook his head. "Sorry. It took some longer than others, but sooner or later, just about everybody who ever knew him wanted him dead. He managed to screw everybody—usually in more ways than one."

"I heard he went to school here," I said.

"Got his Bachelor's. Got bounced a couple of months before he would have gotten his Master's."

"Psychology?"

"That's right. Headgames 'R' Us."

"What happened?"

He fiddled with his notebook. "Some kind of research project. It was titled the Parker Principle, but he called it the Great Brain Fuck. He and Alan were working on it. Alan Keating."

"I've met him."

"He and Sebastian go way back. In fact, Alan practically lived at our house. Tells you something about his home life, doesn't it? That our sad little family seemed preferable?"

"Did he . . . ?" I made an ambiguous gesture.

"Molest me? No. I think he and Sebastian may have had something going for a while, but I don't think they've had that kind of relationship for a long time."

"What can you tell me about this research project the two of them were working on?"

"Not much. It had something to do with behavioral psychology, and there was some question about ethics. I remember right after it happened, after he got expelled, Sebastian kept ranting about the narrow-minded morons running the department. Said he and Alan were working on the most daring project ever done at this school."

"But he didn't tell you what it was about?"

His gave me a chilly smile and said, "Sebastian liked his secrets."

"So how come Razor got expelled and Alan got to stay?"

"I couldn't say. Maybe somebody recognized that Alan was just a puppet. You wouldn't believe how he used to do whatever Sebastian said."

"Used to?"

"He got over it." He stood up, picked up the notebook, tapped it against his thighs. "I think that's why Sebastian kept him around. He wanted to see if he could get that old Alan back. Or maybe part of it was that Alan loved him. Not just some queer thing. I mean, really loved him. And Razor didn't believe in love."

"Medea said something along those lines."

"Yeah, he used to say it all the time. Nobody really loves anybody. And I think he needed to prove to himself that he could kill that in Alan. Or that he couldn't. You know, wanted to prove he was right and wanted to prove he was wrong at the same time."

"It didn't bother him that Alan got to stay in school?"

"It bothered him. But he got over it. He always did, with Alan."

"You loved him too."

His eyebrows shot up. "Who? Alan or Sebastian?"

"Both."

"I hated my brother's guts, and that's the truth. I'd have killed him myself if it wasn't for Mother."

"Hate. Love. Sometimes it's a fine line."

He looked out into space. "Yeah, well. It's nothing a few more years of therapy won't take care of. Until then . . ." He raised an invisible glass. "To my brother, Sebastian. May he rot in Hell."

CHAPTER TWENTY-THREE

I called Alan Keating from my cell phone. Kirsten put me right through.

"The Parker Principle," I said when he answered. "The Great Brain Fuck."

There was silence on the other end. Then, "Mr. McKean," he said.

"This research project. What was it about?"

"It has nothing to do with Bastian's death."

"I'll find out one way or another. It would be easier if you'd just tell me."

"Did it ever occur to you I might not exactly be proud of it?"

Shades of Dennis Knight. "You know what they say, Keating. Honest confession's good for the soul. So spit it out."

There was an uncomfortable silence. Then he said, "You've heard of the Stanford Prison Experiment?"

"Psych experiment. Half the students are guards, and the other half are inmates. It didn't go well."

"They called it off. They had to. It got to be too much like a real prison. The guards started acting like tyrants, the prisoners didn't seem to realize they could just go home."

"I remember."

"The guy who ran it wrote a book about how good people turn evil. Bastian was always fascinated by that kind of thing. Good and evil. He had a theory."

"A theory."

"Beneath the surface, everyone is evil. He thought if you knew enough, you could manipulate almost anyone into doing almost anything. People were marionettes, and all you had to do was find the right string to pull. To prove his theory, we . . . manipulated people. Bastian kept a journal with all the different tales he'd tell people and all the different things he could get them to do."

My gut felt like it had been filled with shaved ice. "What kind of things?"

"Sexual favors, mostly. He was intrigued—and infuriated—by how many girls would cheat on their boyfriends. And how many straight men would perform homosexual acts, even when they were supposedly in exclusive relationships with women."

"Nobody loves anybody," I said.

"Then you know. He had a thing about that. It was like he needed to prove love was a lie."

"He was bisexual."

He laughed without humor. "He was a sexual omnivore. But his machinations weren't limited to sex. Someone would be upset about some perceived slight and he'd suggest some retaliation for it. Just pranks, mostly, but some of them were pretty cruel."

"What was your part in it?"

"I lent an air of credibility, I suppose. I went out with a few of these women, but I wasn't very good at it. Not as charming or believable as Bastian."

"What happened?"

"One of the girls attempted suicide. It came out, what we were doing."

"And Razor got expelled."

"That's right."

"But you didn't. How'd you manage that?"

He was quiet for a moment. "I don't know if you can understand how I felt. It was like some evil spell had been broken and I could see what a terrible thing we'd done. I pleaded for another chance. Broke down and cried like a baby, which also doesn't make me proud. I guess my advisor believed I was sincere."

"Were you?"

"I've never meant anything more."

"That doesn't exactly answer the question."

"I was sincere, all right? What do you want from me?"

"The truth."

"It happened years ago. It has nothing to do with what happened to Bastian."

"So you say. But you lied about the day he was killed, so why should I believe you now?"

He was silent for a beat. Then he said, "What?"

I wasn't certain—all I had were the missing initials on his calendar—but I played the card anyway. "You canceled your appointments for that afternoon. You had plenty of time to get to Razor's and kill him before Byron got home."

When he finally answered, his voice was so quiet I had to strain to hear him. "And why would I do that?"

"You tell me."

"Goodbye, Mr. McKean," he said. And the line went dead.

CHAPTER TWENTY-FOUR

When I got home, the horses were standing by the pasture gate. Their breath billowed out into the chilly evening air, and the snow around the gate was pocked with hoof prints. Churned-up patches of dark earth showed through. Tex whickered softly and pawed at the ground as I approached.

"Hey, fella." I scratched the flat place between his eyes, and he heaved a sigh that warmed my face and drained the tension out of me. By the time I'd brushed the three of them and dropped a flake of hay into each of their stalls, I felt almost human.

Inside, the drone of voices and a flickering light came from Dylan's room, followed by a spate of canned laughter. I peered in and saw Jay slumped in the recliner, eyes closed, head lolling onto his shoulder. Dylan lay back against a stack of pillows, the comforter pulled up to his chest. Beside him, Luca the papillon pup gnawed at a dried ostrich tendon as long as he was tall.

The pup looked up. The tendon dropped from his mouth and he bounced across the bed, wagging from the shoulders down. I scooped him up a heartbeat before he tumbled off the edge, and he licked my chin and squirmed against my shoulder like a fur ball filled with Jell-O.

Dylan opened his eyes and said, "Long day."

"Couldn't sleep?"

"Plenty of time for that, right?" He tried to laugh, but it sounded more like a wheeze. "Nothin' but sleep for a long, long time."

"Can I get you anything?"

"Twenty more years. Barring that, I could use a glass of OJ."

"Juice I can manage."

He forced a smile and closed his eyes. "So, are you the husband in this cozy little arrangement? Because I know Jay's got to be the wife."

I felt the muscles of my face tighten. "I'm a friend."

"Oh, yes. The straight friend. He's made such a point of it, I wonder can it possibly be true? Personally, methinks he doth protest too much."

"He said I was going to like you in spite of myself."

"And you don't?" He gave a dry chuckle that ended in a long, rattling cough. I glanced at Jay, whose eyelids fluttered open, then dropped closed again. Too tired to wake himself up. "I must be losing my touch."

"I'll get you that juice," I said, passing the puppy back to him. It gave a little whine, then sighed and settled down. In the kitchen, I took a few deep breaths, poured a glass of orange juice, and took it back down the hall.

I placed the glass in Dylan's outstretched hand, which dipped dangerously at the sudden weight. He strained to lift his head from the pillow and brought the glass to his lips. Juice spilled around the corners of his mouth and trickled down the sides of his chin.

"Shit," Dylan said. "You know what, Straight? Dying sucks."

I slid one hand under his shoulders and lifted him to a sitting position. Then I took the glass from his hand and held it to his lips. He sipped, swallowed, sipped again.

When he'd finished, he turned his face away and coughed. "Needs vodka," he said. "I don't guess you'd . . ."

I eased him back onto the pillow. "Let me guess. You're not supposed to mix alcohol with your meds."

"What's it going to do, kill me?"

He had a point. I took the OJ into the kitchen and laced it with two ounces of vodka. Then I went back into his room and helped him take a few more sips.

"Don't you die on me now," I said. "Not with this stuff in your system."

"Why worry?" he said. "The most they could charge you with is mercy killing."

"Illegal," I reminded him.

"How about if I promise not to die until the alcohol's out of my bloodstream?"

I agreed that would probably be a good idea.

I was pretty safe, though, because a few swallows of the drink were all he could manage. When he'd finished, he sank back into his pillow and closed his eyes.

"You're a good man, Straight," he sighed. The rattle in his voice suggested some congestion in his lungs. "Jay's a lucky guy."

—⚏—

On the way upstairs, I glanced at the hall table, where the first one home drops the mail. Nothing. It was possible the box had been empty, but this time of year, it was unlikely. Jay must have gotten busy, forgotten to pick it up. I trudged back down to the end of the driveway to check the mailbox. Cable bill, electric bill, three Christmas cards addressed to Jay and one to me. And a plain white envelope, no stamp, no address, just my name printed in heavy block letters across the front. I worked open a corner, then slipped my thumb under the flap. Inside was a piece of white typing paper with the same kind of unidentifiable block lettering I'd found under my windshield wiper.

Second warning, it said. Below the writing was a primitive drawing of a snake. Three tiny circles at the end of the tail identified it as a rattler.

The skin on my forearms prickled with gooseflesh.

The son of a bitch knew where I lived.

I tiptoed into Dylan's room and nudged Jay's shoulder. "Wake up."

He followed me blearily into the kitchen, and I handed him the note. He looked at it for a long time, then laid it on the coffee table and said, "How dangerous is this guy?"

"I wish I knew. My guess is, you're not on his radar. The snake was in my truck, the note has my name on it. But if you wanted to, you and Dylan could go to a hotel until we catch him."

"I'd rather no one was on his radar. And I'm not running off to a hotel while some psychopath threatens you. What can I do to help?"

"For now, just keep your eyes peeled. Doors and windows locked. And take this." I pulled the Glock out of my shoulder holster and held it out to him, butt first.

He raised his hands and took a step back. "You know I can't use that thing."

"I.Q. of a million, and you can't point and shoot?"

He shook his head, but I popped the magazine out and made him practice putting it in, sliding off the safety, and racking the slide.

"I'm not shooting anybody," he said.

"I know," I said. "If we're lucky, you won't have to."

CHAPTER TWENTY-FIVE

The next day, I was back in Razor's neighborhood. Interviewed a couple of folks I'd missed the first time around and learned nothing useful from any of them. It was five o'clock by the time I finished, and since I was in no mood to sit in traffic, I swung by the office to wait it out. Write a report. Do some background checks. Think things through. The front door was locked, most of the other businesses in the building already shut down for the day. A thin band of light streamed out from under the Strip-o-Grams door, and a dance tune heavy on the bass filled the hallway.

The hall light on my floor was off, and only the light that spilled from the stairwell illuminated the dim corridor. I flipped the switch. Nothing.

The light had been fine last night. Maybe it had just burned out, but . . .

I slipped the Glock from under my jacket. Scanned the corridor. Empty.

Maybe I was just being paranoid.

There were no scratch marks on the doorjamb or around the keyhole. No sign of forced entry. I jiggled the handle. Locked. Still uneasy, I opened the door and flipped on the light switch.

Nothing.

A shadow in the corner moved. I swung to face it and caught a glimpse of urban camouflage, a flash of ribbed ski mask. Then a heavy weight slammed into my gut and drove me back into the wall. With a sharp crack and a shower of plaster, the drywall caved. My arm went numb and the Glock skittered across the floor.

I gasped for breath, smelled sour sweat and Ivory soap. Felt like I'd been hit by a cannonball.

Rough hands fell on my shoulders, and a framed Frace print shot toward my face—or maybe it was the other way around. I squeezed my eyes shut and turned my head in time to save my nose and teeth. Glass splintered. A sharp pain shot through my cheek.

Damn.

I slammed my head backward into his face. Bone cracked and he let out a yell, and a warm wetness gushed into my hair. My blood, or his. I couldn't tell.

"Son of a—" He rammed my head into the glass again. A flare of pain. More shattering glass. This time, I tasted copper.

I jabbed an elbow into his stomach and stamped hard on his instep. He bellowed a curse and threw a kidney punch that made every synapse in the right side of my body fire. If I survived this, I'd be pissing blood for a week.

"I told you to let it go, asshole," he growled.

The voice seemed familiar, but I couldn't place it through the ringing in my ears.

"Let what go?" I twisted away, nearly slipped out of his grasp. My hand scrabbled at his face, found the woolen ski mask.

He jerked away. Grabbed a fistful of hair and smashed my forehead against the wall. A burst of pain, and behind my eyes, a curtain of red. Something wet and warm streamed down my face. The world shifted. Tilted. Bile rose in my throat, and I choked it back down.

"Son of a bitch deserved to die." The breath beside my face reeked of beer, and I fought the urge to retch. "Just let it go."

Let the Parker thing go.

I groaned and let my body go limp. Held my breath until I heard the air rush out of him and felt his muscles relax. When he shifted his grip, I twisted suddenly in his arms and pushed off hard with my legs. A sharp pain shot through my calf. I ground my teeth together and pushed past it. The intruder toppled, off balance, and I drove my right fist into his throat.

He gasped like a landed carp, gave a guttural cry that was mostly rage, and swung a meaty fist toward my head. The blow glanced off my left ear, made it ring.

"What about Absinthe?" I asked. "Just let her take the fall?"

"Screw Absinthe," he wheezed. "Who gives a shit about that fat little fuck?"

He rammed me again, and again the nausea roiled up in my gut. Dizzy with vertigo and blinded by blood, I threw another punch. He stumbled clear and caught me with a blow to the belly that brought me to my knees.

Downstairs, the music stopped.

Someone called, "What's going on up there?"

My assailant leaned closer, his breath warm against my ear. "You keep on, you're gonna get somebody hurt."

I heard the clump of heavy footsteps on the hardwood floor give way to the pounding of feet on the stairs. A woman cried out. The front door slammed. By the time I stopped retching, he was gone.

I took a deep, painful breath and used the wall to pull myself to my feet. It felt nice and solid. I decided to lean against it for a while.

As my head cleared, I tried to put it together. Too tall to be Byron. Too stocky for Keating. I thought of Chuck. The height was about right, but his soft, going-to-seed physique bore no resemblance to the intruder's. Besides, I could have hammered Chuck like a tent peg.

Whoever it was, he'd picked the lock to my office without leaving a trace. Just like the guy who'd put the snake in the Silverado.

Another set of footsteps. Lighter, quicker steps, the staccato sound of spiked heels. A statuesque platinum blonde careened around the corner and pulled up short when she saw me. She was wearing a silver-sequined bikini with a top at least a size too small. One of Strip-o-Gram's regulars. I fished in my brain for a name, came up with one: Chantal. The sight of her cheered me up a little.

"My God," she said. "Are you all right?"

"Maybe you should call the police." I touched a hand to my forehead and it came away red. I grimaced and gave her a number. "Ask for Frank Campanella." It wasn't exactly his department, since I was still breathing, but I trusted him. Besides, it appeared to be related to his homicide. Or rather, his precinct's homicide, which was the same thing as far as I was concerned. I sure as hell wasn't going to call Gilley and Robbins.

"You need an ambulance?"

I shook my head and immediately regretted it. "I can drive."

She touched the tips of her fingers to my face. "Maybe someone should take you."

She was dabbing at my forehead with a damp cloth when Frank arrived. He gave her a long, searching look, then turned to me with raised eyebrows and a hint of a grin.

"As a way to meet women, this seems a bit drastic," he said.

"As a way to meet women, it sucks."

He pulled out a pocket steno pad and a pen, and I dutifully described the attack. Then I thanked Chantal for her help and limped out to the weathered Crown Victoria Frank had bought new in 1988.

The passenger door stuck, and I had to yank it hard enough to send a shock wave blasting through my skull. I said, "When are you going to lay this thing to rest?"

"You should be so lucky as to have a car like this," he said. "This car is a classic."

"Coca-Cola is a classic. This car is an antique. Every time it passes a cemetery, the transmission slips. Ever think it might be trying to tell you something?"

"This car will outlast you and me both, Mac," he said. The pounding in my head suggested that he might be right.

He drove me to the emergency room at St. Thomas, where— after a two-hour wait—a doctor who reminded me of Sammy Davis Jr. injected a painful dose of anesthesia into my forehead and stitched me up.

"You're a lucky guy," he said. "Mild concussion. No permanent damage. And even if it scars, your hair will cover most of it." The rest of the cuts on my face looked bad, but none were deep enough for stitches.

"You want to hear the bright side of all this?" asked Frank.

"There's a bright side?"

"Of course." He tossed me my bloodstained shirt. "They only beat the shit out of you when you're on to something."

CHAPTER TWENTY-SIX

"You look like hell," Jay said. He took a bag of frozen peas from the freezer and handed it to me, then took a bottle of aspirin off the counter, tipped three into his palm, and gave them to me as well. "Can't you ever work a case without getting beaten to a pulp?"

"Apparently not." I tried flexing various muscles, and ripples of pain shot through my whole body. "Son of a bitch. I can't believe I walked right into him."

"Your spidey senses must have malfunctioned."

"I should have known he was there." I popped the aspirin into my mouth, swallowed them dry, then pressed the frozen bag to my lip. "Hell, I *did* know something was up, and he still got the jump on me."

"Whatever you say." He brought his meds to the table, pulled out the chair beside me, and washed down the pills with a few sips of purified water. I looked at him more closely. His face looked thin, and there were dark circles under his eyes.

"You don't look so great yourself," I told him. "How's your T-count?"

"I'm fine. Just tired."

"Dylan have a rough night?"

"Hallucinations. Last night, it was Chippendale's dancers. This morning, a Marine. He finds it all very amusing when he's lucid."

It was a bad sign, though. One of the symptoms of end-stage AIDS.

Jay gave me a wan smile. "I wonder what I'll see when it's my time."

"That's a long time away."

"Of course it is." He rubbed an invisible spot on the table. "I'm torn between wanting you to be there and not wanting you to see me like that."

I said, "Are you sure I'm the one you're worried about?"

He picked at a thumbnail. "It's Eric, I guess. I don't think Dylan's his problem. I think it's the disease. Watching someone die. Knowing sooner or later, it's going to be me. You can't blame him for not wanting to go through that."

"Yes, I can." I smiled, but there wasn't much humor in it. Besides, smiling hurt.

"It's hard to love someone under those conditions."

"It's hard to love someone under any conditions."

He took another sip of water. "I don't think he'll be back."

"Give him time."

"Maybe it's better if he doesn't come back. Not if he's just going to leave again when I get . . ." His voice faltered. "When things get bad."

"You want me to talk to him?"

"What, you're going to drag him back here in a sack? I don't think so."

We moved to safer subjects. The Christmas party he was planning for Dylan, my weekend with Paulie. Whether or not I should pull that little strip of paper out of my wallet and call Elisha.

"You're crazy if you don't," he said.

"Josh said the same thing."

"So what's stopping you?"

"I don't know," I said. "There's a lot of stuff still up in the air."

"Too much stress. I don't suppose I can talk you into taking tomorrow off."

"I have to talk to Hewitt," I said. I told him about the attack on Judith.

"Poor woman," he said. "You think Buddy Hewitt may have killed Razor to avenge his wife? Or is it something she could have done?"

I thought it over. "A woman could have done it. At least the initial cutting. But the guy was strung up, bled, and gutted. That would have taken more muscle than most women have."

"You sure? I've known some pretty stout women."

"Judith Hewitt isn't some kind of Amazon. I'd put her on the smallish side. But her husband could have done it. Or his buddy. Elgin Mayers." I pictured the two of them in my mind, Hewitt lean and wiry, Elgin a massive wall of muscle. I replayed our conversation, focused on Elgin's voice. I imagined what his bulk would feel like barreling down on me like a bull rhinoceros. "I think Elgin may have been the one who paid me that little visit."

"Did you tell Frank this?"

"Not yet. I'm not a hundred percent sure."

He squeezed his eyes shut and shook his head. "You are not going to go and confront these people, Jared. That's insane."

"I didn't say I was going to confront them."

"You didn't have to. After all these years, you think I don't know how you think?"

"You worry too much," I said.

—m—

I slept in the next day, finishing my barn chores just in time to call Eric the Viking and meet him at a Chinese restaurant not far from downtown. We greeted one another awkwardly. Then he nodded toward my face and said, "No offense, man, but you look like crap."

"Hazard of the trade," I said.

We each ordered the buffet and piled our plates with lo mein noodles, cashew chicken, lobster rolls, and some of the best crab rangoons in town. Then Eric slid into the booth across the table from me and poured himself a steaming cup of green tea.

"I almost didn't come," he said.

"I almost didn't call."

"Why did you?"

"Call it curiosity. You know us detective types. We never know when to mind our own business."

He made a sound like a game show buzzer. "Wrong answer. Try again."

"All right. Maybe I don't get how you could just walk away. I thought things were going pretty good with you guys."

He frowned into his cup. "He's the one who brought his ex-lover back into the picture."

"His ex-lover is dying," I said. "He's no threat to you."

"It's not about threat. He brought this into our lives without even asking me how I felt about it."

"He thought you'd understand."

Eric speared a floret of broccoli. "My boyfriend is living with another man. I think that's enough to understand."

"Dylan's end-stage. It won't be long."

"I wasn't talking about Dylan."

"There's nothing between Jay and me."

"You keep saying that and maybe someday someone will believe it."

"Eric—"

"No, no. I know you're straight. But he isn't. And he loves you. Don't you think that's enough to deal with without bringing lover boy back into the picture?"

"That's what this is about? You think *I'm* the threat?"

"You are the threat." He traced invisible patterns on the linen tablecloth. "If you'd asked me a month ago, I'd have said it wasn't a problem. But you know what? I can't handle all this. You. Dylan. Jay being sick."

"And if I left?"

He laughed. "Sweetie, you and I both know you aren't going anywhere. Even if you were, what would it change?"

"I'm not going to drop out of his life, if that's what you mean."

"Exactly." He pushed his rice around on his plate. "I can't explain it. I'm not even sure that's the problem. In a way, I'm glad you're there. It means . . ." His voice trailed off.

"It means you don't have to be."

"That sounds pretty damned shallow, doesn't it?"

I didn't deny it.

"Look," he said, "I've nursed friends through this disease. It's ugly, it's messy, it breaks your heart. I'm not sure I can go through it with Jay. I'm sure as hell not willing to go through it for Dylan."

"I'm not moving out if you're not going to be there for him."

"I'm not asking you to." He sighed and rubbed his hands over his face. "I'm just not sure I can handle it. He lights up when you come into the room. Where does that leave me?"

"He's crazy about you," I said. "He's faithful to you. What more do you want?"

His smile was sad. "He's crazy about me and in love with you. And he still cares for Dylan. A whole damn crazy quilt of emotions. Oh yes, and he's dying of AIDS."

"Not for a long time yet."

"From your lips to God's ears."

"He's afraid you won't be able to handle it when—if—he does get sick."

He looked down at his lap. "Maybe he's right."

"Well," I said. "I don't have your experience with this disease, but I know this much: if you can't handle it, maybe you're right to stay away. It'll hurt him in the short run, but better now than later."

"That what I was thinking."

"It wouldn't be worth it to me, but maybe you're made of sterner stuff."

"What are you talking about?"

"He loves you," I said. "Seems to me you love him too. So you run away. You miss the bad part. The ugly, messy part, as you put it. But you miss all the good stuff too. And for the rest of your life, you have to live with knowing you ran out on him."

"I know that, dammit. Don't you think I know that? But . . ."

"But?"

He poked his fork at a bit of water chestnut, raked the tines through the rice. "It scares me," he said softly. "Helping my friends through it . . . that was awful, but I wasn't involved with them. And I wasn't . . ." His voice trailed off, and he took a shuddering breath before plunging on. "I wasn't sleeping with them. I knew I couldn't get it."

I nodded. That was a fear I could understand, and there was nothing I could say in the face of it.

He slid out of the booth and picked up his jacket. "I gotta go," he said. "I just wanted to find out how he was."

"He misses you," I said. "That's how he is."

CHAPTER TWENTY-SEVEN

Frank wasn't in the office, so I left a message and drove over to Hewitt's with Jay's warning echoing in my head. As usual, I ignored it.

This time, when I pulled into Hewitt's driveway, his truck was there. From where I was parked, I could see that the hood of the maroon Grand Prix was up. I went around to the back, where he was bent over the engine, straining against a rusted bolt with a crescent wrench that seemed just a fraction too big.

Elgin was nowhere to be seen.

I lifted the latch on the gate and let myself in.

Hewitt looked up, pushed his orange toboggan farther up on his forehead. "What's the matter?" he asked. "Didn't get all your insults in last time?"

"I was just asking a few questions," I said. "I didn't expect you to get so bent out of shape."

"You practically called me a murderer." He reached for a grease-stained towel and wiped his hands on it. "Looks like I'm not the only guy you've pissed off."

"What? These?" I indicated the bruises and cuts on my face. "Love taps."

He laughed and tossed the towel over the fender of the car. "Whatever you say."

"Where's your buddy?"

"Who? Elgin? At his school, I guess. He teaches self-defense."

"I know. I got a crash course."

He squinted at me, then leaned his hips against the side of the car and folded his arms across his chest. "You saying Elgin did that to you?"

"He told me to back off on the Parker case. Any idea why he might have a problem with my investigating Parker's death?"

"No. Other than the general idea that whoever did Parker should get a commendation, not a jail term."

"Deserved what he got, right?"

"You said it, not me."

"I'd feel the same way if someone had done to my wife what Razor and his buddies did to yours."

His tongue flicked across his lips and disappeared behind his teeth. "What are you talking about?"

"Don't tell me she never mentioned it to you," I said, but I saw it in his face.

The flush started somewhere below his collar and crept upward until his whole face was the color of a country ham. He pushed himself away from the car and said, "You're a damn liar. She'd have told me."

"I'm sorry," I said quietly. "I thought you knew."

"Hell with you," he said. "It didn't happen."

"Why don't you ask her?"

He turned away and slammed the hood of the Grand Prix. "Shit," he muttered. "Why wouldn't she tell me a thing like that?"

I jammed my hands in my pockets and cast about for answers. "Maybe she thought you wouldn't feel the same about her."

"That's bullshit," he said.

"I'm just saying, sometimes that's how it happens."

"Son of a bitch," he muttered again, and I wasn't sure if he meant me or Razor.

He shot me a hateful look and started toward the back door, wiping his hands on the sides of his jeans. I tagged along, even though I hadn't been invited.

I paused long enough to wipe my feet on the mat inside the door. Hewitt charged on, tracking bits of dried grass through the kitchen and onto the living room carpet. Judith sat curled into a corner of the couch, a Maeve Binchy novel in one hand. She looked up as we entered the room. When she saw me, a hint of alarm flickered in her eyes.

"What is it, Buddy?" She looked from him to me and back again. "What's he doing here?"

He sat down beside her, his forearms on his knees. He looked at the floor, glanced at me, shifted his gaze back to her face. "He says . . ." His voice faltered. "He says they hurt you. Parker and some of his friends. He says . . ."

She gave me a look of betrayal that felt like a punch to the stomach.

Hewitt noticed it and swallowed hard. "So it's true."

She closed the book, drew her legs out from under herself, and perched stiffly on the edge of the couch. Hewitt reached toward her, then pulled back his hand and laid it on the cushion beside her. As if she might break. "Why didn't you tell me, baby?"

"What was I supposed to say? They didn't even leave bruises." Tears welled in her eyes. "I didn't even fight them off. How was I supposed to tell you what they did to me when I didn't have a mark on me?"

"They had knives," I said. "They threatened your life."

She gave him a pleading look, and tears spilled down her face. "They said if I told you or called the police, they'd come back and kill us both. They'd have done it, too."

His arms went around her. "You should have told me."

"Why? So you could kill him?" She stopped suddenly and pulled away from him. She looked at me, and one hand flew up to cover her mouth. "I didn't mean that."

Hewitt looked at his feet. "I *would* have killed him, if I'd known." He looked up at me with deadened eyes. "Do you mind? This is kind of a private thing."

I nodded. "Just one more thing I have to ask."

"Fuck." He sighed heavily and rubbed his hands over his face.

I directed the question to Judith. "You didn't know how to tell Buddy, but it was a terrible secret to keep. It must have weighed on you."

She nodded, eyes lowered.

"Did you tell anybody? Anybody at all?"

A small nod. Almost imperceptible.

"Who, Judith?" I asked, as gently as I could manage. "Who did you tell?"

"Elgin," she whispered. "He came over right after it happened. He and Buddy were going to work on the car, but Buddy wasn't home yet." She gave Hewitt another pleading look. "I was crying. Upset. I wouldn't have told him, but . . . he was going to go over there and make them tell him what happened. I was afraid. They said they'd—" She blinked back tears and forced the words out. "I was afraid of what they'd do."

"You made Elgin promise not to tell Buddy," I said. Hewitt gave me a dark look. Judith covered her face with her hands.

"Do you know if he ever confronted Razor?"

"I made him promise not to."

I nodded as if I'd gotten some satisfaction from the conversation, but the truth was, I felt dirty myself, as if I'd taken part in Judith's violation. There was another question I wanted to ask. Needed to ask. But I didn't. Maybe I wasn't ready to hear the answer.

Instead, I caught Hewitt's attention and jerked my head toward the door. His expression was sullen, but he followed me out to my truck.

When we were out of earshot, I scrawled a name on the back of a business card and handed it to him. "Why don't you have her give this lady a call? She's a rape counselor, a damn good one."

He glowered at me. "You come in here and open this can of worms and now you're telling me how to take care of my own wife?"

"I'm sorry about the can of worms," I said. "I wouldn't have brought it up if I'd realized she hadn't told you. But it doesn't change the fact that she needs some help dealing with what happened."

"I can give her whatever help she needs."

"No, Hewitt, you can't. You can stand by her and support her and let her know none of this changes the way you feel about her. But you can't understand what she's feeling. She's got a lot to work through. Get the lady a counselor."

"Go to Hell," he said, but as he turned and walked stiffly back to the house, he stuffed the card into his pocket.

Under the circumstances, it was the best I could have hoped for.

CHAPTER TWENTY-EIGHT

Elgin Mayers ran a self-defense course called "Urban Survival: Staying Alive on the Mean Streets," and an internet search turned up a web page complete with biography, testimonials, recaps of his adventures (the ones he could share without having to kill you), and a photo gallery. According to his bio, he was born Elgin Donald Mayers, in Madison, Tennessee. Enlisted with the Marines at eighteen, received a commendation for his service in Desert Storm at thirty-three, made master sergeant a year later. At thirty-eight, he retired with twenty years and fell off the face of the map. Five years later, he reappeared in Nashville and opened his self-defense school, claiming to have spent the missing years fighting as a mercenary in the jungles of South America.

The accounts of his adventures were vivid and witty, with an occasional turn of phrase that said either someone else did his writing for him, or he was more than the blunt instrument he seemed.

The photo gallery showed pictures of Mayers clad in combat fatigues and demonstrating various combat moves. His flyers offered to transform his clients into "The Baddest Beasts in the Asphalt Jungle."

It made me feel slightly better about having the shit beat out of me.

An hour before Elgin's first class, I arrived at the survival school, a squat brick building in a run-down strip mall on Dickerson Road. Beneath the lettering for Urban Survival, traces of the previous owner's logo etched the plate glass window like ectoplasm. It said, "Ta ni g Sal n."

The school was flanked by a shoe repair shop on the left and an empty building on the right. There was no sign of Elgin, so I locked the doors of the Silverado, swallowed two more aspirins, and settled in to wait.

I punched the radio channel button, and a burst of Christmas music filled the truck. Johnny Cash singing "Little Drummer Boy." I half-listened while the other half of my mind worried at the case like a tongue at a missing tooth.

The logistics were simple enough. Whoever had attacked me either was or knew Razor's killer. Elgin was my assailant. Ergo, Elgin was my primary suspect.

But if it had been Elgin, working with or without Hewitt, why had Keating lied about rescheduling his appointments on the day of Razor's death? And why had he hung up on me when I brought the lie to his attention? Was there a connection between Alan Keating and Elgin Mayers? Or did Keating have a perfectly innocent reason for his lie?

I didn't know what Keating's motive for killing Razor might be, but I was sure he had one. Everybody else did. I ticked them off on my fingers. For Absinthe, it was being supplanted by Medea. For Byron, it was exploitation; for Barnabus, rivalry; for Medea, madness; for Chuck Weaver, revenge. Same for Elgin Mayers and the Hewitts. Even the victim's brother had hated him.

When Elgin arrived twenty minutes before class, I was no closer to a solution than when I started. I turned off the radio, climbed out of the Silverado, and started toward his truck, a black Ford pickup with a camper top. I stopped short, the hairs on my arms prickling. On the side of the camper top was a Marine Special Forces design—an eagle with a rattlesnake in its beak.

It had one of those camper tops with a picture on the side, Caitlin had said the day Josh had slashed his wrists. *Something with an eagle.*

The door of the Ford swung open, and Elgin climbed languorously out of the driver's seat, swollen lip curled upward in a smile, one eye bruised black and shot with blood.

"You son of a bitch." I stepped closer, blood pounding in my ears, fists so tightly clenched my nails dug half-moons into my palms. "What did you do to Josh?"

"Josh?" He raised an eyebrow.

"You remember him. You picked him up on the street, gave him a ride home from school."

"Kid jumped out in front of me. You're lucky I didn't run over him." He slung the strap of his duffel bag over his shoulder and slammed the door of the truck. "Hell, you oughta be thanking me."

I took a long calming breath and forced my fingers to uncurl. Storming the ramparts would get me nowhere with Elgin. "You just happened to be driving by."

"Lucky for him."

"Bullshit. You were stalking him."

"Stalking's an ugly word. I prefer 'reconnaissance.'"

"Why were you doing reconnaissance on a sixteen-year-old boy?"

He jiggled the key impatiently in the lock. "I don't know why you're so bent out of shape. He needed a ride, I gave him one."

I said, "Ten minutes in your truck, and he comes home and tries to kill himself. What'd you say to him?"

"You don't put that on me. Kid was a mess." He jiggled the key again, and this time it twisted in the lock and the door popped open. "Bawling like a little girl about how he's no damn good, the world would be a better place without him."

A dull ache started behind my eyes. "You try to talk him out of it?"

"Not my job, really."

"Neither was giving him a ride."

He grimaced, gestured for me to enter. "Guess I'm just a nice guy."

I stepped past him into the front office, where a particleboard desk sat in the middle of a musty brown carpet that smelled of mold. Photographs covered the walls. Mayers in the jungle carrying an AK-47, Mayers shaking hands with an affluent-looking Latino man, Mayers sitting on the hood of an olive-drab jeep, Mayers brandishing a survival knife with serrated edges.

Much like the one that had gutted Razor.

"Nice," I said.

He chucked the duffel onto an ugly green couch and crossed his arms. "So," he said. "What happened to you? You look like you've been gored by a bull."

"Ambush. Some chicken-shit bastard hid in the shadows and took me by surprise."

"Mm." He grunted. "You should be more alert."

"The guy who did this warned me off the Parker case. Can you figure why anybody'd want some poor confused kid to go to prison for a murder she didn't commit?"

"You're one of those bleeding heart liberals, aren't you?"

"Are we talking politics now? Because politically speaking, I consider myself a moderate."

"Most everybody does. But you . . . you're no moderate. You live with a couple of homos. You a homo, McKean?"

"No," I said, the back of my neck prickling. He knew where I lived. Of course he did. He'd put the note in my mailbox.

"That's funny," he said. "Because I figure any guy who shacks up with a couple of queers has got to be a little light in the loafers himself."

"Haven't you heard, Elgin? Homophobia is a sign of latent homosexuality."

"Homophobia?" He snorted. Picked up an acrylic paperweight with a dead scorpion inside. "What's that? Fear of queers? The faggot ain't been born that I'm afraid of."

"You didn't consider Razor a threat?"

"Razor was a threat to everybody," he said. "Ruined everything he touched."

"He did. Including Judith."

His expression darkened. "What do you know about Judith?"

"I know she told you what Razor did to her."

"Razor and his crew."

"Barnabus and Dark Knight." I left Josh off the list. Elgin gave me a look I couldn't read but didn't correct me. I said, "You know what I find most amazing? That you let it go. No retaliation. Nada. None at all. That doesn't seem like you."

He gave an angry shrug, slapped the paperweight back onto the desk a little too hard. "She asked me not to."

"That might have stopped you for a day or so."

"You think I killed the little shit?"

"I think you care a lot about Judith. You wouldn't let her rapist off scot-free."

His lips parted in a chilly smile. "Everything in its time, McKean."

"You were biding your time."

"Biding. Watching. Learning."

The thought of Josh sitting in Elgin's front seat while Elgin watched and learned turned my stomach to lead. I told myself it meant something that he'd had Josh in his truck and hadn't killed him. But maybe he'd thought Josh would save him the trouble.

"So you waited," I said.

He nodded. "And then some other son of a bitch beat me to it."

"That must have cheesed you off. Here you are, all ready to avenge your buddy's wife, and somebody else gets to your target first. Any idea who that might have been?"

"No." He pushed aside a sheaf of papers and slid his buttocks onto the edge of the desk. "Don't care, either. As far as I'm concerned, whoever did it performed a public service."

"That why you warned me off the case?"

"Did I do that?" He smiled. "Somehow I don't think you have an iota of proof."

I shook my head and forced the corners of my mouth up. "Not even a scintilla."

"Then, if I *had* been the one to . . . re-educate you, it would be stupid of me to admit it."

I decided he probably did do his own writing. Smart guy. Dangerous. What Chuck Weaver might have described as a shark in a people suit.

"I don't back off," I said.

He nodded, rubbing the stubble on his chin. "I can see you're not the sharpest knife in the drawer. I do admire tenacity, but I won't let you ruin a good man's life over scum like Parker."

"Which good man would that be?"

"Whoever killed Sebastian Parker." He reached into the stack of papers, came up with a newspaper clipping with a grainy black and white photo of Razor and his coterie. They looked like ghouls. It was an old photo, and my heart froze as I recognized Josh's sullen face in the mix. Elgin waved the photo in my direction. "They're vipers, McKean. You got to burn out the whole stinking nest."

"They're kids."

"Old enough to know better."

"Anything happens to the rest of Razor's coterie, and you'll be at the top of the suspect list."

"So?" He pointed to the pictures on the wall and gave me a wisp of a smile. "I'm a ghost, man. You can't catch a ghost."

"I won't let you hurt those kids," I said. *I won't let you hurt Josh.*

He laughed and ran his thumb over the edge of an invisible knife. "You ever hear of the Son of Sam, McKean? You know what he said about his victims?"

He didn't have to tell me. I'd heard the quote before. *I didn't want to hurt them. I just wanted to kill them.*

"Come near Josh again," I said, "and a ghost is all you'll ever be."

CHAPTER TWENTY-NINE

I called Frank from the parking lot, and I must have sounded urgent, because Frank promised to put a tail on Elgin. Then I punched in Randall's number.

"I need you to take Wendy and the kids and go somewhere," I said when he answered. "Pick up the kids, rent a cabin. Don't come back until I call you and say it's okay."

"What's going on?"

I couldn't tell him. Not all of it. Instead, I settled for a partial truth. That a former mercenary named Elgin Mayers had a beef with Razor's whole coterie, of which he considered Josh a member. A lie of omission, maybe, but enough to scare him into keeping Josh close to him and far away from Elgin.

"Take your .45," I said. "And do it now."

He didn't argue, and I wasn't sure whether to be worried about that or relieved. I wanted to go with them, to be a part of keeping Josh safe, but he was still a suspect in Razor's murder. He needed me here.

It was Friday afternoon, and I'd promised to pick up Paul. I considered calling Maria and asking to switch weekends, but with Frank on Elgin's tail, Paul would be safe at my place. I could work on the case from my laptop.

My son was waiting for me on the front porch, his chubby arms around the neck of my thirteen-year-old Akita, Queenie. She endured the indignity with characteristic stoicism.

"Daddy!" Paul loosed his hold on the dog and flung himself off the porch and into my arms. "We made reindeer at school."

He squirmed out of my grasp, clumped to his overnight bag, and rummaged through it. Emerged with a reindeer made of three wooden clothespins, a tiny red pom-pom, and a pair of plastic wiggly eyes.

"For you." He held it out as if it were a Pulitzer Prize, and I took it with appropriate reverence. Then I tousled his hair and went inside for final instructions. Queenie hobbled after me.

Maria was in the kitchen, perched on a high stool in the breakfast nook. I felt a pang when I saw her. Remembered sitting beside her at that table a few days after our wedding, a set of 164 Crayola crayons spread in front of us as she quizzed me.

What color is this?

Blue.

Cobalt. And this?

Um . . . Dark blue?

Ultramarine. And this one?

Cobalt?

Cornflower.

I had never known there were so many colors in the world.

"Jared," she said when she saw me, and started to get up. No easy feat, since, at eight months pregnant, she was at the stage she called Beached Whale.

"No, no, stay where you are." I bent to kiss her cheek. She flushed with pleasure or embarrassment.

She reached up, straightened my collar, and smoothed the front of my shirt. Beneath her hand, my heart beat faster. She frowned and pressed her palm to my cheek. "What have you done to yourself now?"

"Technically, I didn't do it." I laid my hand briefly on Maria's bulging belly. "How's your girl?"

"Active." She pressed my hand to her side, where I felt the pulse of a tiny kick. An intimate act, one we'd shared before Paul was born. My throat felt suddenly tight, the flesh of my palm hot.

I drew my hand away. "That's quite a kick."

"She's more active than Paulie was. Do you think that's a good sign?"

I looked into Maria's anxious face and said, "She's going to be fine."

"I haven't developed a photograph since I found out. Just in case the chemicals . . ." She gave me an anxious smile and stroked her stomach. "The ultrasound looked good. Perfect, the doctor said. But I wish she'd hurry up and get here. It will be such a relief to know."

"You and D.W. been going to Lamaze?"

"Lamaze, Parenting classes, La Leche League. Birthing, Burping, and Breastfeeding, he calls it. To be perfectly honest, I think he's scared out of his wits."

"He'll be fine."

"Were you worried? When Paul was born?"

"Petrified."

"And look how well you did."

She gave me the bottle with Queenie's arthritis medicine in it, asked me when I'd be bringing Paul home, and gave my hand a squeeze. "I'll call you if the baby comes," she said. "In the meantime, you guys have a good time."

—✺—

In the morning, Paul helped me feed, water and turn out the horses. Then Jay and I bundled Dylan into his coat and the four of us headed out to the Dickens Christmas festival in Franklin's historic district. It was a clear, mild day, and the temperature hovered in the low sixties. Tennessee weather. Snow and ice one day, outside without a jacket the next.

Jay unloaded a wheelchair from the trunk, and I carefully lifted Dylan into it and tucked his blanket around him. His breath was warm against my cheek. It smelled like boiled corn.

Paul gave Dylan a broad smile and clambered onto Dylan's lap.

"Paul," I said.

Dylan shook his head and edged over to give Paul more room. "He's all right. Not hurting anything."

He was no threat to Paul. I'd read enough books and articles to know the odds of Paul contracting the disease from Dylan were so slim as to be nonexistent. I'd watched my son climb into Jay's lap a thousand times and never blinked an eye. So why was I all of a sudden having visions of killer viruses swarming across the blanket and into my son's body? I gave Paul a quick once-over. No open sores. No scrapes. No scratches.

He was perfectly safe.

I got up and scooped him into my arms. "Maybe another time. When you're feeling stronger."

"Sure." Dylan's voice was bitter. "Whatever you say."

I couldn't meet Jay's gaze.

"Well," Jay said. His tone was conspicuously bright. It made me feel even more like a shit. "Let's get this show on the road."

We spent the morning strolling past carolers in period costume and drinking hot wassail. I pointed out the characters from *A Christmas Carol*, and Paul, having wed himself to the version enacted by Muppets, staunchly insisted that Bob Cratchit was a frog. Dylan, slipping in and out of lucidity, seemed mostly to enjoy himself. A little before noon, he dozed off, snoring quietly, chin on his chest.

As Paul ran ahead to buy a bag of roasted chestnuts, I looked at Jay and said, "About this morning. I'm sorry about—"

"Don't." He looked away. "Can't expect you to be enlightened twenty-four seven."

"I was an ass. It won't happen again."

He forced a smile. "You shouldn't make promises you can't keep."

"I—"

He held up a hand. "It's all right, Jared. Really. You're allowed to be human. Just . . ."

"Just what?"

"Just let's not mention it again."

—w—

Thanks to the miracle of modern cell phones, I called Randall once and Frank twice, was reassured that Josh was safe and Elgin neutralized. I tried to push thoughts of Judith Hewitt, Elgin's threats, and Razor's gutted corpse from my mind and just enjoy my son.

On the way to Pizza Hut for dinner, Paul snuggled in between Jay and me, while Dylan dozed in the backseat, cushioned by pillows, blankets, and the inflatable raft we'd used before.

I glanced into the rearview mirror, and Dylan's eyes snapped open.

"Never seen a gay man sleep before?" he asked. His voice was weak.

"Just thinking, if you're tapped out, we can call it a day."

"No." He cast a wistful glance in Paulie's direction. "I don't expect I have too many of these left."

"These . . ."

"Days," he said softly, and turned his face to the window.

—ᴍ—

Later, while everyone else slept, I booted up my laptop and pulled up a background check program. Starting with Barnabus (birth name Robert Christopher Collins) and Medea (birth name Medina Rhiannon Neel), I worked my way through my list of suspects—criminal records, financial history, driving and employment histories, and more.

Barnabus and Medea came from affluent homes, where youthful indiscretions could be smoothed over with a generous coating of green, but between them, they'd amassed twenty-three speeding tickets and several dozen unpaid credit cards. Barnabus had two arrests—but no convictions—for domestic abuse; Medea had been involuntarily committed to a mental hospital for setting fire to a neighbor's cat. No mention of whether the cat survived. I hoped it had.

Dark Knight was too young, but his mother had a history. Three DUIs, two bankruptcies, and a conviction for passing bad checks. No jail time. No surprises there—it was penny-ante stuff—and there was nothing to make me think she had the brains or the self-control to stage a murder scene like Razor's.

Except for a couple of traffic violations, Hewitt and his wife were clean, but a deeper look into Elgin's past turned up two five-year gaps in which he abruptly ceased to exist. His bio said he'd spent five years as a mercenary, so maybe he'd been out of the country. Or maybe some secret government agency—ours or someone else's—had helped him disappear.

I shut down the computer, my heartbeat loud in my ears.

Elgin Mayers was beginning to scare the hell out of me.

CHAPTER THIRTY

By Monday, the swelling in my lip was gone, and the bruises on my face had taken on a range of hues from greenish yellow to deep plum. As I sat in my office in my ergonomically designed swivel chair with my feet propped on my Wyatt Earp desk, my cell phone rang. I checked the ID. Sherilyn, my friend from the juvenile division.

"Hi, Handsome," she said. "Got something for you."

"Byron Birch?"

"I ought to make you take me someplace nice for this one," she said. "I understand you're working on that vampire killing."

"If this is good, you can name the place."

"It's good," she said. "But I'll let you off the hook this time. Turns out Earl doesn't like me going out with you hot heroic types. Let's just say you owe me one."

"Deal," I said. "What have you got?"

"Mostly small potatoes. Possession of marijuana. Incorrigibility. Picked up a couple of times for solicitation. Ran away from home three times. His caseworker always suspected there was some kind of abuse in the home. One of the stepfathers, probably. There was a whole string of them."

It took me a minute to take control of my voice. "You ever meet him?"

"No."

I said, "Kids like that, they've usually got a shell around them. He didn't seem that hardened to me."

"His case worker thought he was a sweet kid. Charming. But there was something about him. A lot of hurt, way down deep. So I called in some favors, checked a few files. Turns out there was an incident." There was satisfaction in her voice. "No charges were filed. The usual story. Married john, doesn't want his wife to know where he spends his lunch hour."

"What kind of incident? Come on, Sher. You're killing me."

"Oh, all right." She took a deep breath, and I realized I was holding mine. "It happened last spring, and your boy Byron . . ." She paused for effect.

"Go on. My boy Byron, what?"

"He stabbed a guy. Almost hacked his penis off."

I squirmed reflexively. "You're right. That is worth dinner."

"I'll take a rain check," she said. "Who knows if this thing with Earl will work out?"

She gave me the name, address, and workplace of Byron's alleged victim, blew me a kiss over the phone line, and hung up.

I thought about Josh's wry pronouncement at the funeral. *Angel Face was hustling tricks way before he met Razor.* A troubled kid with a history of drug use and sex offenses. Possible abuse, physical and sexual, in the home. The kind of background that was a breeding ground for sociopathy.

I didn't want it to be Byron, but it wasn't the kind of information you could ignore.

I called the number Sherilyn had given me, asked for Kevin Moreland. Married man. Sexual predator. Victimizer. Victim.

The receptionist had a nasal quality to her voice that grated on my nerves. "Mr. Moreland is in a meeting. If you'll leave your name and number, I'll let him know you called."

"Jared McKean. Tell him I'm a private investigator looking for information on an acquaintance of his. Byron Birch."

I left her my number. It took exactly three minutes for the phone to ring.

"My God." His voice was an agitated whisper. "What do you mean, calling me here? Is this some kind of shakedown?" The terminology sounded out of character, as if he'd pulled it from some gangster movie.

"No sir. As I told your receptionist, I'm a—"

"I know what you told her," he said. "A private detective. How did you get this number?"

"That's what detectives do. There's no reason this has to interfere with the rest of your life. I'm curious, though. Why didn't you press charges?"

"I have a wife. Kids." His voice dropped back into the whisper. "My God, I have a *career*. If this got out . . ." His voice cracked, and I imagined the sweat breaking out on his forehead. "Just tell me what you want."

"Just to talk, Mr. Moreland. I'm digging into the kid's history, and here's this . . . incident. Surely you can see why it might be important."

"What? Like some kind of background check? The kid's a psychopath. Simple enough?"

"Like I said, I'd really like to go over the details with you. I'd be happy to come by your house to discuss it." I started to read off the address.

"No!" He cut me off. "Look, I'm in meetings all morning. You know Santa Fe Steakhouse on Music Valley Drive? Twelve-fifteen. I'll meet you there."

"Twelve-fifteen." I wrote it in my appointment book. "I'll be looking forward to it."

CHAPTER THIRTY-ONE

Moreland resembled a weasel with thick, wire-rimmed glasses and a scraggly mustache. He tugged at his tie, smoothed the top of his thinning hair as if to reassure himself that it was still there, and shot a quick, furtive glance around the room. I knew who he was the minute he walked in.

When I waved him over to the table, he ducked his head as if to avoid being recognized and shuffled over. Slid in across from me and smoothed his hair again. I was sure he'd picked this restaurant because, in spite of the lunch crowd, the high-backed booths gave the illusion of privacy.

"Mr. . . . McKean, is it?" he said. "I'm here. Say what you have to say."

"Wouldn't you like to order first?"

"I just want to get this over with."

"Worried about the family finding out, huh?" I shook my napkin out and draped it across my lap. "What I'm wondering is how you managed to keep it from your wife in the first place. A wound like that, I'd think it would be kind of hard to explain."

He averted his gaze. "I told her it was a random mugging, that they never caught the guy."

"A random mugger who just happened to take a whack at your johnson."

"There's an artery in the groin. I told her he was probably going for that."

"Uh-huh. Bet she was real sympathetic too, seeing's how he must've been trying to kill you."

He fumbled with his napkin. Unrolled it too quickly, and the silverware inside clattered to the table. "I don't see how this kind of sarcasm is necessary."

"It makes me feel better." I leaned across the table and stared into his eyes until he looked away. "I mean, you lie to your wife, maybe give her some god-awful disease, and in the process, you exploit some underage kid who's living on the streets."

"It wasn't like that!" His cheeks reddened, two crimson spots against the pastiness of his face. "The Birch kid . . . *he* came on to *me*."

"Yeah, those street punks are like that. Living hand to mouth. Anything for a couple of bucks."

"Exactly," he said, missing the sarcasm this time. "It wasn't like I picked him up off a *playground*."

"So he wasn't exactly an innocent."

"Not at all." The waitress brought us menus and filled our water glasses. When she had gone, Moreland licked his lips and took a sip. "He's been around the block a few times, take it from me. That innocent little baby face? Nothing but pure evil underneath."

"So how'd it happen?"

He took another sip of water and dabbed at his mouth with his napkin. A droplet hung, glistening, in his mustache. "I was on my lunch hour, and I happened to take a walk down around Centennial Park. He stopped me. Asked if I wanted a blowjob. Naturally, I refused."

"Naturally."

He glanced up to see if I was mocking him, and this time I managed to keep my expression neutral. "He came on stronger. Told me he hadn't eaten in two days, really needed the money. So finally, I agreed."

"So it was a humanitarian gesture."

"Exactly. I was just trying to help the boy out."

I refrained from asking why he didn't just hand the kid a twenty.

"So we go to the back of the park, to the little island in the middle of the duck pond. It was spring, and there was a lot of vegetation, so we were pretty well hidden. He . . ." Moreland coughed, glanced away. "He unzipped my pants and started to . . . you know."

I nodded.

"I had my eyes closed. Enjoying it." He had the decency to look embarrassed. "And all of a sudden, I felt this horrible pain. I thought he'd bitten it off." He shuddered at the memory, and I felt my own testicles draw up in sympathy.

"So much blood," he said.

"What did he do then?"

He gave an angry laugh. "Took my wallet and ran away. I managed to staunch the bleeding and stagger to the parking lot, where someone was kind enough to call 911."

"You told the police this?"

He shook his head. "I told them the same thing I told my wife. That it was just a mugging. I went so far as to identify him in a photo lineup. But they knew I hadn't told the whole truth. I could tell. I realized if I testified, it would all come out, how it had happened. I'd be ruined, you understand? My marriage, my career . . . I might even be charged with statutory rape." His voice faltered, and his fingers tightened on the edge of the table. "I told them I didn't want to press charges, that I wasn't certain enough of the identification."

"But you were."

"How could I not be certain? It was broad daylight, for God's sake. And . . . he's not exactly forgettable."

"Right. I'm curious about something else, Mr. Moreland. When you made your complaint, you identified Byron by name. How'd you know it?"

He gave me a baffled look. "He told it to me."

"Kid carries a knife to a public place, intending to slice off a man's penis, and then tells the victim his name?" It seemed a bit unusual, and I told Moreland so.

He dismissed it with a shrug. "Kid's a psycho, like I said. Probably high on something too."

"All the same, it doesn't seem well thought out. Did you say or do anything that might have set him off?"

"Of course it wasn't well thought out." He lifted the napkin in his lap by two corners and snapped it straight. "I keep telling you, the boy is a head case. Why else would he do a thing like that?"

"I don't know." I toyed with my butter knife. "I think I'll ask him."

A flush crept up Moreland's neck. "The little bastard *stabbed* me, for Christ's sake. What makes you think he'll tell you the truth?"

"I don't expect him to. I expect him to lie. And when everybody's lies are on the table, I'll be able to figure out what happened."

"I don't like your implication." He crushed the napkin into a wad and flung it onto the table. The muscles in his jaw twitched like stranded tadpoles. "Are we finished here?"

"Whenever you say so."

"And I won't hear from you again?"

I took a moment to consider the possibility. "I think you've told me everything I need to know."

"Good." He was already halfway to the door when he said over his shoulder, "See you in Hell, McKean."

I lifted my water glass and quietly toasted his retreating back. "Not if I see you first."

CHAPTER THIRTY-TWO

That night, after I'd taken care of Dylan's puppy and the horses, I tossed my wallet onto the table beside my bed and thought about the scrap of paper with Elisha's number on it.

No time like the present, right? What exactly was I waiting for? I made the call. She sounded glad to hear from me.

"Have you eaten?" I asked, after the small talk.

"You mean, ever?"

English teachers. Sheesh. "I mean tonight."

"I was thinking of heating up some chicken noodle soup."

"I think I can do better than that."

———

We met at La Hacienda, a little Mexican restaurant not far from Percy Priest Lake. I'd changed into khakis and then back to jeans, exchanged my flannel shirt for a tan blazer over a white dress shirt, decided that looked too yuppie and exchanged that for a navy crewneck sweater over a denim work shirt.

I got there in fifteen minutes, had hardly closed the Silverado door before she pulled in, scanning the lot for a space. She saw me and waved, flashed a broad grin when I went to open her car door.

A mustached waiter led us to a table near the big screen television and seated us beneath a super-sized mural of Carlos Santana. Flames billowed from the neck of his guitar and mingled with loops and swirls that represented sound waves. Elisha peeled off her coat, draped it and her purse over the back of her chair, and then slid into the seat. Beneath the coat, she was wearing a royal blue sweater and black pants. A chunky lapis and gold bohemian necklace dangled between her breasts; gold gypsy earrings peeked out from a torrent of molasses-colored hair.

Maybe I should have stuck with the tan jacket.

"I wasn't sure you'd call," she said.

"I had it on good authority that I'd be crazy not to."

She laughed. "That's gratifying, I suppose." She brushed a hand lightly on the wall beneath the mural. "Nice."

The waiter brought chips and salsa, took our drink orders. When she left, Elisha said, "What happened to you?"

"You know how it is. Bad guys."

"Maybe it's your approach."

"Maybe it's just that they're bad guys."

She reached for a chip and scooped up a generous dollop of salsa. "I don't know how you stand it. All that ugliness."

"Sometimes you get to make a difference."

Elisha nodded and reached for another chip. "Mmm. Still warm."

The waiter took our orders—a chicken chimichanga with extra cheese sauce for her, a Number Four combo for me.

Elisha brushed a strand of hair away from her face and smiled. "Ten years ago, I'd have ordered a salad, then stopped for a burger on the way home."

"More confident these days," I said. "I like that."

"Not that confident." She reached over, straightened the condiments, fiddled with the salt shaker. "I changed clothes six times."

I smiled. Thought of the tan blazer. Said, "I like that, too."

CHAPTER THIRTY-THREE

Early the next morning, I drove downtown to The Body Shop, Byron Birch's gym. Squeezed between a bicycle store and a shop devoted to computer software, it was close enough to Vanderbilt University to attract a clientele of body-conscious young men and women armed with their parents' credit cards. Razor had paid for Byron's membership, supposedly a gift to Byron but more likely a gift to himself.

The front door opened into a reception area, where a bored-looking woman in an electric pink leotard sat behind a kidney-shaped pinewood desk. She perched on a high stool chomping on gum, reading an outdated copy of *Vogue* magazine, and filing a set of Manchurian fingernails.

A clipboard with a sign-in sheet lay on the desk, three-quarters filled with signatures. I couldn't tell if they were behind the times or if the low-tech method was supposed to represent a more human touch.

Hell, maybe they just had lousy computer system.

I signed Byron's name to the clipboard, along with the time, and walked into the back as if I belonged there. Nobody seemed to know—or care—otherwise.

The carpeted hall ran past the dressing rooms, men's to the left, women's to the right. Then a water fountain and two battered vending machines, one offering water and fruit juices, the other advertising Coca-Cola and Mountain Dew. Sugar and caffeine, twenty-first-century health foods.

Just beyond the vending machines, the strip of carpet cut between two plate glass windows separating the handball courts from the free weights and exercise machines. There was a line waiting for the machines, where hard-bodied women in exercise garb chatted up muscle-bound men between sets. Both handball courts were in use.

I watched through the window for a few moments, then pushed open the door and went inside. A cute brunette in a black thong leotard was doing hamstring stretches while she waited for the Stairmaster. Over twenty-one, I thought, barely.

I went over and said, "You know a kid named Byron Birch? He's a regular here."

She looked up with suspicious eyes. Obviously a girl who was used to being hit on. The cuts and bruises on my face probably weren't very reassuring, but she didn't mention them. "Nope," she said. "Don't recognize the name."

"He's about fifteen. Blond. About so tall." I indicated with my hand palm-down at the tip of my nose.

"Doesn't ring a bell. But not many kids that young come here." She brushed a stray strand of hair away from her face. "This kid. He's, like, Greek god handsome?"

"That seems to be the general consensus."

"I've seen him around. In a couple of years, he's gonna be so hot."

"Do you know if he comes around on Fridays?"

"I think so, but I couldn't say for sure. Lotta people come and go."

It was the same story all around the room.

Yeah, I've seen him around.

Naw, I wouldn't know if he was here on any particular day.

I made a quick canvas of the pool area, looked longingly at the hot tub, and went back to the front desk. The clock over the desk said one-fifty. I signed myself out at four P.M. and left. Nobody seemed to notice, which pretty much blew Byron's alibi out of the water. It didn't mean he'd killed Razor, but it didn't prove he hadn't.

It was easy to imagine Byron killing Razor in a sudden fit of rage—or fear. But disinfecting the tub, smearing the footprints, vacuuming the room, wiping the prints, and then remembering to carry the evidence and his cleaning materials away for disposal just didn't

- 177 -

fit his style. Those were the acts of a precise, analytical mind. Byron was a bright enough kid, but precision and analysis didn't seem to be his strong points.

Keating, on the other hand . . . I thought of the neat rows of toys in his office, the books evenly aligned, the way he'd unconsciously straightened the edges of his sheaf of papers. Precise was Keating's middle name. Then there was the psychology experiment Keating had shared with Razor. Manipulation. People as puppets. Razor had been forced to leave the university. Keating had managed to avoid expulsion. So who was the master manipulator?

Had he somehow manipulated Byron into killing Razor?

The scene showed two completely opposite methodologies—the vicious initial attack and the painstaking attempt to obscure the evidence.

Opposite patterns. Chaos and Reason.

Byron and Keating?

Or Elgin and Hewitt? Either scenario was plausible, but I couldn't make them mesh.

I was worrying at the problem when my mobile phone rang.

It was Frank.

"Bad news, Cowboy," he said.

"What's that?"

"Your suspect. Elgin Mayers. He made the tail. I guess he fig-ured we were onto him." Frank sounded disappointed. "No sign of him since lunch."

"Shit," I said. "Have you told the others? The ones on his list?"

"That's next on *my* list. But you'll never guess what we found in his house."

"Don't tell me," I said. "Rattlesnakes."

Silence. Then, "Rattlesnakes, copperheads, corals. Scrote-bag had about a dozen tanks full of 'em. What they call 'hot' snakes. How'd you know that?"

"Lucky guess," I said, and broke the connection.

CHAPTER THIRTY-FOUR

So Elgin was running. It didn't make him guilty, but it sure as hell didn't make him look innocent. He could be halfway to Mexico, but somehow I didn't think so. He'd made that crack about burning out a nest of vipers, and he didn't seem the type to leave a job half done.

When Frank signed off, I called Miss Aleta and filled her in. Then I called my brother and made sure he and the family were staying put.

"Look," he said, "there are worse things than taking the wife and kids to a nice B&B, but this is getting old. Wendy's worried out of her wits, and I can't stay home from work forever. Are you sure this guy is coming after Josh?"

"Not a hundred percent. Maybe ninety-five."

"Ninety-five is high. It pisses me off, to tell the truth."

"It pisses me off too."

"You're working on it?"

"Frank had a tail on him, but they lost him. I don't know what we can do until he resurfaces. Just stay low until we get him."

"I want to help."

"This guy is good. If he finds out where you are, you need to be there to stop him."

There was a brief silence on the other end. Then he said, "You stop this guy, Jared. And keep me posted."

"Love to Josh and the girls," I said.

"I'll tell them," he said, and hung up.

—◦◦◦—

I hadn't heard from the Hewitts. Since they were the only connections I had to Elgin, I stopped by their house. Judith answered the door, her face pale.

"What do you want?" she asked.

"Heard from Elgin lately?"

"No. And if I did, I wouldn't tell you. Why don't you leave us alone?"

I caught the door before she closed it. "Just tell me this. Is Elgin in the wind because he killed Razor or because he plans to do something to those kids?"

Her jaw tightened. "They weren't such kids when they raped me, were they?"

"They didn't all have a hand in that."

Josh didn't have a hand in that.

She didn't answer, but her eyes were hard.

I felt my own jaw twitch. "Look. If you care about Elgin at all, you'll rein him in. Because if anything happens to those kids . . ." I took a deep breath. *If anything happens to Josh.* "If anything happens to those kids, I will cut out his heart and eat it. You got that?"

"I'll give him the message," she said. "But I wouldn't want to be you when he gets it."

—◊◊◊—

Since I had no idea where to look for Elgin, I drove back to The Body Shop, parked in front of the bicycle store, and waited until seven-fifteen, when Alan Keating's silver Skylark pulled up in front and Byron got out of the passenger side.

I gave Keating time to pull away before I went inside. The receptionist, the same bored-looking woman I'd seen before, looked up from her magazine and said, "You have to sign in."

I scrawled something illegible on the register and ducked into a men's dressing room crowded with milling bodies in various stages of undress. Edging between a row of lockers and the sweaty paunch of a middle-aged man with a towel knotted around his hips, I spotted Byron's blond hair and changed my trajectory to head in that direction.

He had one foot propped on a wooden bench and was bent over it, tying the laces on a thick-soled athletic shoe.

I clapped a hand on his shoulder, and he looked up, startled.

"Hey, buddy," I said. "Let's go for a run."

He looked like he was about to object, then shrugged and tossed a towel over the back of his neck. "What the hell? Think you can keep up?"

Neither of us bothered to sign out as we passed the reception desk. I trailed Byron into the parking lot and followed his lead in a series of light stretches.

"Where to?" he asked.

"How about the park?"

He trotted off in that direction. I jogged along beside him. For the first few minutes, I thought he was going to take it easy on me. Then we turned into Centennial Park, and he picked up speed.

He was fifteen and in good condition. I was twenty-one years older, with my ego at stake. A sharp pain sliced through my calf; I gritted my teeth and pushed through it, knowing I'd pay for my hubris later. I kept up with him, barely.

We made five laps around the park, our breath streaming out behind us like exhaust fumes. Then I veered off and headed for the duck pond. He followed me across an arched wooden bridge that led to an island about the size of a two-car garage. Ducks nested here in spring, but now it was a drab tangle of brown vines and fallen logs amid a copse of bare trees.

I leaned against one to catch my breath.

"Not bad for an old guy," he panted, pulling the towel from around his neck to wipe away sweat.

"Thanks." I didn't have a towel, so I pulled up the collar of my T-shirt and wiped my face with that. The sweat was already beginning to evaporate, and the chill air made my skin feel clammy. "You recognize this place?"

Byron looked around reflexively. "Sure. I been here a few times." "With johns?"

He gave me a narrow look. "Sometimes. Why?"

"You remember a john named Moreland?"

"I don't know. How many guys you know'll tell a hustler their names?"

"Not many. But I bet you remember this guy. He's about five-ten, skinny, wears glasses, got a little pencil mustache."

He laughed. "Half the johns in the city."

"This one's a little different. You almost cut his dick off."

"Oh. That perv."

"So you did cut him."

He gave an angry shrug. "So? It was an accident. He didn't press charges."

"He's still not. But it wasn't an accident. He says you stabbed him for no reason."

"Yeah. Right."

"What'd he do? Try to stiff you?"

"Tried to stiff me all right, but not the way you mean." He kicked at the base of a tree. It was about the diameter of his arm and grew out of the side of the island, jutting almost straight out over the water. "We dealt for a blowjob. Then he decides he wants more." He tested the trunk for strength, then stepped out onto it and balanced there. Bounced on the balls of his feet, as if on a diving board. "I don't do that shit, man."

"Not even with Razor?"

"Razor never touched me."

"The hell he didn't."

"Seriously." He gave a self-conscious little laugh. "He said I was too beautiful just to fuck."

"Yeah. That Razor—he was a real do-gooder."

He shrugged. "He liked to look. To watch me while I worked out, took a shower, whatever. I don't know why he didn't want to screw. He said something about the sweetness of anticipation, whatever that means. I got no problem with that. But hey, he paid the bills. He wanted to do me, I would've let him. At least I'd've gotten something for it. But this guy . . . Moreland . . ." He stomped at the branch, lost his balance, windmilled, and recovered. "Stupid son of a bitch. I say no, and he tries to make me."

"Not so smart," I said.

"Damn straight. Little weasel like him. Like I couldn't take him."

"Why'd you use the knife, then?"

He bounced on the trunk again, lightly this time. "I wasn't thinking, I guess. It was like—" He stopped suddenly.

"Like?"

"Nothing, man. I just got scared, is all."

I could have finished his sentence for him. *It was like when my mother's boyfriend . . . like when my uncle . . . like when my stepdad . . .* I'd heard it a thousand times, and it never got any easier to listen to.

"You ever get scared of Razor like that?" I asked.

"No." He walked heel-to-toe halfway out the trunk of the tree and bounced again. Good balance. If it had been Paulie, I'd have called him back in, but what the hell? The water was shallow, and the worst that could happen would be he'd fall in and I'd have to haul him out. "Like I said, he hardly touched me. He was nice to me. He gave me things. Let me drive his car."

I bit the inside of my cheek to keep from saying the wrong thing.

He answered my silence anyway. "I'm not stupid. I know he wasn't a saint. But there was something about him. Nobody messed with him."

"Somebody killed him."

"Yeah. Well." He stared out over the pond. "The world is full of messed-up people."

CHAPTER THIRTY-FIVE

I was halfway home to change clothes and feed the horses when my cell phone chirped. It was Elisha.

"I hope it's not a bad time," she said.

"It just got a lot better."

"Flatterer. I wanted to thank you again for dinner the other night. I had a good time."

"Me too."

"And I was wondering . . ." Her voice trailed off.

"You were wondering?"

"How you feel about chicken curry."

I smiled, even though she couldn't see it. "I live for chicken curry. You have a place in mind?"

There was a brief silence. Then she said, "I was thinking of eating in. I make a mean Kerala chicken."

"She cooks?" I said. "Be still my heart."

"She cooks. But he's expected to bring the wine."

—ɯ—

I stopped to buy flowers, then pulled into J. Barleycorn's and picked up a bottle of Shakespeare's Love, a fruity white wine the manager assured me was a perfect complement to Indian cuisine. Then home to take care of the horses, check in on Jay, and drive to Elisha's split-level brick house a few miles from the high school. A warm light glowed from behind wispy curtains the color of saffron, and an array of security lights flared to life as I eased the Silverado into the driveway.

Elisha met me at the door. She was barefoot, dressed in jeans and a red turtleneck with white rhinestone snowflakes at the neck and cuffs. Her hair was damp, wispy across her forehead, the sides swept loosely into a silver clip that freed the rest to tumble down her back. I felt better, seeing her.

When she saw the flowers, she flashed a smile and clapped her hands like a child. "Christmas roses! I didn't think men did things like this anymore."

"I aim to please."

She kissed my cheek, and I smelled her shampoo, a sweetly exotic scent like jungle flowers and vanilla. It mixed well with the ambient aroma of simmering spices. "This is a good start. Come in. I'll put these on the table."

I followed her into the kitchen, where she gave me a wooden spoon and instructions to stir the curry while she poured wine and tended to the roses.

"They say there's a language of flowers," she said. "What do these mean?"

"I thought you might know," I said.

"Sorry." She smiled. "French and Italian. A soupçon of Latin. But no flower."

"No interest?"

"Not much opportunity." She opened a blond wood cabinet and took out two long-stemmed glasses. "My ex-husband wasn't much of a romantic."

Sensitive territory. A make or break moment?

I asked, "How long were you married?"

"Six years." She uncorked the wine and poured us each a glass. "But he checked out long before that."

"You tried to make it work."

"Too stubborn to quit." She took the spoon from me, tasted the sauce, and tipped the spoon toward me, her other hand held beneath to catch the drips. "Does this taste right to you?"

"Just about perfect."

She shot me an impish grin. "Just about?"

I put my hands on her hips and pulled her close. She didn't pull away. "Delectable," I said. "Elixir of the gods. Spiced ambrosia. How's that?"

"Getting there." She pecked my chin with her lips and slipped out of my arms, blushing. "I'm being too forward. This is going too fast."

"It's the curry." I turned away to hide my erection, annoyed with myself for rushing things. "They say hot foods do that."

"I'm too comfortable with you," she said. "And not comfortable enough. You make my brain all fizzy. Maybe it's your aftershave."

My brain was feeling pretty fizzy, too. "I'll change it, if you want."

She brushed the back of my hand with her fingertips. "Don't you dare."

She transferred the curry into a serving dish and carried it to the table, where a tossed salad and a loaf of King's Hawaiian Bread were already waiting.

The curry was delicious, the wine light and sweet. I tried not to gorge. Elisha ate with gusto. She either exercised a lot, or she had a good metabolism.

She refused to let me help clean up. "There's nothing to do," she said. "Everything just goes in the dishwasher. Anyway, I'd rather talk. I have thirty student journals to read, but I can put it off for about an hour. Do you have to go right away?"

"I'm in no hurry."

We sat on the couch like a couple of awkward teenagers, thighs touching, my arm draped across the back of the sofa behind her shoulders. Close enough to feel the heat of each other's skin. Wanting.

Holding back.

She talked about school, her students, the ones she delighted in, and the ones she cried over at night. She talked about PTA meetings and empty supply cabinets, dress codes and anti-drug programs. We talked about Josh, his poetry, his artwork.

"You know him pretty well," I said. "You read his writing, you know how he thinks."

"A little. But I can't discuss specifics with you. Not without his parents' permission."

"I know that. I just need a general impression. If someone said he was part of something—something bad—would you believe it?"

She laid a hand on my arm. "You're not looking for a general impression. What's this about?"

"I can't go into it. I'm sorry." I held her gaze, but it took some doing.

"He's a good kid," she said at last. "It's not in him to hurt anyone but himself. Is that what you wanted to know?"

The knot in my gut loosened a hair. "I think so."

"There's no one more vulnerable than a Goth kid. I always worry about them, because when you're smart, sensitive, and disillusioned, the world can get pretty harsh."

"I think Josh's friends were beyond Goth. Goths are stylers, right?"

"Mostly. But there are fringe groups. Can I do anything to help him?"

"I don't know."

Her hand slid down my arm. I turned my palm to meet it so we ended up with our fingers entwined. After a moment, she leaned her head against my shoulder and said, "We've talked about my life *ad nauseum*. It's your turn to spill."

I told her about Paulie, skimmed the details of my work. Took a chance and invited her to the Christmas party Jay had planned for Dylan. Told myself I didn't care if she accepted and grinned like a schoolboy when she said yes.

An hour later, she tilted her head up and pulled mine forward for a long, deep kiss that tasted of wine and spices and left us both breathing hard. She rocked back, away from me, and searched my face with her eyes. "Are you going to be mad if we stop now?"

"I'm a big boy," I said. "I can wait."

"I'm sorry. I shouldn't have . . ." She looked down at her lap, fiddled with the hem of her sweater.

"Nothing to be sorry about," I said. "I'm glad you did."

"It's been a long time since I was with anyone. I'm not sure what the rules are anymore."

I cupped my hand under her chin and tipped her head up. "No rules. Let's just take it as it comes."

"You're sweet." Her eyes filled. "And I'm ruining everything."

"Not even close. It's not a good time for me either, to tell you the truth."

"My husband . . ." Her hands worked at the hem of her sweater, twisted, clutched. "Ex-husband. He wasn't sweet at all."

"I'm not him," I said.

"Neither was he," she said. "At first."

CHAPTER THIRTY-SIX

It was late when I got home, but Jay met me in the front hallway. "You have a message from a Miss Aleta."

He followed me into the kitchen, where I replayed the voice-mail message. "Hello, Mr. McKean. You'll be pleased to know the judge set bail for Laurel O'Brien."

"Laurel O'Brien," Jay said. "That's the girl who confessed, right? What's going on?"

I set the receiver gently in its cradle and said, "Absinthe's out." She would have been safer inside.

—⚭—

Elisha and I, Fabulous Greg and his partner, and three gay couples I didn't know gathered at the house for an early celebration. A contingency, in case Dylan didn't make it until Christmas. Nothing sadder than a stack of presents that would never be opened.

I took the pup outside for a quick pee. Then Jay and I helped Dylan dress, eased him back onto the bed, and played with the controls until we found a comfortable angle for him.

"I feel like Barbie," Dylan groused. "Where are my red pumps?"

At six, we all gathered around Dylan's bed in the living room. Jay had set up a refreshment table and piled gifts under the tree. "Looks like Santa came early," he said, passing out red felt stockings stuffed with Silly Putty, bubbles, Duncan yo-yo's, and a variety of inexpensive puzzles and toys. Kid stuff. We were old enough to appreciate it.

Elisha pulled a plastic wand from a bottle of bubbles. "I haven't done this since I was a little girl," she said, and blew a stream of bubbles my way. One settled on my shoulder, and she poked it with a lacquered fingernail. I felt a heat, low in my belly.

It was understood that the contents of the packages were unimportant. An incense holder and a bundle of incense, three T-shirts with X-rated slogans, a wine and fruit basket with a signed photo of Divine, and a plastic singing fish mounted on a plaque that said *Billy Bob Bass*.

Dylan rested his hand on the neck of the wine bottle and looked around at the offerings. "Nothing from Straight," he said. I hadn't expected him to notice, but he seemed genuinely hurt. "Still haven't learned to love me, huh?"

"I couldn't wrap it," I said. "It's not that kind of gift." I left the room and came back with a fishbowl, where a blood-red beta with a navy-streaked tail drifted above a layer of electric blue gravel.

Dylan's eyes misted, and his sudden smile reminded me of Paulie's. "Aw, Straight, I knew you cared."

Jay set the bowl on the end table so Dylan could see it from the bed. "Look at this haul," he said. "You must have been an awfully good boy this year, Dyl."

"That's a myth, you know," Dylan said. "It's all bullshit."

"No!" Jay raised his eyebrows and covered his mouth in mock surprise. "No Santa?"

"Not that part." Dylan's voice was a whisper. He cleared his throat and tried again. "Not that part. The part about the good little boys and girls. Truth is . . . Santa doesn't give a shit."

"Truth is," Jay said softly, "Santa only sees the good things."

Dylan leaned back into the pillow and closed his eyes. Guilt? Regret? "Nice trick," he said. "If you can manage it."

"We'll let you get some rest." Jay motioned to the other guests, who filed out of the room, pausing only long enough to squeeze Dylan's hand or shoulder and wish him a merry Christmas.

I sent Elisha ahead and stayed behind to place Luca on Dylan's lap and clear the gifts off the bed. He stroked the puppy's head, and the pup curled against his body and licked his hand. "Feels weird," he said. "Like being at your own funeral."

"I don't think they meant it that way."

"I know. It's all right. Damn waste to wait until I'm dead, right?" His gaze went to the door, where Jay had vanished. "I should have stayed with him, shouldn't I?"

"Twenty-twenty hindsight," I said. "But yeah. You should have."

He gave a rattling laugh. "That's what I like about you, Straight. No bullshit."

"Hey, you got a chance to make it up to him." I poured a cup of eggnog from the refreshment table and offered him a sip. "Not everybody gets that much."

He swallowed, coughed, and dabbed at his lips with the sleeve of his pajama shirt. "How? By letting him watch me die?"

"By letting him help you. It means a lot to him."

"Yeah? What's that called? Killing me with kindness?"

"It's called forgiveness, Jackass."

He smiled at the epithet. "So, Jay-o's forgiven me, has he? For dumping him, or for killing him?"

"Both, I guess."

"And you?"

"I don't have anything to forgive you for, Dylan."

He looked away. "Yeah. Right."

"But for what it's worth, if Jay's okay with you, there's no reason for me not to be."

He looked away, toward the fishbowl. "Thanks, Straight. You're a pal. Now I can die in peace, knowing you and I are on good terms."

"Fuck you too," I said, but we both smiled.

—⁂—

Later, with Dylan asleep and the others in the kitchen sipping Long Island Teas and talking politics, Elisha and I scraped the remains of strawberry crepes and vegetarian pigs-in-blankets into the disposal, piled the soiled dishes in the sink, and filled the basin with suds. She glanced around and plucked a dish towel from a hook by the sink. Tossed it to me.

"I'll wash, you dry," she said.

Snippets of conversation from the other room drifted into the kitchen as we worked.

"It was nice of you to do this," Elisha said.

"I'd like to take the credit, but it was Jay's idea."

"Still." She flicked suds in my direction. I dodged, snapped her rear with the towel.

We laughed, made small talk punctuated by companionable silence. Our fingers touched as she handed me the dripping plates. Pulled away. A ballet of heat and electricity, skin against skin.

As I put away the last of the dishes, she busied herself with something behind my back, came up beside me and snaked an arm around my waist. "Look what I found." She dangled a sprig of mistletoe over her head and batted her eyes.

I kissed her, gently at first, then harder. My arms went around her and she clasped her hands at the small of my back, pulling me closer, the zipper of my jeans pressed against her belly.

"God, you smell good," she said. She nuzzled my neck. "What *is* that?"

"Patchouli," I mumbled. Maria had given it to me.

I pushed that thought from my mind and slid my right hand forward, stroked the curve of Elisha's breast with my thumb. She shifted toward my touch and arched into my palm, her breath catching in her throat.

Then she broke away. "Bad idea," she said. "On so many different levels."

I agreed, but that didn't stop me from feeling a pang of disappointment.

"I mean, it's way too soon." She toyed with the buttons of her blouse. "Don't you think?"

I nodded. "It's too soon."

"You've heard that 'three dates, no sex' rule? No sex by date three, and there's no date four?"

"I've heard of it."

"I don't believe in that." She looked into my eyes. Gnawed her lip. "I'm sorry."

"Nothing to be sorry about. I told you that before." I stroked her cheek. Ran two fingers through her hair. Brushed her lips with mine.

From somewhere far away, I heard a shrill, relentless ringing.

"The phone," she murmured.

"Let the machine pick up."

She put her hands on my chest and pushed away. "No," she said. "Jay."

We stepped apart just as he came into the room.

"Well, well, kiddies, having fun?" he asked. Elisha blushed and smoothed her hair. Jay grinned and picked up the phone.

"Hello?" He listened for a moment, then held out the receiver. "Darlene O'Brien."

"Absinthe's mother," I said. I put the phone to my ear. "Mrs. O'Brien—"

"I got your number from Miss Aleta," she said. "Laurel's gone."

"What do you mean, gone?"

"I mean gone! Run away. We came back from a party and she wasn't here. Maybe I should have taken her car keys—you know, in light of the troubles—but I thought we'd put all that behind us."

"Was she at home alone?"

"Yes. I had a date." She made a small hiccupping sound. "Oh, I know, maybe I shouldn't have left her. But she's almost seventeen. Shouldn't she be old enough to stay home by herself for one evening?"

"You'd think so. But what makes you think she ran away? Couldn't she just have gone off with some friends?"

"She packed a bag. Clothes. Toothbrush. Mr. Flumpy."

"Mr. Flumpy?"

"Her stuffed rabbit. She's had him since she was three. That's how I knew she hadn't gone out with friends. She wasn't ready to give him up, but she wouldn't have taken him to a friend's. That would have been . . ." She paused. "Uncool."

"Did she leave a note?"

"No." She drew in a long, ragged breath. "Won't you come over, Mr. McKean? I just know you can find her."

"Have you called the police?"

"Yes. And they're doing all the usual things. Amber Alert, the whole shebang. But they don't really seem to be taking it very seriously. After all this trouble . . . well, they seem to think she's just trying to get attention. That she'll just turn up somewhere. Please," she said again. "I don't know what else to do."

I looked at Elisha. Too soon, she'd said. Too soon for both of us. But just because we weren't going to make love didn't mean I was in any hurry to end the evening.

She gave me a tentative smile.

I sighed and said into the receiver, "I'll be right over."

CHAPTER THIRTY-SEVEN

Absinthe and her mother lived in a two-story, Norman-style brick manor in Brentwood, an upscale community south of town. The average house in the area cost upwards of half a million dollars, and the O'Brien house, with its arched entryway and low-walled brick terrace, was somewhere north of average. I eased the Silverado up the drive, passed a Venetian-style fountain draped with colored lights, and parked behind a shiny black BMW that reminded me of a cockroach in a tuxedo.

According to the Parker file, the BMW belonged to Absinthe's mother. No dad in the picture, just two stepfathers, one of whom had died almost a year ago.

I picked my way up a flagstone path slippery with frost, past a life-sized Italian-style Nativity and up the front steps to a doorbell camouflaged as Rudolph's nose. I pressed my thumb against it, and eight tones sounded, simulated hand bells. A small dog yapped somewhere in the back of the house, followed by the click of high-heeled shoes on a hardwood floor. Then the door cracked open with a warm gust of cinnamon-scented air, and a wan face peered out.

"Mr. McKean?" A layer of makeup, expertly applied, softened but could not quite hide the worry lines around her bloodshot eyes. The top of her head was even with the center of my chest.

"Mrs. O'Brien," I said.

"It's Miz." She extended a hand, ragged nails gnawed to the quick. Like mother, like daughter. "Twice divorced and couldn't be happier. But please—call me Darlene."

She moved aside to let me pass, and I stepped into her hallway. Every available surface, nook, and cranny was crammed with plush toys and figurines: toy mice with candy canes, polar bears on ice-skates, rosy-cheeked elves dancing polkas. The place looked and smelled like Christmas Village.

A tiny head poked from beneath the hall table. Pricked ears, tousled hair, a pair of eyes like black beads wedged into a gray dust mop. Darlene scooped up the dust mop, a cairn terrier with its tiny nails painted a glittery purple.

"Laurel's work," Darlene said, nodding toward the dog's paws. "She has a well-honed sense of the dramatic." She gave a shrill, nervous laugh, and pressed her hand to her mouth as if to stuff the laughter back in. "I'm sorry. I'm rattling on. I don't know what to say. What to do. What do you need me to do?"

"I need to see her room."

"Of course. This way." She set the dog down and started up the stairs. The dog trotted behind her, wagging its stump of a tail.

I followed the dog.

Absinthe's room was, much like Absinthe herself, a study in opposites. White satin coverlet with a pattern of pink embroidered roses. Matching canopy arched across the bed. Three teddy bears, a mouse puppet, and a stuffed dragon arranged neatly on the pillows. Black walls, decorated with glow-in-the-dark, stick-on stars and posters of bands I'd never heard of. Arkham Asylum, Butterfly Messiah, Cult of the Psychic Fetus.

A tangle of necklaces dangled from the mirror of her antique white French Provincial dresser, some carved with runes, others made from different colors of crystal. I remembered a few from the books she'd recommended. Rose quartz for love. Amethyst for wisdom.

On her nightstand were an incense holder with a smoldering cone of sandalwood, a crystal ball, and copies of *I, Dracula*, *The Witches of Eastwick*, and something by Frederick Nietzsche.

Under her mother's worried gaze, I searched the drawers and closets, her desk, under the bed, and between the mattresses. Then I carefully took each drawer out of its slot, emptied it systematically, and searched for false bottoms and hidden compartments. In the bottom of her underwear drawer, I found a stack of granny panties, a couple of plus-sized satin thongs, and a plastic sandwich bag filled with something that looked a lot like oregano. Beside it was a pack of rolling papers and a book of matches.

Darlene looked away, embarrassed. I handed her the bag. She carried it down the hall between two fingers and a thumb and flushed the contents down the toilet.

I finished my search of the room, but turned up nothing that might tell me where Absinthe might have gone.

"Did the police check the doors and windows for signs of forced entry?" I asked.

"They didn't find anything," she said. "They seemed pretty sure she was a runaway. But where would she go? She doesn't have any money, and I took away her credit cards when all this happened."

The police had made a reasonable assumption, but I looked again anyway. Faint scratch marks marred the paint around the front door. Easy to miss, especially if you were already convinced there was nothing there.

Elgin Mayers? Leaving the marks on the door seemed clumsy for him. He hadn't left any trace when he'd broken into my office, which would have been more of a challenge.

"I'll keep looking," I said. "I'm sure the police will too. You should try and get some sleep. And stay here until we find her. Just in case she calls."

Darlene forced a smile. "I can take some time off from work, if I have to. Just . . . please find her."

I got a description of Absinthe's car—a red Corvette—and her license plate number. Then I climbed into the Silverado and pulled out of the driveway, not sure where to start. Where did a teen-aged girl with no credit cards and no money to speak of go after midnight?

As I merged onto I-65 North, my cell phone buzzed. I groped across the seat for it and was greeted by a breathless, teary voice.

"Mr. McKean?"

"Absinthe."

Something rattled in the background, followed by a heavy thump. "I'm at Dark Knight's," she whispered. "You have to get here right away. It's—" There was another bump, and she gave a muffled little shriek. "I have to go. They're here!"

There was a clatter, followed by the sound of running footsteps and a sharp cry cut off abruptly.

I dropped the phone onto the seat and punched the gas. Dodged a gray Cadillac and a tomato red Mitsubishi, then pushed the Silverado up to one-twenty and hurtled down the Interstate. I drove with one hand, punched 911 on my cell phone with the other.

I couldn't offer much information. Just an address and that a girl was in trouble. But I knew all the right codes, and the dispatcher, probably thinking I was an off-duty officer, assured me she would send the nearest patrol car ASAP.

I hoped they'd beat me there.

As I swung onto I-40, a patrol car cut in after me, blue lights flashing. I pretended he was answering my 911 call and kept my foot on the accelerator.

I squealed onto the Donelson Pike ramp, shot past a row of restaurants, a pawn shop, and a funeral home, the patrol car on my tail. With a prayer to the patron saint of reckless drivers, I screeched onto Dark Knight's street. The Silverado fishtailed, then recovered. I didn't need to look for the Knights' duplex. The blue flashing lights led me there.

There were two patrol cars parked outside. A red Corvette with Absinthe's license tags was parked between them. The Asian family huddled on their porch, watching the proceedings with wide eyes. A pair of uniformed officers stood to either side of the Knights' front door.

How long since Absinthe had screamed?

Not long.

Too long.

I parked the Silverado and got out with my hands up.

The patrol officer who'd been following me scrambled out of his car, gun out.

"What's your hurry, Mister?" he asked.

Slowly, I turned to face him. "There's a kid in there who may be in trouble."

"And you'd know this, how?"

I told him.

When I'd finished, he said, "Nice story. We'll see if it checks out." He moved closer and I checked out his nametag. T. Brandt. "In the meantime, how about showing me some ID? Slow and easy now."

I nodded and reached for my wallet, careful not to expose the shoulder rig. I eased the leather case open so he could see my identification and held it out.

He spared it a glance. "You think that license means you can blow off the speed limits?"

"No, sir." I glanced up the steps, where one of the two policemen was pushing open the door to the Knights' apartment. It was unlocked. Not a good sign. "I just wasn't sure how close you guys were. Can I put my hands down?"

"You armed?"

"I have a Glock forty caliber in a shoulder holster. I have a license to carry it."

"Why don't you just slowly put it on the hood of the truck and back away from it?"

I did as he asked.

"Now," he said, "put your palms on the side of the truck and spread your legs."

I let him pat me down.

"Okay." He stepped away and lowered his gun. "You can put 'em down."

There was a tense silence. Then one of the uniforms came outside and nodded to Brandt. "Got a couple of D.O.A.s in there," he said.

For a moment, I couldn't breathe. "The girl?"

He gave me a blank stare. "Female, mid-thirties. Teenage male."

"Shit." I pounded the side of the Silverado. "What happened?"

Brandt stepped closer. "Better call this in," he said to the uniformed officer. To me, he said, "Maybe you should tell me everything you know about what happened here."

I filled him in. Twenty minutes later, Harry Kominsky arrived with the M.E. and a host of forensic detectives and I went through it again.

I was glad it was Harry. The guys on the Job called him Lurch, because he was the tallest man in the department and had a stiff, uneasy way of moving, as if his joints had been welded together; but he'd been on the Job for forty years, and Frank and I had worked with him enough to know he knew his stuff.

He listened to my story without interrupting, then rubbed his gaunt face with his hands and said, "Sit tight."

He disappeared inside, leaving me in T. Brandt's capable hands.

A few minutes later, he opened the door and waved to Brandt. "Give him his piece back and let him come up." When I joined him on the front steps, he said, "Don't touch anything. I guess I don't need to tell you that."

"How bad is it?" I asked.

He hunched his big shoulders and shoved his hands into his pockets. "Not as bad as it could be," he said. "But bad enough."

CHAPTER THIRTY-EIGHT

I opened the door and stopped short, hit by a blast of frigid air laced with the pungent scents of stale urine, excrement and rotting meat.

The kid and his mother had been dead awhile. Probably killed not long after I'd last talked to Dennis. I breathed through my mouth and told myself it wasn't my fault.

I moved further into the apartment, sidestepping a woman taking photographs of the scene and a man dusting for fingerprints. Tara Knight's bloated body was sprawled in the recliner, an afghan draped across her lap, sightless eyes riveted on the television. The bruises that circled her neck were punctuated by darker marks where her killer's fingers had dug into the skin.

See enough dead bodies, and they start to look unreal, more like movie props than people. I waited for that familiar detachment to set in, but knowing the victim made it harder. Tara Knight had lived a hard life, and a sad one. I'd have wished her a gentler death.

I followed Harry down the hall, where Dennis Knight lay sprawled on his back, his bare legs stretched beyond the threshold of his bedroom, his head resting near the open bathroom door. He wore a pair of soiled navy blue cotton briefs and a Marilyn Manson T-shirt with a dark, rust-colored stain that started at the collar, spread across the shoulders and chest, and darkened the carpet around his upper body. The left side of his face was pressed against the carpet, throat gaped open, one long gash from ear to ear. The edges of the wound were beginning to turn black.

Through the open bedroom door, I could see that one of the shelves was off-kilter, cartoon characters scattered on the floor below. Elmer Fudd and Wile E. Coyote tangled with Daffy Duck and Marvin the Martian.

I resisted the impulse to pick them up and put them where they belonged.

"Must've gotten up to investigate a noise," Harry said. "Or take a leak. Probably never knew what hit him. Killer nailed him as he came out the bedroom door."

He'd been dead long enough for rigor mortis to fade and the blood to settle and turn the backs of his arms and legs a livid purple. The part of his body facing upward was pale in comparison, but the flesh of his head and neck had already turned a greenish red. The body had begun to bloat, escaping gases forming blisters the size of silver dollars on the young man's skin.

Someone, probably the killer, had turned the air conditioner on full blast, presumably to slow decomposition.

"What do you figure?" I asked. I fought the urge to go outside and take a gulp of fresh air. Do that, and your olfactory senses have to adjust to the stench all over again. Better to tough it out, if you can stand it. "Couple of days?"

Harry nodded. "Probably. Though cold as it is in here, it'll be hard to pin down an exact time." He waved a hand in front of his nose. "Another day or so and the neighbors would have been complaining."

"Efficient kill," I said. "Quick. Quiet."

"Must've been. He strangles the mother, then waits for the kid to come out of his room."

"Signs of forced entry?"

"Bathroom window's open, but we're thinking that's where the girl went out." I peeked in. It would have been a tight squeeze, but with a boost from adrenalin, she could have managed it. He said, "We're dusting for prints now."

"Any other sign of the girl?"

"Nada. We'll probably get a match on her prints, though."

I glanced around. "Anything missing?"

"Who could tell? Mom was a pack rat, kid had a lot of junk. Comics and shit. All those little toys. But I'm not seeing this as a robbery."

"No. More like an execution."

"Yeah, but for what?"

I filled him in on Judith's rape and Elgin's vanishing act. Again, I left Josh out of it. "I'm not sure if Hewitt's involved or not, but this looks like Mayers to me."

He rubbed at a spot on the side of his jaw. "Hewitt. We talked to him after the Parker killing. He and the brother-in-law alibied each other."

"Brother-in-law?"

"Mayers is Judith Hewitt's half brother. You didn't know?"

"No." I felt annoyed that I hadn't considered the possibility. Careless. "Different last names."

"He's quite a bit older. Already grown up and out of the house by the time Daddy and his new wife had the girl."

"They're close, though."

"Seems like it. You say Parker and his buddies raped her?"

"Yeah." I looked again at Dark Knight's body. Stupid, senseless way to die. "Better send someone to warn Barnabus. And Medea, too. He's targeted the whole group." I gave him the address.

"I'll see to it." He didn't seem offended that I'd offered the suggestion. "As for you, why don't you go on home and get some sleep? And drive slow, McKean. I don't think Officer Brandt is likely to let you off with two warnings in one night."

My gaze slid back to Dark Knight's body. I resisted the sudden urge to cover him with a blanket.

In the bathroom, another detective was coating the windowsill with black fingerprint dust. A mobile phone with lots of chrome, probably Absinthe's, lay on the floor beneath the window. It looked like a crushed beetle. I watched the technician for a few moments, then went back into the living room. The scene was abuzz with detectives and forensic technicians turning the duplex into an efficient and official crime scene.

Harry was kneeling beside Dennis Knight's body, talking quietly to the medical examiner. I gave him a quick nod on the way out. He nodded back.

I stepped out onto the porch and came nose to eyebrows with Kelly Malone. Her hair was tousled, her face bare. I guessed she'd gotten the call at home, no time for makeup.

She crossed her arms and said, "What are you doing at my crime scene?"

"Nice to see you too, Detective."

"Answer the question. I said—"

"I know what you said. The girl called me. Absinthe—Laurel—O'Brien."

"So?"

"She's in trouble. Her mom hired me to find her."

"Then unless she's hiding in the closet, this is not your business. I suggest you get out of here before I have you arrested."

"For what?"

"For being a pain in the ass."

"I don't think there's a law against that. Did you call Frank?"

She looked like she'd swallowed a slug. "I'll call Detective Campanella when he learns what a chain of command is. And you. Go home."

"Stellar idea," I said. "You'll be happy to know Detective Kominsky gave me the same advice."

"Good. Maybe I won't have to fire him." She uncrossed her arms and stepped forward as if she might walk through me. I moved aside and let her pass, even though I knew she'd consider it a sign of weakness. But this was a battle I could only win at Harry's expense. And Frank's.

Absinthe's Corvette was still parked in front, one front tire on the curb. A quick glance told me Officer Brandt and the other two uniforms were gone. Back on patrol, I assumed.

I peered through the window of Absinthe's car. Nothing out of the ordinary inside. McDonald's wrappers, a half-empty bag of Cheetos, a stack of library books.

I tried the door. Unlocked. A quick toss of the car turned up no clues as to where she might have gone.

Damn.

I rubbed my eyes as if I could wipe away the fatigue and turned back toward the Silverado just as Malone came back outside. She fumbled in her pockets, came up with a pack of cigarettes, and tapped one out. Placed it between her lips and stuffed the pack back into the pocket it had come from. Even in the dim light, I could tell her hands were shaking.

I went over and stood next to her. "You okay?"

"You're still here?" she said, her voice strained.

"This your first?"

"Is it that obvious?"

She pulled out a disposable lighter and flicked her thumb across the spark wheel. After the third try, I reached across and took it from her. This time, the flame caught. I shielded it with my cupped hand and held it out so she could light her cigarette.

Still trembling, she took a long draw from the cigarette, blew out the smoke through her mouth, and said, "You get used to it, I guess."

"Some do." I handed her the lighter, which she pocketed. "Some just aren't cut out for it."

"I thought I should see what it's like. My detectives have been having a hard time. Tough guys, I'd've said."

"They probably are."

"They're falling apart."

"It's a different kind of toughness. Your guys—Gilley and Robbins?"

She nodded.

"I bet they could take on a bunch of bikers, talk some hophead down from a building, walk into a domestic disturbance and stay cool, even with some jerk-off waving a shotgun around. Am I right?"

"I'd've thought so. But this . . . Gilley looks like he hasn't slept in weeks. Robbins acts like he's sleepwalking all the time. And Harry's in there cool as Christmas, like he's looking at a frozen turkey instead of a murdered boy."

"You have to turn it off, that part of you that says this is a murdered kid. Not everybody can do it. You'll just end up unraveling guys like Gilley and Robbins and wasting guys like Harry and Frank."

"The policy—"

"The policy is bullshit."

She looked back over her shoulder, toward the apartment. "Something to think about," she said. She ground out the cigarette on the sole of her shoe, field stripped it, and put the butt in her pocket. "Don't be here when I come back out."

I nodded. Waited until the door closed behind her. Then I called my brother. I told him what had happened, told him to stay put, and snapped the phone shut before he could argue. Then I stopped at a Quik Sak for a box of NoDoz. I popped two into my mouth and washed them down with a cup of tepid coffee.

No rest for the weary. Absinthe was still out there somewhere. And Elgin wanted to kill her.

CHAPTER THIRTY-NINE

It was close to dawn, but the lights were still on at Barnabus's. It was possible the police had been here before me, but I rang the bell anyway. No answer. I rang again. The door opened a crack and Barnabus's pale, sharp face peered out.

"What do you want this time?" he asked.

"Feeling peckish, are we? The police been here yet?"

A muscle in his cheek twitched. "Why would the police have been here? And why the hell are you?"

"I wanted to know if you knew where Absinthe might be."

The heavy lids looked suddenly less drowsy. "What makes you think I'd have any idea where Absinthe is?"

"She's not at home. With Dark Knight out of the picture, that leaves you and Medea."

"Haven't heard from her. Is that all you wanted?"

"How come you didn't ask me why Dark Knight was out of the picture?"

His nostrils flared. He wavered for a moment. Then he said, "Hey, you say he's out of the picture, he's out of the picture."

"When I say he's out of the picture, I mean he's dead. Murdered."

"Oh." He pressed a finger to his lips.

"Could be you and Medea are next."

"Are you threatening me?"

"Not threatening. Warning."

He gave a nervous titter. "Why would anyone want me and Medea dead?"

"Judith Hewitt."

"That again. If we raped her, how come there was never a mark on her?"

"You threatened her at knife-point."

"Says who?"

"Dark Knight says. Judith confirmed it."

He smiled as if he'd caught me in a mousetrap. "But Dark Knight's dead. That makes it her word against mine."

"Wonder who they'll believe." I pushed the door open a little wider and shouldered in past him. "And if you have any ideas about shutting her up, I'd forget it. Anything happens to her, cops'll be all over you like maggots on carrion."

"Lovely image."

"What I'm saying is, the police are not your biggest problem."

"And what, exactly, *is* my biggest problem?"

"Big guy. Mustache. Scar on his cheek. Same guy who killed Dennis Knight and his mother. He's a martial arts expert and a trained sniper, but he's partial to knives. And for you, I think he'll want to get in close."

His lower lip quivered. He closed his upper teeth on it. "Hey, man, she wanted it. Couldn't get enough."

"Somehow, I don't think he'll buy it. Look at the bright side, though. Maybe it's not him. Maybe it's just some freak with a jones for vampires."

"I can take care of myself," Barnabus muttered, but his gaze jumped around the room as if Elgin's form might coalesce from the shadows.

"No worries." I tucked my card into his shirt pocket and breezed out past him. "Just get Medea to whip out a couple of protection spells and I'm sure you'll both be fine."

CHAPTER FORTY

I drove a grid through downtown, north to south, east to west, saw no sign of Absinthe. Made one last stop on the way home. This time, I didn't worry about waking anyone. The guy I'd come to see was always up before dawn.

I turned the Silverado onto Broadway and followed it to Third Avenue, made a series of convoluted turns to navigate a maze of one-way streets and came back past the bus terminal. Kaizen, the rehab center run by my good buddy Billy Mean, sat on the opposite corner. Kaizen was a Japanese term. Billy said it meant improving by a small amount each day. Miniscule was good enough, as long as you kept moving forward. It was Billy's philosophy about sobriety.

It seemed like a pretty good way to get through life.

Back in the early seventies, Billy had been in Vietnam. Special Forces. He'd had trouble adjusting when he got back home. Black days. Bad choices. Ended up in prison, somehow managed to get his head on straight, and started a shelter for other lost veterans. Kaizen offered three squares a day, job training and transportation, business wear for interviews and the workplace, and classes in goal-setting, anger management, and overcoming addictions.

He was my first client. I'd found his estranged daughter, arranged a reconciliation. For this, he declared me a friend.

I pushed open the door to the shelter, and a burst of warm air teased me with the scents of fresh coffee and frying bacon. Billy stood behind the serving table, plopping heaps of scrambled eggs and hash browns onto plastic trays. His paunch strained beneath a dingy white apron speckled with grease. When he saw me, his face broke into a grin, his teeth gleaming white amidst a wiry tangle of beard.

"Jared, my man!" He waved me over with his serving spoon. "Grab a plate and join us for a bite."

I eyed the eggs, clumps of congealed yolk floating in a watery soup. "Truth to tell, I'm not all that hungry."

"Since when?" He guffawed, tugged off his apron, and came out from behind the serving table. "You look like you ran into the wrong end of a lawnmower."

"Got a job for you and some of your boys, if you're interested."

"Always interested." He waved at a grizzled man with a nearly empty plate and tossed the apron to him. "Here you go, Arnie. Make yourself useful."

I nodded to a familiar face across the room, a Vietnam vet with his dog at his feet. Then Billy and I walked out the back door into the courtyard, a twenty-foot cobbled square surrounded on three sides by gray brick walls. The fourth side was separated from a narrow alley by a wrought-iron fence with spikes at the top. Billy's clients had laid the cobblestones, built the slatted benches lining the walls, dug the tiny pond with the Japanese-style fountain, and planted a red twig dogwood on either side of each bench. The trees were bare this time of year, but the deep red branches gave a splash of brightness.

Billy dropped onto one of the benches, which creaked beneath his weight.

I stayed standing. "Got a lost girl," I said. "I can't hunt for her twenty-four seven, thought you and your guys might take up the slack." I gave him a description of Absinthe and a quick run-down on events to date.

When I finished, he leaned back and spread his arms out across the back of the bench. "You got any idea where this kid might be?"

"Not really. Might check out the Goth hangouts. There's a dance club on Second, used to be called the Underground. And a club off Elliston that caters to the vampire crowd. The Masquerade."

"I'll see what I can do."

"I appreciate it."

"Pleasure's all mine." He heaved himself to his feet. "You know, we got extra beds if you need to crash for a while."

"Thanks, but I better get home."

"At least let me send a cup of coffee with you. That way, when you fall asleep at the wheel and smash face-first into an eighteen-wheeler, no one can say it was my fault."

I gave him a weary grin. "Billy, my friend, you're all heart."

—⁓—

Maybe the coffee helped. I nodded off twice on the way home, came awake with a start, and jerked the pickup back into the center of the lane. When I got home, Jay was fixing breakfast and Elisha was curled up on the couch. I bent down and kissed her on the forehead.

Her eyes fluttered open, and she gave me a sleepy smile. "I was worried about you."

"Sorry."

She sat up, looked around blearily, and rubbed her eyes. "It's daylight already."

"Things got complicated."

"Is Absinthe all right?"

"I don't know. We haven't found her yet."

Jay popped his head in and gave me a relieved smile. I shot him a thumbs-up signal. He nodded and disappeared down the hall.

"Well." Elisha stood up, smoothing the front of her blouse. "Now that I know you're okay, I should probably get home."

"Be all right if you stayed," I told her. "There's plenty of room."

"Jared—"

"Don't worry. I'm too tired to do anything but sleep."

I didn't tell her about Dark Knight's death, or about the cartoon figurines or the comic book collection or how young he'd seemed. I didn't tell her that I should have been able to stop it. Something must have shown on my face though, because she put her arms around my waist and looked up at me. "All right. I'm still pretty wiped out myself."

I laid my palms against the sides of her face and stroked her cheeks with my thumbs.

Beautiful.

I closed my eyes and saw Absinthe's face. Lost and afraid. Running. Hiding. *They're here*, she'd said. But who were *they*? And what would happen if they found her first?

"Maybe I should—" I started.

"Sssh." Elisha placed two fingers over my lips. "Even Superman has to sleep sometime."

"I'm Batman," I said. "Randall is Superman."

"I always liked Batman best."

She hadn't brought a nightgown, so I gave her one of my flannel shirts. It came almost to her knees. I slept in a pair of gym shorts and a T-shirt with a picture of a rearing stallion on the front that Maria had given me.

I fell asleep quickly, but not deeply, drifting at the edge of consciousness with unsettling images scuttling through my dreams. When I finally awoke, Elisha's back was pressed against my stomach and I was holding onto her like a drowning man.

I lay there for a long while, not moving, afraid I'd wake her. Then she stirred, stretched, and rolled over to face me.

"Morning." She smiled.

"Morning."

"Or maybe I should say afternoon." She snuggled into the crook of my arm. "This is nice."

"Very nice."

She trundled off to take a shower while I went out to do the barn chores. As I passed Dylan's room, I heard him say, "You shouldn't be here. What if someone reports you?"

I peered inside and saw him sitting up in bed, eyes focused on the corner of the room opposite the Christmas tree. There was no one else in the room.

I stepped inside and leaned against the doorframe. "Who are you talking to?"

He looked up. Saw me. "Just that damn Marine. He comes here all the time."

"Really."

"Today, he's supposed to have inspection and then a five-mile run. But he came here instead."

"He say why?"

Dylan laughed. "He's hot for me is the real reason. But he says he's here to help me on my way. Earlier this morning, he even brought a friend. A lot more solid than most of my hallucinations."

The hairs on my arms stood up. "What did he look like? This friend?"

"Big. A little scary. He had a scar." He traced a line from the corner of his mouth to his jawline.

"Did he say anything?"

"No, he waited over by the barn." Dylan's bony fingers plucked at the blanket. "I like it better when the children come. I like to see them play."

I kept my voice neutral. "They come here a lot?"

"Not so often." He chuckled. "It's all right, Straight. I know they're not real. It's just that I can *see* them. I'd heard about the hallucinations, but no one ever told me what a hoot they can be."

My mouth felt dry. "It's good you can appreciate them."

He picked at a scab on his ear. "You're stuck with them either way, right? Might as well enjoy them."

"Good point."

"I didn't used to be so philosophical, but what the hell, right? Dying kinda puts things in perspective." His gaze drifted to the beta. "I named him Straight. After you."

"I'm honored."

He smiled. "Before you go, would you tell that Marine to get on home? I don't have time to fool with him."

"I'll tell him."

"Good." He lay back and closed his eyes. "He's not bad looking. But he's really not my type."

CHAPTER FORTY-ONE

From Dylan's window, it was easy to see where the hallucination must have stood. I crunched my way across the frozen grass to a small depression near the corner of the barn. A few shreds of tobacco and a smattering of ash had been ground into a partial heel print. Someone, probably Elgin, had field stripped a cigarette here.

Dylan's Marine might be a hallucination, but his guest this morning had been all too real.

A slow burn started low in my stomach. The son of a bitch had been in my yard. He'd seen Elisha's car and probably taken note of her license plate. Then he'd skulked away like the ghost he claimed to be. But he'd left a trace of himself behind. The carelessness was uncharacteristic, and I wondered if he'd left the tobacco and ash on purpose as a message or a warning. *I can get to you at any time.*

I sent Elisha home and made Jay practice with the Glock again. Then I called to update Frank and Harry. Frank was heading up the surveillance on Barnabus's place and seemed almost chipper.

"We've got uniforms outside," Frank said. "No sign of the girl-friend, and Collins looks scared."

"Malone brought you in on this?" I said.

He chuckled. "Harry brought me in. Malone's pretending not to know."

It was a start.

Billy's search for Absinthe had been fruitless. "We looked everywhere you said, man," he told me when I picked him up. He sounded as bummed as I felt. "No luck. 'Course, it's a big city."

I nodded. "Too big, sometimes."

It was probably overkill, but Billy and I started over, from Dark Knight's duplex to Barnabus's house, to Absinthe's. At sunset, we tried the Underground and the Masquerade, then prowled downtown until our eyes were red with cold and our fingers and toes were numb.

No luck.

A little before midnight, I turned to him and said, "I have an idea."

"Good. If it doesn't work, can we go home and get some sleep?"

"I have to make a phone call."

I punched in a number, woke Heath Parker out of a sound sleep, and told him I needed the key to his brother's apartment and why I needed it.

"Sure, man," he said, proving that blood is not destiny. Billy and I made a detour to Heath's apartment to pick up the key, and thirty minutes later, we pulled Billy's van, the one with the painting of Van Gogh's "Starry Night" on the sides, into Razor's driveway.

"You want to go around back?" I asked Billy. "I'll take the front."

He nodded and ambled around the corner of the house. He was a big man, fifty extra pounds of weight around the middle, but you could still see the Special Forces in him when he moved.

I opened the front door and stepped into Razor's living room.

It was much as I remembered it, decorated in late *Dark Shadows*, early *Addams Family*. It had a certain morbid elegance, from the deep purple velvet draperies to the red satin throw pillows on the black velour sofa. In front of the sofa was a smoked glass coffee table with a crack in it, and to the right of that was a black acrylic curio cabinet, shelves full of occult knick-knacks. Tarot cards, a crystal ball, a gold goblet shaped like a dragon's claw, a jar full of colored crystals, a shrunken head.

On the mantel, two gold candelabras flanked a leering human skull. It looked real, but a tap with a fingernail said it was fiberglass.

Since I'd been there last, he'd added a print of a crucified Jesus and attached a Groucho Marx nose and mustache to the face.

I was no saint, but it pissed me off anyway.

The room had been awash in blood. The stains were still visible, Rorschach blossoms on the pale carpet. Across the walls, dark, angry splashes bled long vertical drip marks. In front of the stairs, the bloody imprint of Razor's body lay across a pentagram the color of rust.

The Parkers hadn't hired a cleaning crew yet. I wondered why. Apathetic brother, mom in denial?

I closed the door behind me and stepped in, careful to avoid the dried pools of blood. "Absinthe? It's Jared McKean."

No answer.

I made my way through the house, turning on lights as I went and turning them off as I finished with each room. In the kitchen sink, someone had left a spoon and a cereal bowl with a trace of milk still in the bottom. The milk was still fresh.

In the upstairs bathroom, a 2X Guns N' Roses T-shirt hung over the curtain rod. It was damp.

The bedroom window was open. I leaned out and called again.

No answer. I combed the house again, just to be sure she wasn't hiding in a closet or under a bed. Then I went around to the back and called again. "Billy? Where the hell are you?"

Finally, Billy trotted out of the shadows in the backyard, breathing hard. "Lost her," he said. "She dropped out of that tree there beside the house and took off like a scared rabbit. Fast little sucker, ain't she? For a fat kid."

"Probably went out the bedroom window as soon as she saw the van."

"Least we know she's close."

I nodded. "Tell you what. You take the van and see if you can spot her on the street. I'll cut through the yards and try to catch her on foot."

We spent the next four hours searching Razor's neighborhood, but there was no sign of the missing girl.

Like Elgin Mayers, she was a ghost.

Finally, Billy drove me back to the shelter to pick up my truck, and I promptly drove it back to Razor's.

I mean, why waste a perfectly good key?

This time, I took my time.

The footprints Frank had described were between the curio cabinet and the glass-topped coffee table. They had been smeared beyond recognition and more blood splashed over them. A crescent-shaped stain indicated where the killer had dropped the knife.

Razor had probably been killed here. The rest of the scene—pentagram, blood splashes, charred heart—were all designed to obscure that fact. But between the crime scene photos and the pattern of stains, a decent investigator could pretty much read the story of Razor's death.

His killer had been standing beside the curio. The first slash, the one to the throat, had caught Razor by surprise. He'd jerked away from his attacker, widening the gash, and thrown up his hands to protect himself. Arterial blood spurted from his neck, drenching himself and his attacker. Spraying the white carpet with red.

The knife wrenched free, sliced through the webbing between his ring and middle fingers, cut downward across the palm, and bounced across the forearm, leaving the defensive cuts we'd seen in the photos.

Razor stumbled backward and tripped over the coffee table. He'd fallen into it, leaving a hairline crack in the glass.

He would have died quickly after that.

I stepped over the pentagram and went upstairs to the bathroom. Byron's chin-up bar, where Razor had been hung to bleed out, stretched across the door. It would have taken a long time, during which the killer had probably gone back downstairs to smear the footprints and use the vacuum.

The anxiety must have been unbearable.

What if a neighbor had wanted to borrow a cup of sugar? What if someone had come by selling Girl Scout cookies or collecting for UNICEF?

The bathtub looked pristine, but I knew that under the right light, I would see traces of glowing violet.

I went back downstairs to look at the pentagram.

It had been drawn inside a six-foot diameter circle. The edges were straight and the angles symmetrical. Either a measuring device had been used or someone had a good eye for geometry. Like draining the body, this had taken some time.

The killer, or killers, must have spent hours in the house after Razor's death.

The body had been placed on the pentagram and eviscerated, the heart burned, and the blood splashed around the room.

Why?

If they'd left the scene the way it was, there was a good chance it would have gone down as a drug-related crime or a burglary gone bad. That told me that the killers had left clues—or thought they had.

I was still thinking of two separate killers. Killer One, who had initiated the spontaneous and clearly disorganized attack, and Killer Two, who had painstakingly analyzed and staged the scene.

Had Killer One acted on his own impulse, snatching up the athame as a weapon of opportunity? Or had Killer Two somehow choreographed it?

Too many questions. Not enough answers. I pushed Razor's murder to the back of my mind and called Absinthe's name again.

Why had she come here? Because it was empty and familiar? How had she felt, passing the pentagram every time she crossed the living room? And who had frightened her away from home?

They're here, she'd said. But who were "they"? Elgin and Hewitt? Byron and Keating?

Barnabus and Medea?

I'd beaten the police to Barnabus, and yet he'd shown no surprise that Dark Knight was dead.

Because he'd already known? Followed Absinthe to the Knights' and seen the bodies then?

But why go after Absinthe in the first place?

I shook my head. I had nothing but conjecture, and it was getting me nowhere.

I started in the kitchen and went through the house, searching it much as I'd searched Absinthe's room. The police had already covered this ground. The drugs had been confiscated, and the black residue of fingerprint powder clung to shelves and countertops and lingered in the crevices around the doorknobs.

In Razor's walk-in closet, I rifled through rows of leather pants studded with silver, long silk shirts with puffy sleeves, vests and evening jackets made of velvet and velour. There were condoms in some of the pockets, and I didn't like thinking about who he'd planned to be with when he used them.

The floor was lined with polished boots, mostly calf-length, some with buckles or chains. On the top shelf was a row of books. *The Prince* by Machiavelli, a collection of works by the Marquis de Sade, several treatises on psychology and the workings of the human mind.

I reached up and pushed on the ceiling panel with my fingertips. It tilted under the pressure, and I extracted it easily. Behind the false ceiling was another shelf that ran the length of the closet. I ran my fingers around the edge and into the corners, but there was nothing there.

Probably where he'd stashed his dope. By now, the police would have impounded it.

I put everything back the way I'd found it and left the house, locking the door behind me.

CHAPTER FORTY-TWO

I was sure Frank already knew about Razor's secret hiding place, but I called him in the morning anyway.

"You searched the house," he said. Disapproving.

"Brother Heath gave me a key."

"Right." I heard him shift the phone to the other ear. "And he gave you permission to toss the place."

"He didn't tell me not to."

"Right," he said again. "You're gonna give me ulcers."

"So, what was in it?"

"What? The hidey hole?" He was quiet for a moment, as if trying to decide whether or not to tell me. Then he said, "Nothing. It was empty."

"The drugs?"

"Underwear drawer, coat pockets, bedside table. Pretty much everywhere *but* there."

"Any chance he didn't realize it was there?"

"I wouldn't think so. It seemed new, not like it came with the house."

So Razor had a secret compartment built into his closet and then forgot to stash anything in it.

Frank's gravelly baritone broke into my thoughts. "We found the girl."

"Absinthe?"

"The other one. The older one. Medina Neel."

I heard it in his voice. "Medea. Is she—"

"Single slash to the throat. Very clean." He wasn't referring to the scene. There would have been a lot of blood. "Found her car in one of those pay-by-the-day parking garages downtown. Security guard noticed a bad smell coming from the trunk. When he got close, he saw a blanket draped over the front seat, but there was blood on the floor and around the dashboard. Lotta blood. Looks like the killer was waiting in the backseat of her car. Killed her quick. Put her in the trunk. Covered the bloody seat with the blanket."

I shook my head. A quick glance in the back before she got in the car, and Medea might have survived. I thought about reaping and sowing, about the Rule of Three. "Witnesses?"

"None that we know of."

"Prints?"

"Wiped clean. No hair, no fibers. Guy's a fucking ghost."

"So he says."

Frank heaved a sigh. "We're sitting on Collins now. Piece of work, isn't he? Scared out of his wits and still talking trash. Says he can take care of himself, we're *cramping* his *style*."

"He gave me that same line," I said. "About being able to take care of himself."

"What can I say?" Frank said. "The world is full of stupid people."

—✺—

If Elgin Mayers was a ghost, Absinthe had become mist. Her teachers had no idea where she might have gone. Her classmates knew her only as an odd girl who claimed to be a witch. The Goth kids down on Elliston were no help: she was finding her path, she was following the great wheel, maybe she'd hitchhiked to California.

I left a trail of business cards around town, all bearing the same message: "Absinthe, call me, 24/7." By then I was just going through the motions. I only hoped that Elgin Mayers was having no better luck.

—✺—

On Thursday morning, while Jay finished the last of his Christmas shopping, I stayed with Dylan. He spent the morning dozing and conversing with his invisible Marine. The two of them seemed to have developed a companionable relationship, and I was glad of it.

For lunch, he managed to swallow a few mouthfuls of Campbell's cream of mushroom soup. Then he turned his head away from the spoon and waved it away with his hand. Two sips of water and he was done.

"You're good with kids, aren't you, Straight?" he asked. "I always wished I'd had some. Too selfish though, I guess."

"They're a big commitment," I said. "Nothing's quite the same after you have one, that's for sure."

He smiled and pointed toward the window. "I like that little blonde girl with the ponytail. I see her here a lot."

"Do you?" I glanced toward the window as if I might actually see her there.

"I think they like it here. Lots of light, and Jay's Christmas tree. Do you think that might be it?"

"Maybe they just came by to say hello."

"Maybe so." His smile was wistful. "I think they like me, Straight. I can't imagine why the hell they would. Maybe they just come to see this little guy." He scratched the pup's oversized ears. Then he murmured, "I keep forgetting they're not real."

I wasn't sure how to respond to that, so I tapped a few fish flakes into the fishbowl instead. The beta darted up to the surface after them.

"Straight?" Dylan said.

"Yeah?"

"I've got to take a piss."

I was rinsing out the urinal when Jay came in. His cheeks were flushed with cold, his arms full of department store bags. Rolls of metallic wrapping paper jutted out of one of them.

"How is he?" he asked.

"Seems okay."

He nodded toward the urinal. "Sorry you had to do that."

"Not a problem."

He held up the bags. "This should do it for me. What do you have planned for the rest of the day?"

"Thought I'd go sit around and watch Barnabus's place."

"Don't the police have that covered?"

"Beats asking the same two hundred people if they've heard anything from Absinthe."

He shook his head. Tsk-tsked. "I'll leave you some dinner in the fridge if you want it."

"Could be a long time. Maybe a couple of days."

"I'll take care of the horses while you're gone."

I thanked him and grabbed my jacket. "Call me if there's a problem. Anything."

As I started out the door, I heard Dylan call out, "Come on, children. It's time to go home."

CHAPTER FORTY-THREE

Movies notwithstanding, there's nothing fun about stakeouts. Muscles aching, bladder swollen. Nothing to read. Nothing to do. No heat or air conditioning, because sitting in a parked vehicle with the engine running draws the wrong kind of attention. In fact, sitting in a parked vehicle at all gets to look suspicious after a while, which is why tinted windows are a good thing.

Trying not to eat or drink, because intake leads to output. I had an empty plastic jug on hand for emergencies, but obviously that wouldn't cover all contingencies.

I drove by once, spotted the unmarked across from the house, two plainclothes cops slouched inside sipping coffee and looking bored. Two. So one could watch while the other took a piss.

Lucky bastards.

I sighed and parked a few blocks over. Circled wide through the neighbors' yards and came around the back. No cops here. It looked sloppy. Since Frank was anything but sloppy, it told me he'd put his men inside the house instead.

Even at this time of year, Barnabus's yard was an overgrown tangle that stretched back two hundred yards and ended at the edge of a wooded tract that probably belonged to someone else. I hunted around until I found a deadfall I could sit behind and still see the back of the house without being spotted. Then I hunkered down behind a rotting log, put my phone on vibrate, and burrowed into my parka.

It wasn't cold enough for frostbite, but it was cold enough to numb my fingers and toes. I spent a long, unfruitful night. Then in the morning, stiff and cranky, ears burning with cold, I went to a nearby Waffle House for a bite of breakfast and a real restroom. I called Jay at home, but got no answer. On the way back to Barnabus's, I picked up a few packs of peanut butter crackers and two bottles of water.

It was past time to give up. Frank had everything under control, and the smartest thing I could do would be to go home and take a long, hot shower. But I'd reached that stubborn stage, where, when nothing is working, you dig in your heels and hang on until something gives.

Someone had killed Tara and Dennis Knight. Slashed Medea's throat. With Absinthe in the wind and Josh under wraps, that same someone was coming after Barnabus. Maybe later, maybe sooner, maybe Mayers, maybe someone else, but he was coming. I intended to be there.

At suppertime, I broke out a pack of peanut butter crackers and took a few sips of water.

I waited. Took a leak. Checked my phone. No messages. Waited some more.

Night fell. The lights came on in Barnabus's windows, and I felt a surge of resentment that the master vampire was inside all warm and cozy, while I was skulking around in the woods pretending to be Supercop.

It got colder. I lowered myself to the ground, leaned my back against a tree trunk and shivered, tucking my hands under my arms.

I must have dozed off sometime after midnight, because suddenly my eyes snapped open and I came fully awake. A sharp cry came from inside the house, followed by the crack of a pistol. I scrambled to my feet and felt for the Glock. Moved in closer for a better look.

There was a flurry of movement behind the curtains. Then the back door burst open and a man plunged out into the darkness. He sprinted for the woods, arms and legs pumping. In the dark, I couldn't see his features.

I moved to intercept him, the Glock pointed at the center of his chest, and said, "I'd stop if I were you."

He skidded to a halt and cocked his head to one side. His gaze flicked left, then right, settled on my face. Up close, I recognized the pitted cheeks, the long scar, the heavy mustache. A Ruger double-action revolver dangled from one hand. I could see him thinking about it.

"Don't do it, Elgin," I said. "Bad idea."

He sank into a combat stance but didn't raise the gun. "I can take you," he said.

I held the Glock steady. "Could be."

"Pansy." He spat at my feet, but cast a glance over his shoulder, where two men carrying sidearms were scrambling out the door. In the illumination from the porch light, I recognized the one in front. Kurt something or other.

The man in back was limping, a bandana knotted around his thigh just above a dark wet stain.

Kurt said something into his radio and started in our direction.

"Why don't you put that popgun down?" Elgin said. "You and me see who's the better man, McKean. Mano a mano."

I laughed. "That only works in the movies, pal. I do something that stupid, I deserve to get my ass whipped."

He glanced behind him again. "Oh well. Worth a try."

He let the Ruger fall to his side.

Kurt paused at the edge of the woods and peered into the shadows. I had a better view of him than he did of me.

"Kurt?" I called. "It's Jared McKean. I've got your guy here."

"Zat so?" He advanced noisily, leading with his 9mm. "What're you doing here?"

"Same thing you are," I said.

"Dying," Elgin said, and snapped up the Ruger.

I dove to the side, firing two shots at his center of mass. His first bullet grazed my shoulder as I fell.

His second spatted into the ground beside my head.

My next shot caught him in the chest as Kurt emptied the 9mm into his left side.

The Ruger swung toward Kurt—my God, how could this guy not be dead?—and I fired again.

Elgin looked down at the crimson flowers spreading across the shoulder and sleeve of his jacket. The hand with the Ruger hung limply at his side. "Damn," he said. He sounded bewildered, like a child awakening in a strange place.

I pointed the Glock at the center of his forehead. His pale eyes were clear and cold. My finger twitched on the trigger. He'd murdered three people and shot a cop; one look at Kurt's face told me I could end it here and walk away clear. No chance Elgin would hire some shit-for-brains defense attorney and get off on some technicality, no chance he'd ever come for Josh.

Elgin's hand, the one with the Ruger, still dangled, useless. The viper defanged. Finished.

I slid my finger off the trigger.

Elgin smiled. "Took two of you," he said and sank to his knees.

CHAPTER FORTY-FOUR

The lights were on when I got home. From force of habit, I looked in on Dylan before I went upstairs. The hospital bed was gone, the medicines and Dylan's gifts piled into a box and pushed against the far wall.

Damn. Damn.

Damn.

I found Jay in his room, the plastic monster models he'd made when we were kids lined up on the desk in front of him like toy soldiers. Dylan's pup lay at Jay's feet. It stretched, yawned, and blinked up at me with sleepy eyes, tail thumping.

"Why didn't you call?" I asked.

Jay looked up, his face tear-streaked. "What could you have done?"

"Been here."

He gave me a sad smile and turned back to his desk. He ran a finger lightly across the Wolfman's face. "Did you catch the bad guys?"

"I think so. One of them, anyway."

"Good."

I sat down on his bed and looked around at the walls, which were covered with posters from his favorite old movies. *Casablanca. Creature from the Black Lagoon. Abbott and Costello Meet Frankenstein.* "When did it happen?"

"Yesterday. I started to call you, but then I thought, what the hell for, you know? You were doing something important."

"I would have come home," I said.

"I know," he said. "That's why I didn't call."

—◊◊—

With Elgin neutralized, Randall and his family finally came home. On the phone, I told them about Dylan.

"Give Jay our sympathies," Randall said. "And tell him y'all can come over to our place after the service."

The arrangements had been made months before. Dylan had chosen a sleek copper casket for himself, and the music was a non-traditional mix apparently designed to impart his final message to the world. At the first strains of "Don't Fear the Reaper," the mourners looked at one another and tried not to chuckle. At "Don't Pay the Ferryman," the minister began to look uncomfortable. But when Arlo Guthrie came across the speakers singing "Alice's Restaurant," it was all I could do to keep from breaking into a belly laugh.

I glanced over at Jay and saw that he was biting his cheek. "Dyl's last little joke," he whispered.

At the gravesite, I looked up and saw Eric standing in the back, looking like a little lost boy in his navy suit. When I met him, he'd been Eric the cad. Then he'd become Eric the *mensch*. Now it looked like he was Eric the cad again.

"Jay." I nudged him and nodded in Eric's direction.

"Oh, God," he said. "Why now?"

"You want me to get rid of him?"

"No. I'll do it." He looked at Eric, hurt and hunger in his eyes. "It's not that I don't want to see him. It's just . . ."

"I know."

"I can't deal with him right now."

"Tell him that."

He nodded and slipped out of his seat. Eric saw him coming and straightened his shoulders. Jay said something to him, and he looked away into the distance, nodded, gave a vague smile. Jay put a hand on Eric's shoulder. Eric pressed his palm to Jay's cheek, then turned and walked away.

After the funeral, we gathered at Randall's place, where Wendy had prepared a covered dish dinner. I could smell fried chicken halfway across the yard. Frank was waiting for us in the living room. After he'd paid his respects, he clapped me on the shoulder and steered me into Randall's study.

"Didn't expect you here," I said.

"Nah. Don't care much for funerals." He put his hands in his pockets and strolled around the room, running his finger over Randall's military history books, pausing to peruse the tactical maps that covered the walls.

Randall joined the Air Force at eighteen, planning to add his own medals to the ones Dad had brought home from Vietnam. Instead, our mother died of cancer, and Randall applied for a hardship discharge so he could come back home and finish raising me. He'd planned to re-enlist later, but an accident on a construction site left him with a bad back and a trick knee, and that was the end of Randall's dreams of military greatness.

"He ever play those war games?" asked Frank. "You know what I mean? With the little lead guys?"

"He used to, when we were kids. But you know Randall. If it isn't real, he's got no use for it." It was more complicated than that. Games were fine when he had a shot at the dream, but once the dream had ended, games were no substitute. But Frank hadn't called me in here to talk about Randall.

"What's going on?" I said.

"Your boy, Mayers. He's hanging in there. Got him under guard."

"Tough son of a bitch."

"In spades. But the vest he was wearing probably helped some too."

That explained a lot.

Frank picked up a paperweight, a gold doubloon in an acrylic pyramid, and turned it over in his hands. "You did okay out there."

"Your guys would have gotten him."

"Maybe. Maybe not. Malone is pissed about you being there. 'Free country,' I said." He studied the paperweight, set it back down where he'd gotten it. "They've closed the Parker case."

I nodded. I'd expected it. "Mayers?"

"Yeah. How you feel about that?"

I thought it over. "He could've done it. He had motive, the skill to dress out the body, the physical strength to arrange it. But . . ."

"But?"

"Maybe I've just gotten used to the idea of multiple killers."

"Could be. But you still said *but*."

"Okay ... all three died from slashed throats, right? Razor, Medea, and Dark Knight."

"Right."

"With Dennis Knight, the cuts were clean. No struggle. Lots of blood, but controlled. The killer probably didn't even get any on himself. And he didn't try to cover up what he'd done. Took pride in it, actually."

Frank nodded. "True."

"Same with Medea. But Razor's murder was different. It was messy. Then someone came along and tried to make it *look* controlled."

"That's what I'm thinking too," Frank said. "You should be a detective."

"I figure Elgin did Medea and the Knights, but somebody else did Razor. Then either they came to their senses and tried to muddy the waters, or there were two of them and the second guy staged the scene."

"You figure Mayers for the second guy?"

"Could be. But were the other two murders to draw attention away from Killer Number One or to take revenge on the coterie for Judith's rape?"

"Maybe both. If he survives, I'll ask him. You figure Hewitt for Razor's murder?"

"Maybe. Hewitt sounded genuine when he said Judith hadn't told him about the rape. But Elgin said I'd be ruining a good man if I kept on with the case. Could be he meant Hewitt."

"Be a kicker if it *wasn't* Hewitt, wouldn't it?" Frank mused. "Mayers does all this to protect him and it turns out he didn't do it."

"Somehow I doubt he'd appreciate the irony."

Frank's cell phone rang. He took it out of his pocket and listened for a moment. Then he turned to me and said, "That kid, Byron. He's in the hospital. Tried to off himself."

CHAPTER FORTY-FIVE

I debated whether or not to tell Josh, decided he might hear it from someone else and think I'd kept it from him.

I found him outside pushing Caitlin on the tire swing. She clung to the tire with mittened hands, lifted one in a welcoming wave when she saw me. She laughed, and her breath burst out in a cloud of steam. Rina waited her turn on the sidelines, clutching a ragged sock doll. I kissed the top of her white-blonde head and then turned to Josh, "Got a minute?"

He gave Caitlin a final push and followed me up to his room, where I filled him in. When I'd finished, he said, "I have to show you something."

He shoved aside a stack of pen-and-ink drawings on his desk and unearthed a leather-bound sketchbook. Flipped to the middle, where, tucked between the pages, was an ivory parchment envelope. Across the front in bold spiky letters were Josh's name and address. "Here," he said, handing it over. "Read this."

I lifted the flap and pulled out a sheet of heavy linen paper emblazoned with the same fierce handwriting.

Dear Joshua, it said.

I am sitting at my bedroom window, looking at the moon and wondering if it is the same moon you see.

I know you are disappointed and confused by all that has happened between us. I am disappointed as well. After all, don't you have plenty of which to be ashamed? You, better than anyone, know the pervasive power of secrets. In fact, your whole life is a secret, isn't it?

Your parents don't know who you are. If they did, do you think they would look on you with pride? Or would you see only disappointment in their eyes? Do you think they would forgive you? I know you, Josh. And I know that hidden darkness within you as well as, or better than, you know it yourself.

You and I are two of a kind. Kindred spirits, so to speak. The flesh dies, but the soul endures, loves forever, can be joined forever, and that is the only forgiveness there is. Free your soul from its prison of guilt and flesh and come home to me. Death lasts but a moment. Undeath, like love, is for eternity.

Anxiously Awaiting Your Return,

Razor

I looked up at Josh. "When did you get this?"

"A couple of months ago."

I took a chance. "After Judith Hewitt's rape." He made a strangled sound, and I said, as gently as I could, "What does he mean, you have plenty to be ashamed of?"

He looked away, eyes welling. "I should have stopped them."

Should have stopped them. Suddenly I could breathe again. "Tell me what happened."

He dug at the carpet with the toe of his shoe. "You remember how it was. I wasn't supposed to be seeing Razor, you know? Not without a chaperone. Dad and Mom fought about that, like, all the time. Dad didn't want me seeing him at all, but Mom thought I'd go behind their backs and hook up with him if they tried to cut things off completely. But whenever we'd get together—Razor and me—things felt really weird."

"Go figure."

"I know, I know." He looked miserable. "I thought it was because we were never alone. So I sneaked out a couple of times and hitched downtown to see him."

"Exactly what your folks were trying to avoid."

"I was an idiot."

"So the day of Judith's rape, you went downtown to see Razor."

"Right. Barnabus and Dark Knight and Medea were hanging around, and Razor looks out the window and sees Mrs. Hewitt run past in that little pink jogging suit. She did it every day, you know? And Razor says we should go out and talk to her. Let her know her husband's behavior is . . ." He wrinkled his nose and grimaced. "Not acceptable. Then he pulls a knife out of his pocket, and the three of them hustle her inside."

"The three of them."

"Razor, Barnabus, and Dark Knight. I know what you're thinking. Why didn't I do something?"

"You're wondering it yourself. Did you come up with an answer?"

"At first I thought he was just going to scare her. Then things got totally out of hand. Barnabus started saying things like, *let's show this bitch what a real man is* and *let's do this bitch*. It was like it was his idea, but I could tell it wasn't, that Razor was leading him into it. Why would he do that?"

"It was how he got his kicks."

"I told them to stop, and Razor—" Tears sprang to his eyes, and he wiped them away with the palms of his hands. "He laughed at me and said I should take a turn, that it would make my father proud if I did it with a woman."

He closed his eyes, reliving it, and I saw it through his eyes—Judith pale and shivering, trying to cover herself with her hands. Medea laughing. *Give it to her. Show her she can't mess with us!* Dark Knight sobbing as he took his turn, his pimpled face red and slick with snot and tears.

Josh opened his eyes and said, "I kept thinking, Uncle Jared would make them stop. My father would—" His voice broke. "A real man would do something. But it was like I was rooted to the ground."

"They had knives," I said without conviction. "They could have killed you."

He looked down at his lap and said, "I tell myself that. But so what? Even if it was true, it wouldn't have stopped you. It wouldn't have stopped Dad."

"Maybe. It's hard to say, until you're in that situation. But you didn't call the police afterward either."

"I know. I kept telling myself that if she came forward, I would too, that I'd back her up. But she never did. Too scared, I guess."

"Or too ashamed."

He nodded. Couldn't meet my eyes.

I thought of a dozen things to say, tried to decide which one would make things right. Knew none of them would. After an awkward silence, I said, "You didn't show the letter to anybody?"

"Like who? Dad? He wanted to kill Razor as it was." He shifted in his seat, averting his eyes. "I knew it was stupid, what Razor wanted me to do. But it made sense, too, in a way. So I kept the letter, so I could think about it for awhile."

A dull ache settled in the pit of my stomach. "And that's why you did what you did? Because of this letter?"

"Not at first. Because I got the letter, and then he hooked up with Byron and I thought, eternity hell, he couldn't even wait for me two months. But then he . . ."

"Then he died."

"And I felt like maybe it was because of what we did, and that would make it partly my fault. And I couldn't handle it, that I was part of that too, part of killing him, I mean. And now Byron's in the hospital, and maybe that's my fault too."

Because of what we did. It was a poor choice of words, that was all. He felt guilty, like he was part of it because he hadn't stepped up. He hadn't stopped them. That wasn't the same as helping them.

I put my hand on his shoulder and said, "None of that was your fault."

He reached for the letter. "If I'd shown you this earlier—"

"It wouldn't have made any difference. Razor's dead. I still wouldn't have thought Byron was in any danger."

"But—"

"You're showing me now," I said.

He looked at me with pleading eyes. "Are you going to tell Dad?"

"It isn't mine to tell," I said.

He gave me a grateful smile, and I forced myself to smile back. I knew what this knowledge would do to my brother. It would break his heart.

Josh said, "You think I should tell the police, don't you? About Mrs. Hewitt. What they did to her. But what good would it do? Razor and Dark Knight are dead."

"You have to decide that, son," I said. "But yeah, I think you should tell." I gave him a quick hug and stood up to leave.

He stopped me at the door. "Do you hate me, Uncle Jared?"

I thought back to a game we played when he was small. *I love you to England. I love you to France. I love you to the moon and back again.* "I love you to the stars and back again," I told him. "I could never hate you."

In the living room, I passed Frank. He perched on the edge of the leather sofa, a platter of potato salad and chicken wings teetering on his lap.

"Can you give Jay a ride home?" I asked him.

He looked up. "Going to the hospital?"

"Not just yet."

He frowned. "Do I want to know what you're up to?"

"No," I told him. "Definitely not."

CHAPTER FORTY-SIX

Breaking and Entering is a serious crime. I have a rule about committing serious crimes. It involves not committing them.

But Absinthe and Benjy were missing, Chase was dead, and Byron was in the hospital. Josh had almost been among them.

This was no time for protocol.

Josh had kept his letter for almost two months, weighing his options, trying to decide. Could Byron have done the same thing? Would Razor have sent a letter like that, with Byron still living with him?

Getting tired of Angel Face? Looking for someone younger and less jaded?

Had Chase Eddington received a letter? Or Benjy Savales?

If there was a letter, it was probably at Keating's. I thought about the Great Brain Fuck. Maybe Keating hadn't been as sorry as he claimed. Maybe he and Razor had never stopped playing their nasty little game.

I looped around to the north of town and the small Nashville suburb known as Madison. From there, I turned onto a two-lane highway that was once an old bison trail, past the Tennessee Christian Medical Center, and then onto the smaller road that led past the hospital and to the tree-lined suburban street where Alan Keating's gray brick house huddled against a backdrop of oak and evergreen. A fat, tinseled fir tree draped with multicolored lights peeked through a gap in the living room curtains.

No sign of his Skylark.

I climbed out of the truck and glanced around. The street was empty, the neighbors driven indoors by the cold. A wooden privacy fence surrounded the backyard. I got out and tried the gate. Locked.

I didn't peg Keating for an animal person. Both times I'd seen him, his suits had been spotless, not so much as a stray cat hair to tarnish his image. Still, I tapped on the gate and listened. No barking, yapping, or snarling, so after another quick glance around, I scaled the fence and dropped into the yard on the other side.

Even in the dead of winter, Keating's backyard was as kempt as the rest of him. The grass was brown but trimmed, and the flower-beds were covered. The back door was a heavy wooden one with three vertical squares of leaded glass. No sign of an alarm.

Flexing my fingers inside my gloves, I thought about the consequences of what I was about to do. Jail, maybe. The loss of my license. Then I thought of Byron lying in a hospital bed, of Keating's connection to Razor, the Great Brain Fuck, and the empty secret compartment in Razor's closet.

I took a deep breath and punched through the glass with my gloved fist. It was no harder than breaking a cinder block in half at the dojang. Inside, shards of glass tinkled to the floor.

Careful not to cut myself on the jagged edges, I reached through and unlocked the door. Keating would know he'd had a break-in. But I was willing to bet he wouldn't call the cops.

The house, like his yard and his office, was impeccable. Dark leather furniture, gleaming glass-topped coffee table, polished wood bookcase filled with leather-bound books, and beside it a wooden sculpture of what might have been an eagle. Lots of swooping curves, abstract paintings, and high-priced free-form sculptures.

The kitchen was open and airy, with walnut cabinets and an unopened bottle of Dom Pérignon on the counter.

The guest room bed was made but rumpled, as if someone had been lying on top of the covers. Byron's jacket hung over the bedpost, and a set of hand weights and an exercise band lay on the floor beside the bed. The room stank of bile, and a pool of vomit oozed into the carpet on the floor at the end of the bed. A few half-dissolved tablets were identifiable in the puddle. A few feet away was an envelope addressed to Byron and forwarded to Keating's house. I picked the envelope up by one corner and looked at the handwriting, the same sprawling script that had been on Josh's. There was no return address, and the postmark was dated less than a week ago.

A week ago, Razor was already dead.

There was no letter inside. Maybe Keating had taken it. I put the envelope back where I'd found it and moved on to Keating's study.

Bookshelves lined three of the walls. More psychology texts, philosophy, religion, sociology, anthropology, history. There were books by Steven Hawking and Khalil Gibran. Like my brother, Keating apparently had no use for fiction.

A teakwood desk held a PC and printer on one side and a stack of leather-bound notebooks on the other. I picked one up. It said, *The Parker Principle: An Experiment in Human Emotion.*

There were eleven volumes in which Razor had recorded his experiment. Compelled, perhaps, by the same pathological need to preserve or justify that had made the Nazis put their crimes in writing. Beginning with the exercises in manipulation and betrayal he and Keating had begun in college, Razor had filled three volumes with raw notes for his thesis, then carried his obsession off-campus and continued to dip out his cup full of midnight.

Five months after his expulsion, Razor began Volume IV of the Great Brain Fuck.

Today, I met a man who calls himself Barnabus, a narcissistic personality with a coffin in his bedroom and custom-made porcelain fangs. He is a living caricature, fascinated by Darkness and enthralled by my vampire persona. I'm not sure there are any limits to the things I can persuade him to do . . .

Between entries, he delved into the psychology of his "subjects" in language that slipped from overblown to conversational to psychobabble and back again. I skipped ahead.

I've assembled a small collection of misfits. Some are very young—pimple-faced Dark Knight and the porcine Absinthe—but that's for the best. Young minds are very pliable, and these have such fragile egos, I believe I could tell them anything, and they would believe it. As for Medea the psychotic and Barnabus the sociopath, I find them fascinating, all id and no superego to speak of. I know I'm not a vampire in the traditional sense, but if the essence of the vampire is his ability to peer into men's souls and bend them to his will, perhaps I am a vampire after all . . .

And later:

. . . I believe Absinthe would die for me if I asked her to. There is something precious and fragile in her devotion to me. I adore her for it, but I also can't help despising her weakness. She brought me a gift today, though she doesn't know it, a beautiful dark-haired boy named Benjy Savales.

I looked up from the book and took a deep breath. I'd promised Benjy's mother I would find out what had happened to him, but was it better to know, beyond all doubt, that there was no hope? If it were my son, would I prefer to tell myself he'd been taken by a kindly couple and was living a good life in a cozy home a couple hundred miles away?

Hell, no. I'd want to know.

I looked back at the book. Skipped ahead again until I found November third, the day Benjy Savales walked off the edge of the earth.

CHAPTER FORTY-SEVEN

The journal read:

Barnabus has grown into his fangs. I knew he would be the first, but it was Benjy's fault. His imbecile mother convinced him to end our relationship. I called and told him I had a few of his things and would like him to come and get them, intending to get him here and then persuade him to reconsider. But he was completely unreasonable and threatened to have me arrested if I ever came near him again.

Naturally, this was not acceptable.

Not acceptable. The same words he'd used just before persuading Barnabus and Dark Knight to rape Judith Hewitt.

We were all there: Barnabus, Absinthe, Dark Knight, Medea. When Benjy started for the door, I cried out, "Stop him!" Barnabus picked up the crystal ball and bashed Benjy in the back of the head with it. There was hardly any blood, but Benjy dropped like a sack of wet sand and didn't move.

He was still breathing, but at that point, it no longer mattered. Once Barnabus had hit him, we had to kill him. So I ordered Barnabus to cover Benjy's face with one of the sofa pillows. He held it there until Benjy was finally dead.

Absinthe began to blubber and pound Barnabus with her fat fists. Dark Knight and I had to hold her down with our hands over her mouth until the deed was done. For the next half hour, all she did was weep. I was terribly disappointed in her.

I thought of the marks on Absinthe's doorjamb. Too clumsy for Elgin. Razor and Dark Knight were dead. But Barnabus and Medea had reason to silence Absinthe. A broken Absinthe confessing to murder was no threat to them; an Absinthe free of the law and free of the coterie was another story. No wonder Barnabus hadn't been surprised by the news of Dark Knight's death. He'd seen the bodies when he followed Absinthe to the Knights' duplex.

I felt a stab of pride and pity for Absinthe. She'd tried to save Benjy, and that was something. But the feeling was tempered by the knowledge that she hadn't gone to the police. Or even extricated herself from Razor's murderous little group. No wonder she'd felt guilty enough to confess to Razor's murder.

The journal went on:

I have mixed feelings about all of this. Regret, because after all, I did care for Benjy, in my way. Chagrin at Barnabus because his actions put us all in danger and deprived me of the chance to win back Benjy's loyalty. And, of course, elation. Because, on my word alone, one human being has actually killed another. The Ultimate Expression of the Parker Principle. Only one thing dims my excitement: there was hardly any challenge to it at all. Like a scorpion that is bound to sting, Barnabus was destined to kill. It was only a question of who and when.

To make someone who is not a murderer at heart kill—now, that would be a wonder.

I sank down on the bed, the journal's leather cover clammy in my sweating hands. All the times Josh had crept out to see Razor. They might have killed him any time, just for the fun of it. I forced myself to read the rest.

I told the others we were all guilty of Benjy's death—that the police would never believe we had not all been a part of it. I told them this was a fortuitous accident, as I had recently learned a new ritual, one that would show their commitment to Darkness and Undeath, honor Benjy, and bind us all to one another.

We all sliced our palms and squeezed a small amount of blood into the dragon claw goblet. We added some of Benjy's blood to the mixture. Then I invented the Ritual of Transformation to the next level of Consciousness, what I called the Second Ring.

Absinthe balked until I reminded her that, in the eyes of the law, we were all culpable in Benjy's death and that if she ever spoke of this, we would all swear that it was she who had murdered Benjy. That shut her up. She drank from the communal cup, and the thing was done, though, of course, I could not allow her to be Transformed. Not after such treachery.

They'd wrapped the body in garbage bags and carried it out to Barnabus's hearse. Then, while Absinthe and Medea took Benjy's car to the Greyhound station, the men bought garden tools at Walmart and cruised the outskirts of the city, looking for the perfect place. It took them most of the night to find what they were looking for, an out-of-the-way cemetery with a freshly dug grave. They buried Benjy in the grave and replaced the sod so no one would notice. Razor thought it was a fine joke. He even wrote down the name on the tombstone.

I committed the name to memory, then found the rest of what I was looking for.

Last week, Chase's parents forced him to sever all ties with me. This was unacceptable, as, by controlling his life, they were trying to control mine as well. Chase is mine, now and forever, and I crafted a letter telling him so and inviting him to spend eternity with me. Yesterday, he opened up his veins, proof that my influence over him was stronger even than that most basic human instinct—survival. I didn't expect it to work. I just wanted to see what he would do. Maybe it's true what they say. We really do have the power to cloud men's minds.

Ten more pages. Twenty. When I got to the part where he talked about Josh, I had to steady the book against my stomach. I skimmed through Judith Hewitt's rape, pausing only long enough to verify with a sense of relief that Razor's version meshed with Josh's.

. . . I am disappointed in Joshua. I sent him The Letter over a month ago and he still fails to act on it. Maybe my success with Chase made me overconfident . . . Perhaps I should send another.

- 243 -

Blood hammered in my ears, and my chest felt tight.

We'd come so close to losing Josh.

Eyes burning, I flipped forward and looked at the date on the final entry, a rambling treatise about the beauty of death and the hypocrisy of love. It had been written the morning of Razor's murder.

So how had the notebooks ended up in Alan Keating's study?

CHAPTER FORTY-EIGHT

Tennessee Christian Medical Center was less than a mile from Keating's house, which had probably been a lucky thing for Byron.

I passed under an awning shaped like an artist's palette into a circular lobby with a round marble fountain in the middle. The receptionist's desk was off to one side, and behind the desk, a woman with a graying Prince Valiant haircut looked up and smiled. I asked for Byron's room number, and she tapped something into her computer and said, "He's still in Critical Care. I'm afraid only family is allowed in the room, but you're welcome to wait in the visitor's area."

I followed the signs until I found the Critical Care waiting room, a cramped 'L' with floral-patterned upholstered chairs along three walls and a soft drink machine hulked in one corner. Beside the drink machine, a television set mounted on wall brackets played a black-and-white western with the sound turned off.

Keating slumped in a green vinyl recliner that looked out of place among the florals. His tie was askew, his suit rumpled, as if he'd slept in it. It was the first time since I'd met him that he wasn't pressed and starched.

He looked up at me with tired eyes but didn't extend his hand. "Mr. McKean. Come to pay your respects?"

"How is he?"

"Stable. If he keeps improving, they'll move him to the psych ward later this afternoon." He rubbed his chin, where a sooty stubble had begun to sprout. "Guess he needs a real psychologist."

"I thought you were a real psychologist."

He looked down at his tie, tugged it straight. "So did I."

"How'd you get Child Services to let you have him, anyway?"

His lips quirked upward in a sardonic smile. "He's not a ward of the State. I contacted his mother and asked if he could stay with me. She was happy to be rid of him."

"Where is she now?"

"Who knows? She put in an appearance earlier. Now I imagine she's in some bar crying crocodile tears to some brawny bruiser who will buy her a beer and smack her around."

"Pretty harsh, coming from a shrink. Aren't you guys supposed to be all validating and nonjudgmental?"

"She's not a client. I don't have to validate her."

I sat down in the chair beside him. "Any idea what brought this on?"

He took in a long slow breath through his nose and blew it out his mouth. "He got a letter from Razor."

He'd dropped the 'Bastian.' Distancing himself?

He said, "His executor sent it. Had no idea what was in it, just had instructions to drop it in the mail a couple of weeks after Razor died." He gave a sharp, angry laugh. "One last little yank of the strings."

"Must have been a hell of a letter," I said. "Do you have it with you?"

After a moment, he reached inside his jacket and handed it over.

Dear Byron,

I am sitting at my bedroom window, looking at the moon and wondering if it is the same moon you see.

If you are reading this, I am dead—at least, by ordinary standards. I have tasted the darkness in your soul, and you have tasted mine. Tell me, my lovely young Adonis, was it sweet?

It was different from Josh's letter, tailored to Byron's personality and situation, but the message was the same. Live in shame and guilt, or die and live forever. With me.

An angry pulse throbbed in my temples.

Keating shifted in his seat and said, "He played on all Byron's worst fears. Being back on the streets. Being sodomized by one sick pervert after another. He had Byron so twisted up, talked like dying was just some kind of initiation."

"Doesn't sound all that convincing," I said.

"Not to you, of course not. You're not some messed up little street rat he's been working on for months."

"Byron said Razor never had sex with him. Said he was too beautiful to fuck. You believe that?"

He took the letter back, folded it neatly, and tucked it back inside his jacket. "It's not inconceivable. Razor liked a challenge, and Byron would have—and had—put out for anyone who offered him a Happy Meal and a sofa to crash on. My guess is that, for Razor, not having sex with Byron was the greater challenge. Besides, I think Razor had bigger plans for him."

"How so?"

"I think he meant for Byron to kill him."

Razor hadn't seemed like the suicidal type, or the type to deny himself something he wanted just because it was beautiful. But then, people were complicated. They had layers. I said, "Why would he want that?"

Keating laughed. "Bastian never felt a single noble impulse in his life that he didn't feel compelled to twist into something evil. He felt sorry for Byron—genuinely sorry—so of course, he had to turn it into something ugly."

"He wasn't saving Byron. He was saving him *for* something?"

"Exactly."

"That makes no sense."

"Nobody hates the world that much unless he hates himself even more. I think he planned for Byron to kill him, get the letter, and then kill himself. Go out in a blaze of glory, so to speak. The ultimate expression of the Parker Principle."

"That wasn't in his journals."

Keating looked more resigned than surprised. "I read between the lines," he said. "And you've been in my home."

I put my hands in my jacket pocket and looked at him for a while without saying anything.

His shoulders sagged and he sank back into the chair, fingering the edge of a blue silk tie stamped with gold koi fish. "You're like a damn snapping turtle. Tell me, what does it take to get you to let go?"

"You want to tell me what happened?"

"There's not that much to tell."

"Did you kill him? Or did Byron?"

He cast an angry look in my direction. "Leave Byron out of this. He was at the gym, like he said."

"So all those plans for Byron to commit a murder/suicide—"

"Something better came along."

"You were the big prize, weren't you?" I asked. "The one he needed to prove something about—or to. Did you kill him because you found out he was responsible for Chase Eddington's death? Or was it still that damn experiment? Were you still part of it?"

"Part of it?" he echoed. "I wouldn't be part of that—"

"But you were," I said. "Back in college. What happened? You found out he was still keeping records and were afraid he might use the diaries to ruin your career?"

"That was all taken care of by the university. I explained to you how it happened. It was a mistake, that was all. A stupid, horrible mistake."

"Costly mistake."

"No one was permanently injured," he said. Then his face crumpled and he rubbed at it with both hands. "Listen to me. Still justifying it after all this time. No, you're right. It was a costly mistake. But I would never have killed anybody over it."

"When did you realize Razor was still trying to prove the Parker Principle?"

"When—" He stopped himself. "First of all, it wasn't an experiment. It was a game. Scientifically, it was full of flaws. There were no controls. Everything was at his whim. He had no real interest in science. It was an ego trip. He did it because it was fun."

"And you knew about it when?"

"He was already dead by the time I found out," he said carefully.

"Why'd you take the books?"

He looked down at his lap, fiddled with his tie. "I didn't want the world to think he was a monster."

"He was a monster."

"People are more complex than that."

There was an awkward silence. Then I said, "He wrote in his journal the day he was killed. The police searched the house right after Byron found the body and the books weren't there then. So how'd you get them?"

He forced himself to meet my gaze. "They were hidden."

"Secret compartment behind a false ceiling in the closet, right?"

His breathing quickened, and I saw his gaze flicker left, then right. Searching for a way out?

"Cops found that," I said. "The day he was killed. It was empty."

"You think Razor had just one hiding place?" he asked, but his voice was weak.

"Come on, Keating. You were in the house between the time Razor was murdered and the time the police searched the house. A decent prosecutor could make a good case that you killed him."

His knee began to jiggle. He noticed what he was doing and stopped. A line of perspiration formed on his upper lip and he licked it away. "I didn't kill him."

"Why did you cancel your appointments that afternoon?"

"I got a phone call from . . . someone in crisis. Not a client, exactly. I cleared my calendar so I could be available in case . . ." His voice trailed off.

"Meltdown."

"Not exactly clinical terminology, but accurate enough."

"This meltdown . . . It had something to do with Razor?"

"I don't think I should discuss it any further."

"Were you afraid this person would kill Razor?"

"That thought never occurred to me."

"But that's what happened, isn't it?"

He slumped further in his seat and pinched the bridge of his nose between his thumb and middle finger. "I loved Bastian," he said finally. "But he was . . . ill. Not evil, you understand. Ill."

"If you say so."

He glanced back toward Byron's room. "In a sense, Razor killed himself."

"Philosophically speaking," I said, "you may be right. But legally speaking, I'd say you're in deep shit."

CHAPTER FORTY-NINE

I might be a snapping turtle, but Keating was just as stubborn, in his own way. Since not even the threat of being charged with Razor's murder could pry further information from him, I left him in the waiting room and dialed Frank's mobile. It took him a while to answer, and when he did it sounded like he'd stuffed his mouth with cotton balls. Or maybe deviled eggs.

"Can you do me a favor?" I asked.

"Won't know 'til you ask."

"Phone records. Alan Keating's office."

"Why? What's going on?"

"I'll let you know when I'm sure. Can you do it?"

There was silence on the line. Then he said, "Might not get an answer 'til tomorrow. How far back you want to go?"

I gave him a date a week before Razor's death.

"You want to tell me where you've been and why you've suddenly got a hard-on for Keating?"

I hesitated. "You really want to know?"

Another pause. Then, "Tell me something I can live with."

"Let's say I went over to Keating's to ask him some questions about Razor. The gate to the backyard was ajar, and when I went back there, I noticed signs of forced entry."

"Let me guess." His voice was dry. "You were concerned for his safety, so you went inside to make sure he was okay."

"Matter of fact, I did. Nobody home, as it turns out, but there were some interesting items in the guest room and the study."

"Interesting items, huh?"

"Notebooks. An envelope addressed to Byron. It's from Razor, but it was sent weeks after he died."

"You're going to give me gray hair, you know that, McKean? I call in this story, are you going to stick with it?"

"I was thinking an anonymous tip."

"You going to make the call?"

"I wouldn't be a very good citizen if I didn't."

"Good. Then I don't want to know any more about it." He let out a guttural growl. "Damn it, Mac. Gotta go. Spilled my potato salad."

—⚉—

It was the middle of the next afternoon before he called. The temperature had plummeted, and the sky was heavy and gray. Occasionally, it spat out a mouthful of icy rain.

Jay and I were in the dining room wrapping presents for Paulie, and when the phone rang, I lunged across the table and snatched up the phone on the first ring. Jay made a face, and I tried to look apologetic.

"Got it," Frank said, without preamble. "You're off the payroll on this one, right?"

"Right. Why?"

"Your guy Mayers is a prosecutor's wet dream. Not only did he do the dirty deed, he admits to it. No question he did the Knights and Medea. And there are two cops who saw him try to take down Collins. But if there's someone else out there . . . You get what I'm saying?"

"Sure. If there's someone else out there, you want him."

"You like Keating for the Parker thing?"

"He was there. Whether he was there from the beginning or got called in afterward, I don't know. My guess is, he came in later."

"Yeah. But either way, we got another guy to catch. Anybody turns up on this list, you willing to wear a wire when you talk to them?"

"Damn straight."

"So why don't you come down here and take a look?"

—⚉—

The calls were listed in chronological order. Beside the numbers of the callers, Frank had listed names and addresses. On the day of Razor's murder, in addition to the outgoing calls he'd made to cancel his appointments, Keating had received a call at 8:16 A.M. from his tailor and one from his dry cleaner's at 10:35. At 11:03, just before the flurry of cancellations, he'd received another call.

The name leaped out at me.

Someone in crisis, Keating had said. *Not exactly a client.*

Beside the phone number on the printout, Frank had scribbled *Doug and Hannah Eddington.* There was another call at 1:15. This one came from a mobile phone assigned to Doug.

I'd've killed the bastard then, if I'd gotten my hands on him.

Keating had told me all I needed to know. I just hadn't recognized it.

Rage.

CHAPTER FIFTY

"Doug?" I said. "It's Jared. Jared McKean. Remember me?"

"Jared. Sure." Wary at first, then a forced friendliness. "What's on your mind?"

"Something's turned up in the Parker case. Would it be okay if I came by? Asked you and your wife a few more questions?"

Silence. Then, "It's really not a good time. So close to Christmas and all. It's been hard on Hannah."

"I understand. I won't take much of your time."

"Your visits upset her. I know you don't mean to. But dredging it all up—"

"This is the last time," I said. "It's important."

"This will get you out of our hair for good and all?"

"Word of honor. This is the last time you'll hear from me."

"Oh, hell. Let's just get this over with."

I'd spent three years in Vice before joining the Murder Squad. Wearing a wire, I'd always felt an adrenaline rush, a tremor of excitement like a bloodhound catching scent, laced with an edgy understanding that today might be my day to die.

This time, I just felt bad.

The center of my chest itched where they'd attached the wire.

I climbed out of the surveillance van and into the Silverado. The surveillance team slammed the door I'd just come out of and revved the engine. Frank gave them a wave and followed me to my truck.

"Be careful," he said. "I don't want to have to explain to my boss how I let you get yourself chopped up into little pieces."

"I'm touched by your concern."

He chuckled and headed for the Crown Vic. He and the surveillance team would park a short distance away so the Eddingtons wouldn't see them and get spooked. I pulled the Silverado all the way up into the Eddingtons' driveway.

Doug Eddington met me at the door. "Hannah's lying down," he said. "I didn't see any need to wake her."

He didn't offer me a drink this time. We went into the living room and sat across from each other in soft, salmon-colored chairs.

"So," he said. "You had some questions."

It wasn't a real undercover operation. Eddington knew exactly who I was and what I was there for. If I wanted the truth from him, I'd have to get him rattled, make him think I had a royal flush instead of just a lousy pair of twos. I didn't think he'd rattle easy.

"Last time we talked, you told me your only contact with Keating was when he was treating your son."

"If you want to call it treatment."

"But actually, you called him twice the day Razor died. Once in the morning and once in the afternoon."

His gaze met mine. Unwavering. Sizing up the enemy? Stalling for time? "You want to know why I called him?"

"The question occurred to me."

He shifted his weight and plopped one ankle onto the opposite knee. Cleared his throat. "Actually . . . The first call was from Hannah. It's a rough time for her, coming up on the holidays. She was clearing out Chase's room and it got to be more than she could handle."

"Why call Keating? Wouldn't he be the last guy she'd want to talk to?"

With one finger, he traced the pattern on the crocheted doily on the arm of his chair. "I guess she wanted to talk to someone who'd known Chase. Then she called me at work and I came straight home. Got her calmed down. I called Keating that afternoon to let him know she was all right and wouldn't be needing him anymore."

It was a good story. I wondered if he'd practiced it.

I wondered if it might be true.

"She found the letter, didn't she?" I asked. "That's what upset her."

Silence. He blinked once, very slowly. Then he said, "What letter would that be?"

"The one Razor sent to your son. The one that told him if he'd take his own life, he'd be one with Razor forever."

A muscle in his jaw twitched, and for a moment his eyes filled with a terrible sadness. Then it was gone. "You think my son killed himself over a letter?"

"I think he was confused. I think Razor had been working on him a long time, got him all tangled up inside. The letter just pushed him over the edge."

"Pretty farfetched theory."

"My nephew got a letter just like it."

He gave me a long, flat look. "Is your nephew dead, Jared?"

"No, but—"

"Well, then."

"It was a near thing."

His fingers drummed on the arms of his chair. "You want me to say Chase got a letter like that and that's what drove him to kill himself? I guess it's possible."

"But you never saw the letter."

"I couldn't say there was one, no."

I couldn't say. Careful words. A careful man. Not a lie, exactly, but not entirely the truth.

"Razor kept a journal. He mentioned sending the letter."

"I see. And you're certain it arrived?"

"Razor seemed to be."

He uncrossed his legs and put his hands on his knees. "You think I had something to do with that man's murder?"

Still couldn't bring himself to say the name. "Didn't it occur to you that one or more of Razor's neighbors might have seen you and Keating at his house that afternoon?"

His smile was forced, but his gaze never wavered. "Eyewitness accounts are notoriously unreliable. Or so I've heard. Besides, they couldn't have seen what wasn't there."

"I know you were careful. But it was the middle of the day on a Friday. How could someone *not* have seen?"

He looked down at his hands. Then he said, "You're bluffing. If I'd been identified by neighbors, I'd be talking to the police, not you."

"Smart man," I said. "I'm impressed. But I think you're going at this the wrong way."

"How do you mean?"

I walked over to the end table and picked up a picture of Doug and Hannah with their son. "It could be argued that Razor was responsible for Chase's death."

He gave a bitter laugh. "It could be argued, yes."

"Wife calls you, tells you about this letter she found that almost certainly contributed to your son's suicide. You go over to confront Razor. Things get out of hand. There's no doubt in anybody's mind that Razor was scum. Any defense attorney with half a brain could convince a jury you were out of your mind with grief when you killed him. Panicked. Called Keating to help you clean things up. That's how I'd go about it."

"Why do you assume I did it?"

I held up the photograph. "You had the best motive."

He plucked again at the frayed patch. "I bet you can't count on both hands the people who wanted him dead. Besides, I heard on the news they got the guy who did it."

"Elgin Mayers. He did some bad things, but he didn't kill Razor. Besides, we know Keating was there that afternoon."

"Then why aren't you talking to him?"

"We did. And we know there are calls from your phone to Keating's shortly before and shortly after Razor died."

"Circumstantial evidence."

"Sometimes that's the best kind. But I agree. You might get away with it, since it'll be easier for a prosecutor to pin it all on Keating. It was an ugly murder. They may even go for the death penalty."

A strangled cry came from the doorway, and I turned to see who had made it. Hannah Eddington stood just inside the room, one hand pressed to her lips, the other gripping the doorframe so hard her knuckles turned white.

"Honey . . ." Doug got to his feet, pushed past me to get to his wife. "You should be upstairs. Resting."

"Is it true?" she asked me. Her knees buckled, and she steadied herself against the door. "Alan is in trouble?"

Alan. Not Mr. Keating.

"He's in trouble," I said.

She started to speak, but Doug put an arm around her shoulders and pulled her in close. His eyes were wild. "Hannah. Don't."

"We have to," she said. "We have to. We can't just let him—"

"Hush," he said. "This guy's grasping at straws."

I took a step toward them. "You remember what you said earlier, Doug? About how if the neighbors had ID'd you, you'd be talking to the police right now instead of me?"

"So?" The affable demeanor was gone and there was nothing in his face now but a smoldering hostility.

I unbuttoned my shirt and showed him the wire. "You are talking to the police."

"Oh, God," Hannah said.

Doug looked at the wire and then back at his wife. All the air seemed to leak out of him, and he suddenly looked smaller.

"All right," he said. "All right. You've worked it all out. I killed him. I thought I'd covered everything, but I guess I was wrong." His hand gripped Hannah's shoulder so hard it must have hurt.

She put her arms around his waist and buried her face in his shirt. Took a deep breath, as if somehow she could draw his strength in through her lungs.

"Sssh," he said, stroking her hair. "It's all right, honey. It will be all right." Then Hannah lifted her face to look at me, and Doug said, "Honey, no, don't."

"It's the right thing," Hannah said. "We should have done it a long time ago."

"No," Doug said, and looked at me. "Turn that thing off, and I'll tell you everything."

CHAPTER FIFTY-ONE

Imagine a Saturday in late November. The air is brisk and crisp. It smells of juniper and burning leaves. Hannah Eddington goes into her dead son's room. Smells the stuffy air and wonders if there still might be some trace of him that she can savor, a breath of aftershave perhaps. Or even a sweaty gym sock. Thanksgiving has passed, one empty holiday over, hundreds left to sleepwalk through. All the Christmases, the Easters, the St. Patrick's Days, all the July Fourth fireworks, all the Mother's Days. Can she be a mother without a child? And if not, what does that make her?

This day is just one more day to get through. Time to let go of the past.

She begins by sorting through his clothes. Throw this away or give it to charity? Ah, this one has a hole in the knee, out it goes. His favorite shirt. Perhaps she'll keep that just a little longer.

Then on to his other possessions. Most of it she gently packs into a box. She'll have Doug take it to the Goodwill in the morning. But some things are too precious to give up. The pennant he won playing Little League. His drama award. A sketchbook full of comic book-style drawings and classical nudes of well-muscled young men.

Her husband can't admit their son was gay, but Hannah knows better. She knew even before what she thinks of as The Terrible Thing. It doesn't matter. He could be gay or straight or bi or non. All she wants is for him to be back.

In the back of his closet, she finds his high school yearbook. Picks it up. Strokes it lightly with her fingers. No way will she give this up. Who except herself would want it anyway? She opens it up, wanting to read the cryptic, silly messages his friends have scrawled inside.

Something flutters out from between the pages. A piece of unlined paper. She picks it up and reads it.

Dear Chase, it begins, *I am sitting at my bedroom window, looking at the moon and wondering if it is the same moon you see . . .*

As she reads, the blood roars in her ears. Her heart races. She can hardly breathe. This letter . . . She is holding her son's death in her hands.

She looks again at the signature. The man is a monster. How could he have done such a thing? Was it a joke, perhaps? She could understand that, a joke gone horribly wrong. She picks up the phone, dials the first three digits of her husband's work number.

Puts the receiver back in its cradle.

No. Doug will kill the man.

Instead, she calls her son's therapist. A nice enough man, she's always thought, though Doug has never trusted him. Now the questions simmer in her mind. *Did Alan know? Could he have stopped it from happening?*

Her conversation with Keating is unsatisfying. He seems horrified at what she has learned. But she still has to know what would drive someone to write such horrid things to her son. She needs to believe it was an accident. At least, that's what she tells herself.

An open wound, she drives to Razor's house and rings the bell. He answers in a black silk robe tied at the waist. As if from far away, she hears herself speak. "I'm Hannah Eddington. Chase's mother."

The weather is brisk, and she has pulled on driving gloves and a light jacket. He doesn't offer to take her coat.

She holds the letter out for him to see. "Why?"

"Oh, that." He laughs. "I just wanted to see if he would do it."

Her face feels warm. Her throat is too tight. It hurts even to breathe.

"Let me get you a glass of water," he says, but his voice is mocking.

She turns away to hide her face. Not a joke, then. Not an accident. In front of her is a shiny black curio, and on it she sees only one thing. A small curved dagger with a black handle. The edge looks very sharp.

She doesn't plan to kill him, even then. It's just a thought, dancing at the edge of her mind. Somehow, the dagger finds its way into her hand. It feels nice there. Safe. With it, she could . . .

No.

She feels his warmth behind her. He seems to radiate a kind of heat. Perhaps that was what first attracted Chase to him. That raw, primal heat. She has to get away from him before she is consumed by rage. Get away. Run away. Put down the knife and tell him she has things to do.

Then he says, "You know what I loved most about your son? He had such a nice tight little ass."

She turns to face him and the knife comes up.

Then there is only blood.

CHAPTER FIFTY-TWO

My cell phone, on vibrate, buzzed against my hip. I closed my hand over it to further mute the faint sound and tugged aside the curtain to wave at the police van down the block.

"He was a monster," Doug said. "Hannah did the world a favor."

"Maybe."

"And if you repeat any of this, we'll both deny it."

"It doesn't matter what you deny," I said. "We have Keating. You think he'll go to prison for you?"

"A good lawyer—" he started, and Hannah laid a hand on his forearm.

"I killed a man," she said. "And it was wrong. We can't let Alan take the blame."

Doug gave his head a heavy shake. Directed his next words to me. "I won't let her go to prison, McKean. You know what it will do to her."

The phone buzzed again, and I tugged it off my belt and flipped it open to see the caller ID. No surprises there. It was Frank.

"I better take this," I said. "If I don't, he'll think I've been taken hostage and storm the battlements."

They nodded in unison, his arm around her shoulders, her hand clamped to his wrist.

I pressed the *talk* button and said, "McKean here."

Frank's dry rasp came across the handset. "Glad you're not dead yet. You got what we need?"

"Almost."

"Get it on tape, McKean. And get out here. Fast."

"What's happening, Frank?"

"Just do it," he said, and broke the connection.

I turned back to the Eddingtons and said, "It's time."

Doug's hand tightened on Hannah's shoulder. "You aren't listening. You charge her, and I'll twist up your case so bad the D.A. will wind up in a straitjacket. You know the evidence is iffy. No one will do a day of time if you charge her."

"A man was murdered. We can't just let that go."

"Turn on the recorder. I'll say I did it. I'll give a detailed confession. Case closed, everybody's happy."

I nodded toward his wife, who clung to his arm as if she might topple. The color had leeched from her face. "Hannah doesn't look that happy."

"Prison will kill her," he said. "I was a POW in 'Nam. I know how to do time. Let me do this, McKean."

"First tell me about Keating. How'd he get mixed up in this?"

"Hannah called me. I called him. It wasn't complicated."

"You hate Alan Keating."

He shrugged. "She'd already called him. I thought there was a better chance he'd keep it under his jacket if he had something to lose too. Besides, he owed us."

Keating must have thought so too.

"Tell me the rest," I said.

When the rage had spent itself, she was horrified by what she'd done and terrified of the consequences. And so she did what she had always done. She called the man who had always been there when she needed him.

Don't move, he said. I'll be right there.

He took the time to shop. A hunting knife, garbage bags, baby wipes, handheld vacuum cleaner, shower cap, rubber gloves. A pair of coveralls for Hannah and one for himself. He knew he was forgetting something, but he had no idea what. He was new to this business of murder.

Once he'd bundled Hannah into her new coveralls and sent her home to shower, he allowed himself to feel the panic. He had no idea where to start. The body, he supposed. And he had to do something about the footprints. And the blood. What else?

Alan Keating.

Doug wasn't a man who would casually ask for help, but the crime scene was beyond him. Keating was a smart guy. He'd know what to do. Besides, if Doug could get Keating involved, he could cover his bases and ensure that the psychologist wouldn't betray Hannah. He called Keating, and Keating, overwhelmed by guilt and by the knowledge of what his friend had done, agreed to help.

Between them, they staged the scene. Vacuumed the living room. Smeared Hannah's bloody footprints. While Doug carved his grief on Razor's body, Keating searched the house for copies of the letter, which would provide the police with a motive for Razor's death. Instead, he found the journals.

When they'd done all they could think of to do, Doug took the garbage bags with the vacuum cleaner bags, the cleaning rags, and the rest of the evidence and burned it to ash. What wouldn't burn, including the knife, went into a landfill.

The journals went home with Keating. A little piece of Razor's soul? A reminder of his fall from grace? Or maybe Keating really couldn't bear to see his friend exposed as a monster. Maybe, after all Razor's talk about the deceptive nature of love, Alan Keating had wanted to prove him wrong.

I wondered about Razor. The last few minutes of his life. When he'd seen Hannah holding the knife, had he decided to try one last experiment? See if he could turn an all-American soccer mom into a murderess? She was a better prize than Byron, who was, after all, slightly tarnished.

As the blood leaked out of him, did Razor actually think he'd won?

My cell phone buzzed again, and I said, "I gotta go. Let's get this over with." I turned the wire back on and said to Doug, "Tell me what you just said about Sebastian Parker's murder."

He leaned toward the wire beneath my shirt and said, "I did it. I killed him. I took that funky little knife off the shelf and almost sliced his fucking little head off."

The front door banged open, and Frank stomped in, trailed by a couple of detectives I recognized from the surveillance van.

"'Bout damn time," he said. He turned to Doug. "These fellas here are going to read you your rights. Then you and they are gonna take a little ride." To me, he said, "Elgin Mayers offed his guard and left the hospital in a stolen BMW. Belonged to some surgeon, I guess. No one noticed he was missing until the relief guard came on."

My entrails turned to water. "How long?"

"Too long," he said. "Come on. I'll drive, and you get Randall on the phone."

CHAPTER FIFTY-THREE

We left the Silverado in the driveway. Frank nosed the Vic onto the street while I tried Randall's cell. Voice mail. I punched in his home phone. Answering machine. Shit.

At Josh's school, a nasal voice on the answering machine said they were closed for the winter holidays.

Shit, shit, shit.

"No use worrying yet," Frank said. "He may not go for Josh at all. He wasn't part of Judith Hewitt's rape."

I could have told him about Josh then, but the words stuck in my throat. There was no way to make it sound good. *He was there, but he didn't hurt anybody.* It was right up there with, *I smoked pot, but I didn't inhale.* It may have been true, but it didn't change anything. The fact remained that Josh had watched a woman being terrorized and done nothing. Not then, and not later. I hated myself for being ashamed of that.

Frank said, "Mayers'll probably try for Barnabus first. Unfinished business, and all that."

I said, "I put four bullets in him. He's going to go for Josh."

"Two bullets," he said. "The vest stopped two."

My phone shrilled, Randall's ring. I snapped it open and said, "Where are you?"

"Why? What's wrong?"

"Are you in the house?"

"Jared—"

"Is anybody in the fucking house?"

"Wendy and the girls are Christmas shopping. I dropped Josh off at your place a couple hours ago."

I groaned. Elgin knew where I lived.

Alarm in his voice, Randall said, "He wanted to watch Christmas movies on the big screen. What's going on?"

Frank switched lanes so fast I had to grab the dashboard with one hand. "Listen," I said. "I need you to go get Wendy and the girls. Take them to a hotel. Someplace safe. Do it now. I'm going after Josh."

"You said you got the guy. So why are we running again?"

"We got him. And then he slipped his leash. Go find the girls. Don't let them go home. He won't go after them, but he won't blink if they get in his way." I hung up and said to Frank, "Josh is at my place."

Frank swung the Crown Vic onto Briley and merged into traffic.

"There's no reason for him to think Josh would be at your place," Frank said.

"He doesn't find Josh at home, where do you think he's gonna look?"

My palms drummed on the dashboard, a rhythmless machine-gun tattoo. Frank reached across with his free hand and blocked mine. "Stop," he said. "It will be all right."

A gap opened in the line of cars beside us. Frank punched the accelerator and wrenched the wheel. The Crown Vic hesitated, wheezed, and shot into the gap. A horn blared. Frank swore softly. A few icy droplets splatted onto the windshield. We swooped around the cloverleaf that looped onto I-40 East, merged onto the Interstate, and barreled—as much as the Crown Vic could barrel—toward the Mt. Juliet exit, where we fishtailed onto the ramp, skidded on a thin patch of ice, and shot past the Providence outdoor mall.

I unclamped my teeth and said, "Can't this thing go any faster?"

"Hold your potatoes," Frank said. "Let's get there in one piece."

As we rounded the last curve, the mailbox at the end of the driveway came into view. A patrol car from the Wilson County Sheriff's office squatted across the entrance, blue lights flashing. A uniformed officer leaned against the passenger door, talking into his radio.

"Tell me you called them," I said to Frank. "They're here because you called?"

Frank didn't answer. He didn't have to. His grim expression said everything.

I unstrapped my seat belt, opened the door while the car was still rolling. The officer pushed away from the patrol car and thrust out a hand to stop me. Frank, wrestling the Crown Vic into park, waved his badge out the window and said, "Let him through."

I darted around the patrol car, bulldozed through a stand of brittle thigh-high weeds, hit the gravel running, and sprinted toward the house. Frank puffed behind.

Through a gap in the trees, I caught a glimpse of flashing lights and ran harder. My boot came down in a water-filled rut crusted with ice, and some distant part of my mind registered the crack of the ice, the splash of freezing water, the sharp pain in my calf that was eclipsed by fear.

Jesus God Jesus God Jesus God.

The place was swarming. Two ambulances, a jumble of patrol cars, a couple of unmarked sedans. Uniforms everywhere. Too much activity. Too many people. *Too late.* I stumbled toward the house, lungs burning, a cold knot in my heart.

A man carrying a memo pad and wearing a Sheriff's Department uniform stepped into my path. *Blankenship,* said the nameplate. "You can't go in there, sir."

I couldn't breathe. Nodded toward the house. "In there. Are they . . .?"

"I'm sorry, sir. If you could just wait over there."

I pressed forward, but Frank dug his fingers into my shoulder. "Hold your potatoes, Cowboy," he said again.

The front door smacked open and a knot of paramedics eased a stretcher through. The wheels left a smeared trail of blood across the porch slats. The paramedics were covered with it. My stomach clenched, and I started forward again, straining against the hands that were suddenly barring my way.

Too many people. I couldn't see the patient's face. But so much blood. An IV bag swayed, and someone grabbed it before it fell.

Snatches of doc-talk cut through the buzz outside. "Stat . . . BP . . .
pressure falling . . . shock . . ."

A second stretcher followed the first, pushed by a pair of EMTs
in blood-splashed uniforms. My stomach sank at their lack of
urgency even before I saw the crisp white sheet draped over the
body. Red stains were beginning to seep through.

A sound tore from my throat, and all the fight drained out of
me. The hands fell away, all but one. Frank's hand, heavy on my
shoulder.

Too late. Too late for one of them.

I couldn't bring myself to ask which one. Knew which I would
choose and felt a wave of guilt and shame, because to hope for one
was to betray the other.

There were noises around me—shouting voices, running footsteps, the metallic bang of ambulance doors, the scream of a siren.
They all seemed very far away.

"Sir, you can't go in there," Blankenship said again, but not to
me.

I shrugged off Frank's hand and willed my feet to move toward
the sheet-draped gurney. My boots were almost too heavy to lift.

One wheel of the stretcher caught on the porch step. As the
EMTs jostled it free, a bloodied hand slipped out from beneath the
sheet.

Around the thin wrist was a frayed gauze bandage.

Behind me, someone moaned. I turned around as my brother,
still breathless from the sprint up the long driveway, sank to his
knees.

"My son," he said, voice breaking. "My son."

CHAPTER FIFTY-FOUR

Sometimes, in His infinite cruelty, God allows us to believe we can protect the things we love. I held my brother as grief shuddered through him and knew that was a lie.

We can protect nothing.

The EMTs were kind. Tried to keep Randall from the broken boy that had been Josh, and when that didn't work, held him at arm's length while they rolled back the sheet. Preserving evidence. Not that there would be any.

Josh's eyes were closed. More likely, someone had closed them. His skin looked almost translucent in the dimming light. There was a smear of blood on his chin, and I wanted to wipe it away. It made him seem even younger than he was.

Randall made a keening sound, stretched out a hand to touch Josh's cheek.

"I'm sorry, sir," one of the EMTs said, easing Randall away from the body. With clinical efficiency, the second pulled the sheet back up and laid it over Josh's face. "I'm very sorry."

I knew they'd taken hundreds of gurneys from hundreds of houses, that to them there was nothing special about this day or this boy. All the same, they were gentle as they eased the stretcher across the graveled parking area and loaded it into the second ambulance. They didn't bother with the siren this time. There was no need.

Blankenship's voice cut through the fog in my brain. He was talking, not so much to fill us in as to bring us back. I knew, because I'd done the same thing often enough, when I was in his shoes. "The call came from a guy named Jay Renfield. Said there was a prowler, they were going upstairs, get his roommate's gun."

"My gun," I said, dully. Saw the speculation in his eyes. Didn't answer the unspoken question. None of his fucking business.

"There was a dog barking on the tape. Some little yappy thing."

"Only dog in the house is Luca," I said. It was just something to say, to keep from thinking about the things I didn't want to think about. "He doesn't bark."

He gave me a brief smile. "Tell it to the dispatcher. She could hardly hear Mr. Renfield for the yapping."

"That's how he knew to call," I said, putting it together. "Jay wouldn't have heard Elgin, but the dog tipped him off."

"Yeah, that's what he told the dispatcher. Then there was a crash and a couple of shots."

Randall looked up. "That's how it happened? He shot my boy?"

Blankenship looked like he wished he were somewhere else. "We don't think so, sir," he said. "We think the shots came from your son or Mr. Renfield. We think the suspect used a knife."

A small sound came from the back of Randall's throat. Then he said, "Was it quick? Did he—did my son suffer?"

"It was quick," Blankenship said. It was the right thing to say, but that didn't make it true. Josh had bled out, and that takes time. I hoped he'd gone into shock quickly. After that, he wouldn't have felt much. I wondered if he'd been afraid.

"There was a struggle," Blankenship said. "Then the cell phone signal got cut off."

I said, "Cut off how?"

"Phone got crushed. We figure one of them stepped on it, probably the suspect."

"Son of a bitch," Randall said. "Son of a fucking—" He stopped. "You'll catch him, right? You'll catch him?"

"We'll catch him," Blankenship said. A raindrop landed on his forehead, and he wiped it away with one hand. "We did a sweep of the area, and we've set up roadblocks on all the surrounding streets."

"Check the driveways and garages too," Frank said. "He's probably in a stolen BMW."

He ran down the case for Blankenship. I tried to focus. Couldn't. I looked toward the pasture, where the horses were milling anxiously in the corner of the field farthest from the barn. Dakota snorted and danced, swinging his head in a broad arc so that his good eye took in both the woods and the driveway. Crockett pawed at the ground. Tex flared his nostrils and tossed his head. He spooked at something and wheeled into Crockett's shoulder. All three of them shied in different directions, then trotted back into an uneasy cluster. Even from this distance, I could see the whites of their eyes.

Frank said to Blankenship, "You just about finished here?"

"Not for awhile. We're still processing the scene."

"You need these guys?"

"Not just now."

Frank turned to me. "Come on, Cowboy. I'll drive you and Randall to the hospital."

It was where I needed to be, but something was buzzing around in my head. I just needed time to think it out.

"You go ahead," I said. "I'll bring Jay's car."

He gave me a look.

I said, "Who knows when I'll get back home? I have some things to take care of here before I go."

Randall stared up at the glowering sky. "I have to tell Wendy. Dear God, how am I going to tell her?"

I opened my mouth to say I'd go with him. Glanced back out at the horses. Then at the barn, which stood, door ajar, at the opposite corner of the pasture. Clamped my teeth together while I thought it through.

The paddock gate was open. From there, the horses could walk right into their stalls. There was hay and water inside, and it was as far as they could get from the chaos in the driveway. It should have been the first place they headed when all hell broke loose.

So why were they gathered in the corner farthest from it?

In the pit of my stomach, something dark grew. But there was no time to think about it. My brother needed me. I tried to think of a good way to keep from asking and couldn't. "Do you want me to go with you?" I said.

Yes, his eyes said. *I don't want to do this alone.* Aloud, he said, "No. It's mine to do. And Wendy will——" His voice broke. "She'll . . . need some time."

"You go on then," I said. "I'll meet you at the hospital. Or at your place. Wherever you want."

"You won't be long?"

"I'll be right behind you."

Frank gave me a hard look. A calculator in his eyes. "What's going on, Cowboy?"

"I just need a minute here, Frank."

Again, the look. "Sure, buddy," he said at last. "You take what you need. Just don't be too long."

I glanced up sharply. Was that a dig? Didn't matter. I didn't need Frank to tell me that my brother needed me now. And I'd be there for him. Just as soon as I dealt with whatever—whoever—had spooked the horses away from the barn.

Randall gave a resigned shrug and said to Frank, "My car's at the end of the driveway. I'll meet you at the hospital."

"Sure you're okay to drive?" Frank said.

"I'll be okay," Randall said. "See you in a few."

When they had gone, I turned to Blankenship. "Any reason I can't go in the barn?"

He thought about it. "Barn's clear," he said. "Guess it would be okay."

"You're sure?" I asked. "That it's clear?"

"We know our jobs," he said, a little sharpness in his tone. "That was the first place we looked, after the house, and we were thorough."

"Don't guess I could go inside a minute?" I nodded toward the house.

"The house is off limits. If you need something—toothbrush, wallet, whatever—let me know and we'll see what we can do."

I thanked him and started toward the pasture, remembered to ask about the papillon pup, and was relieved when he said the little guy was safely stashed in the laundry room. It was a small consolation, considering all that had happened, but, given the circumstances, I'd take it.

The barn was empty, like he said. Nothing but the smells of earth, sweet hay, and horses. In here, the buzz of activity from outside was almost imperceptible. I stood there in the quiet, tears leaking from my eyes, and listened to my heartbeat. It sounded loud in my ears. Strange, that it could go on calmly pounding when my chest was about to crack.

I thought of Medea. Her curse. The Rule of Three.

Think of this when your world falls all to hell.

I didn't believe in curses. I believed in actions and consequences, but what difference did it make when the ends were the same?

I kicked aside a clod of dirt and let myself into Crockett's stall. Closed the sliding door behind me and crossed the stall to the open pasture door. Across the field, the horses raised their heads. They shifted, snorted, started toward me. Then fear got the better of them, and they retreated back into the corner. Tex gave an anxious whicker.

Something about the barn frightened them. Or maybe something near it. I glanced toward the house. Saw Blankenship watching. I gave him a curt nod and stepped back into the barn and pitched out three flakes of hay and whistled for the boys.

The combination of food and the familiar whistle reassured them, and they plodded toward me, casting anxious glances around the pasture. By the time Tex nosed the first flake of hay, Blankenship had gone inside.

I left the horses munching and inched along the fence line, starting at the back wall of the barn and moving up and away from the house. I didn't know what I was looking for, so I scanned the grass inside the fence, the fence itself, and the woods beyond. Even so, in the fading light, I almost missed it.

On the underside of one of the fence slats was a smear of blood.

CHAPTER FIFTY-FIVE

The dark thing in my belly uncoiled. It was a thing of grief and rage and guilt—guilt that I had not killed Elgin when I had the chance. The rage boiled into hatred, and I was glad, because the hatred filled me up and left no room for grief.

I glanced around to make sure no one was watching and vaulted the fence. The horses snorted and raised their heads but settled quickly, ears pricked in my direction. I drew the Glock as I stepped into the deepening shadows. Elgin may or may not have a firearm, but he was plenty deadly with a blade.

A small voice told me I should leave Elgin to Blankenship and the Wilson County Sheriff's Department. But I did not want to sit in a plastic chair in a hospital waiting room while someone else brought in the man who had murdered Josh. I imagined marching Elgin through the trees at gunpoint. I imagined other things too. Snapping bones, bleeding flesh. Elgin's craggy features battered beyond recognition. I told myself I didn't mean them.

There was little wind, but as the light drained away, so did the warmth. The scattered droplets became an icy drizzle that soaked through my jeans and numbed my skin. Fingers stiff with cold, I turned up the collar of my jacket and squinted into the shadows.

For almost two years, I had hiked and ridden through these woods. In the growing darkness, I moved among familiar trees. Bare branches made crisscross shadows on the dead leaves below. Wind rustled in the branches, and muffled voices drifted from the house. The rain on wet leaves made a hissing patter.

A patch of moonlight showed a broken branch, a sheen of black blood. A few minutes later, a heavy footprint marred the earth beside a frozen puddle.

A twig snapped somewhere behind me. I froze. Listened. A deer? One of Blankenship's men? Elgin was in front of me, I was pretty sure. I wiped the water from my eyes with a soggy sleeve and edged forward, more cautiously. Then a shadow moved ahead of me, and I swung the Glock toward it.

"I know you're there," I said. "Might as well come out."

With a burst of ragged laughter, Elgin stepped from behind a stand of cedars. One hand held a hunting knife like the one Doug Eddington had used on Razor. Moonlight and rainwater glinted on the blade. The other hand hung limp at his side. He'd zipped a folded towel into the shoulder of his jacket, but it hadn't been enough to keep a dark stain from seeping through.

"You again," he said. "Come to take me up on my offer? Mano a mano? Me one-handed and all shot full of holes, you might actually take me."

"You must be too stubborn to die," I said.

"Not with unfinished business."

"The kids?"

"Not such kids," he said.

I said, "Josh didn't rape your sister."

He laughed without humor. "You know what they say. 'All it takes for evil to prevail—"

"—is for good men to do nothing,'" I finished for him. "You murdered a bunch of fucked-up teenagers. You don't get to be self-righteous."

"Twelve is the age of accountability," he said. "In all the major religions. Besides, they weren't all teenagers."

While we talked, we circled each other like a couple of alpha wolves.

Searching for weaknesses.

"You're just pissed because you didn't get to kill Razor," I said.

The muscles around his eyes tightened. "Who says I didn't?"

"You're a real dumbass, you know that?" I said. He took a step forward. My finger twitched toward the trigger. "You killed Medea and the Knights the way you did so we'd look at you and not Hewitt. Only Hewitt didn't do it."

A vein in his forehead pulsed. "I'd've done it, if I was him."

"He didn't know about the rape."

"Parker died, I thought Judith must've told him." He took another step toward me.

"That's far enough." I raised the Glock, pointed it at the center of his forehead. A vest wouldn't help him this time. "Drop the knife."

He tilted his head as if weighing his options. He must have seen something in my face because he grimaced and dropped his weapon. It landed in the wet leaves with a heavy splat. "What now?"

"What would you have done if Razor hadn't been killed?"

"Don't be stupid," he said. "They were all dead the minute they laid a hand on Judith. Starting with that asshole, Razor. But I'd've taken my time. Done it up right. Like the fella says, a series of unfortunate accidents." He gave a bark of bitter laughter. "You never would have caught me. Hell, you never would have known."

I was afraid he might be right.

"World's a better place without him in it," Elgin said. "I woulda liked a piece of that. Guess I had to settle for his playmates." He grinned and added, "You gonna take me in, or kill me?"

Then he ducked, feinted, and charged. I got off a single shot. Heard him cry out just before his head plowed into my midsection. It was like being hit in the belly with a bowling ball.

He drove me backward into the rough bark of a black walnut tree, which dislodged a shower of water so cold it felt like ice. My elbow bounced off the tree, and the Glock fell from my hand.

Shit.

He ground his head into my gut as if he wanted to climb inside it. Pain blazed through my lower back, and for a panicked second, I thought he'd snapped my spine.

I cupped my hands, clapped them hard against his ears. He screamed and fell away, clutching an ear with each hand. Blood streamed from beneath his palms and dripped off his jaw.

I slumped against the tree and gasped for breath. A warm wetness trickled down my back. It felt like someone had scraped a cheese grater down my spine. I tried to move, and a wave of pain strong enough to make me retch shot from my shoulder blades to my tailbone.

"You fuck," Elgin said.

Behind us, something large—from the sound of it, something about the size of a small rhinoceros—crashed through the undergrowth. Blankenship, I thought. Here comes the cavalry. I should have been relieved. Instead, it pissed me off.

Elgin was mine.

I braced myself for another wave of pain and pushed away from the tree. Fumbled for my gun. Elgin unfolded himself and scrabbled for his knife. Came up empty and lashed out with a kick that drove the heel of his boot into my injured calf.

My leg buckled. I clamped my teeth on a scream, grabbed the front of Elgin's shirt with one hand, and drove the fingers of my other hand into his left eye. Felt the eyeball give and a rush of hot wetness stream down my hand. Bore him to the ground with the weight of my body. Elgin howled and clawed at my wrist, my face, my eyes.

Another figure burst into the clearing, calling my name. Randall's voice. Randall's bulk, charging through the branches. He'd followed Frank out, hadn't he?

He must have turned back. Made the same connections I'd made. Or read it on my face. Farther behind him, flashlight beams cut the night.

Elgin bucked and writhed beneath me. With one hand twisted in his shirt front and the other plunged into his eye, all I could do was watch his groping fingers find the knife and close around the hilt. The blade jerked up.

"No," Randall said. His boot slammed down on Elgin's wrist and held until the fingers opened.

I dug my fingers into Elgin's bloody socket. He moaned and gagged, then went limp. I rolled off him and curled over my injured leg, retching and sucking for air, shivering with cold and half-blinded by pain.

Randall knelt beside me and asked, "Are you all right?"

I figured he meant, was I going to live. I would have made some wiseass comment, but I seemed to have lost the power of speech. I nodded, tears streaming from my eyes.

Through a haze of pain, I heard him stand. Heard footsteps, followed by the rustle of dry leaves. "Son of a bitch," he said, very quietly.

A single gunshot echoed through the woods.

CHAPTER FIFTY-SIX

I opened my eyes. Elgin lay at Randall's feet, one eye hanging from the socket by a few bloody tendrils, a seeping bullet hole in the center of his forehead. The blood was a pinkish color, already mixing with the rain. Everywhere I looked was blood, mingling with water and washing away. My gun dangled from the end of Randall's fingers.

I staggered to my feet and touched my brother's shoulder. Felt him shivering.

"He had his hand on his knife," I said. "He was about to throw it at me."

Randall stared at Elgin's corpse and shuddered. His lips were blue, and his teeth chattered. "No," he said. "I—"

"Yes." With the flashlights bobbing toward us, I took his face in my hands and made him look into my eyes. We had two or three minutes before they got there. Max. "Listen to me. He was about to kill me. He had the knife in his hand. Say it."

"I—"

"*Say it.*"

"He had the knife in his hand."

We told it the way it happened, except for the end. Blood spatter evidence might have proven us liars, if not for the rain. The beautiful, blessed rain.

—✺—

It was after midnight when we finished at the sheriff's office. The thought of going home made me want to crawl into a bottle of

Jack Daniels and drink myself into a stupor. Bad idea. I knew that. Instead, I headed down to Elliston again. There was no sign of Absinthe, but I left cards in all the usual places, tacked to doors and stuffed in people's pockets. This time the message read, "Absinthe— it's safe to come home."

Early the next morning, she did.

—m—

We buried Josh on Christmas Eve.

Paulie squirmed in my lap while the preacher read a passage from Ecclesiastes and said a few words about stray lambs. Someone played some songs I didn't recognize. Wendy had found them on Josh's iPod. Caitlin read a poem and got all the way through it before dissolving into tears. I was proud of her.

Halfway through the service, I glanced over my shoulder at the congregation. Saw a blur of faces. Strangers, mostly, but a few I recognized. Maria, sobbing against D.W.'s shoulder, fist clenched against her swollen belly. Seeing them together, I felt a weary sadness. Elisha, dabbing at her eyes with a tattered Kleenex. She was beautiful, and she had loved Josh, which made her even more beautiful to me.

Frank and Harry sat together, looking uncomfortable in their funeral suits. Marta Savales. Sherilyn and Earl. Even Miss Aleta and Kelly Malone had made an appearance.

Absinthe sat hunched in a back pew, clutching her mother's hand.

At the back of the chapel, face shaded by a wide-brimmed black hat, sat Hannah Eddington.

Beside me, Wendy sobbed and pounded her thigh with a clenched fist. Randall reached across the space between them, but she moved her hand away before his fingers brushed her skin.

After the service, I handed Paul off to Maria and made my way through a gauntlet of well-wishers. I lost a few seconds in Absinthe's damp hug, then pushed through the chapel doors, and caught Hannah Eddington just as she slipped her key into the driver's side lock.

"I didn't want to intrude," she said. "I wasn't sure you'd want to see me."

"I'm not sure either," I said. "But let's see how it goes."

She said, "Doug is pleading guilty. His lawyer thinks he can get a good plea bargain."

"How do you feel about that?"

"Guilty, mostly. And relieved. Then guilty again."

"Don't," I said. "That isn't what he wants."

Her smile was sad. "We don't always get what we want. You of all people know that. Anyway, I'm sorry for your loss. That's all I came to say. I'm sorry all this happened."

"Josh isn't yours to carry," I said. "Razor set it in motion, and Elgin carried it through. It had nothing to do with you."

She gave me an awkward hug and hurried to her car. I turned to go inside, and came chin to forehead with Marta Savales.

"You found my son," she said. Her eyes were wet. "I didn't believe you when you said you would."

"I'm not sure I believed myself."

She looked off into the distance, a little furrow forming between her eyebrows. Then she gently touched my hand and said, "Thank you."

—⁂—

I found Randall in the meditation room, a tiny chamber with two vinyl chairs and a coffee table with a live orchid in the center. The orchid was from Keating, who had written his message in uniform block letters. BYRON'S WITH ME. I SWEAR I'LL KEEP HIM SAFE. P.S. I OWE YOU EVERYTHING. The thought made me grimace. I didn't want Keating to owe me anything.

I slid into the chair across from Randall. "How you holding up?"

He looked exhausted, and probably was. I wondered if he'd had a full night's sleep since Josh's death. He glanced at me with glazed eyes. "How should I be holding up?"

I couldn't answer that. Instead, I said, "I'm going to see Jay. You want to come?"

He couldn't meet my gaze. "I don't think so," he said.

"You can't possibly be blaming him," I said. "He did everything right. He called 911, barricaded the door. Hell, he even shot the bastard."

"I don't blame him. I just can't look at him. Every time I do, I hate that he's alive and Josh isn't."

"I know," I said.

"You don't know. He's your little faggot friend, and that's just fine, but—"

"What the hell is wrong with you? He tried to save Josh."

"I know," he said. His eyes were wet. "But he didn't. And every time I think of him, I think, my God, Josh had his whole life in front of him, and Jay is—" He stopped.

I said it for him. "Jay is already dying."

"What kind of justice is that?"

"Justice," I said. "What the hell does justice have to do with anything?"

He looked away and said, "Wendy wants me gone."

"What? For how long?"

He gave a small, bitter laugh. "A day, a month, a year. Forever. I don't know. She blames me. Hell, I blame myself."

"You didn't kill him, Randall."

He looked away. "I was thinking Alaska, maybe. Work on one of those fishing boats."

"What about the girls?"

He shook his head. "I'm no good to them. Not now."

I wasn't sure what he meant by that. *Not now, when I'm falling to pieces? Not now, while my marriage unravels like a badly knit sweater? Not now that I've killed a man?*

"When will you go?" I said.

"Soon."

"And when will you be back?"

"I don't know. When she's ready, I guess."

"You guess?"

He shrugged. "We have a lot to talk about. But neither one of us is talking. I can't . . . I just don't have the words."

Maybe he was right. Maybe he needed time to heal. A place to crawl away and lick his wounds like an injured wolf.

"Call when you get there?" I said.

"When I get settled."

"You need anything . . ."

"I know. I'll call."

CHAPTER FIFTY-SEVEN

Elisha was waiting for me beside the Silverado. She handed me a long white envelope. It was sealed. "Frank asked me to give you this," she said. "He said to open it when you're alone."

I tucked it inside my jacket and opened the passenger side door. "I'm going to the hospital. You want to come?"

"Of course."

We stopped at the office on the way. I shoved the stack of Richie Barron photos into a nine-by-fourteen metered envelope and addressed it to Richie's wife, Marissa Barron. Before I dropped it in the mailbox, I scrawled across the flap, *Richie is the Hindenburg . . . Here's your parachute.*

—◊—

Jay was in a private room. Fabulous Greg had decorated it with tropical plants, circus balloons, and half a dozen get-well cards the size of Oklahoma. An outpouring of goodwill from friends and friends of friends.

None of them were from Jay's parents.

When we arrived, the door was ajar. I peered in and saw Eric spooning a block of cherry Jell-O into Jay's mouth.

"Well, well," I said, more heartily than I felt. "Have we declared an armistice?"

Jay looked up and whispered, "I've decided to forgive him."

"New Year's Eve," Eric explained. "He says he needs someone to kiss." He laid the spoon back on the tray. "And now, boys and girls, I'm parched. If you'll be here a minute, I'll go downstairs and get a Coke." He looked pointedly at Elisha. "Be a sweetheart and join me?"

She raised her eyebrows, and he gave her what I surmised was a meaningful smile. "Sure," she said. Gave Jay a peck on the cheek and followed Eric from the room.

When they were gone, I pulled a chair over beside the bed. Thought of the last time I'd stood by a hospital bed. A hundred years ago, when Josh asked me to find his molester's killer.

Jay said, "I'm sorry."

"Sorry for what?" I asked. But I knew.

Sorry for not saving Josh. Sorry for not killing Elgin. Sorry for being the one who survived.

I said, "I'm the one who didn't put Elgin down when I had the chance. If I'd put a bullet in his brain at Barnabus's place . . ." I stopped.

"Don't," he said. "Don't apologize for not being a murderer."

He was my best and oldest friend. I loved him like a brother. He'd have laid down his life for me, and I'd have traded it for Josh's in a heartbeat.

I saw that knowledge in his eyes.

"I'm sorry," he said again.

I forced the words past the tightness in my throat, knowing they were not enough and never would be. "You have nothing to be sorry for."

He turned his head toward the wall and said, "Everyone has something to be sorry for."

—⚏—

I dropped Elisha off at the funeral home and watched until she pulled out of the parking lot. Then I pulled Frank's envelope out of my pocket. Scrawled across the back, he'd written, "This was on the table beside your bed."

Inside was a Xerox copy of a piece of notebook paper, and on the paper was a handwritten message. The writing was Josh's. Swooping and even, almost like calligraphy.

A copy. Of course. The original was evidence.
The note was brief. Only five lines.

> *Dear Uncle Jared,*
> *I'm going to do the right thing.*
> *Love,*
> *Josh*
> *P.S. I wish you were my father.*

CHAPTER FIFTY-EIGHT

Sometimes in the evenings, I sit on the front porch with Luca in my lap and a beer in my hand and wait for the phone to ring, hoping it will be my brother.

It never is.

Two weeks after New Year's, Randall sent a check. It was addressed to me, but it was meant for Wendy and the girls. The postmark was from Omaha. In February, Montreal. In March and April, Nome, Alaska.

There's never a return address, and I don't try to find one. That's the way he wants it.

I carry Josh's letter in my wallet, between Paulie's picture and one of Randall's family, all four of them, taken a few weeks before Josh opened his veins. They look happy.

Sometimes, I think of what might happen if a semi should roll over on my pickup, or a bullet were to shatter my window and drive into my brain. What it would do to Randall to open my wallet and read those words. I think about burning the letter, or shredding it, or dropping it into a landfill. Once, I held it to a candle, watched the edges brown and curl before I yanked it away from the flame. I know the words by heart, but I can't bring myself to destroy the page. It's as if some part of Josh lives in the ink and in the fibers of the paper. As if to destroy the letter would be to destroy all that's left of him.

Jay rarely talks about that night. He bakes cherry cobbler. Plants miniature roses in his garden. Goes to dance clubs with Eric the maybe-*mensch*. On weekends, he sometimes sings my son to sleep. The scar on his throat is fading, but his eyes still carry the scars on his soul.

This is what we do, he says. He hands me another beer and sinks down on the porch step, a glass of lemonade in his hand. This is all we *can* do. We bend. We break. We carry on.